The Love Shack

LORI FOSTER

CANARY STREET PRESS

CANARY
STREET
PRESS™

Recycling programs
for this product may
not exist in your area.

ISBN-13: 978-1-335-51714-2

The Love Shack

Copyright © 2024 by Lori Foster

For questions and comments about the quality of this book, please contact us at CustomerService@Harlequin.com.

TM is a trademark of Harlequin Enterprises ULC.

Canary Street Press
22 Adelaide St. West, 41st Floor
Toronto, Ontario M5H 4E3, Canada
CanaryStPress.com

Printed in U.S.A.

Special thanks to all the readers who enjoyed this series. I love that you cheered on Kathleen, the mascot-mannequin. It's time to say goodbye to the quirky town called Cemetery, where anything could— and did—happen... Even the most unexpected happily-ever-afters.

1

Carrying a colorful bouquet of flowers and a pastry box, Berkley Carr strolled down the sidewalk with her dog, Hero, taking in the sights, sounds and colors of the eclectic little town where she'd recently relocated. A bright afternoon sun heated her shoulders as she breathed in the unique freshness that she'd never experienced anywhere else.

She'd made the right decision when she'd accepted the new job and, basically, a new life. The notoriety that so often haunted her couldn't possibly bother her here, not in this quaint rural setting bustling with activity and filled with kindness.

As she waved to the owner of the sweet shop, and then, on the opposite side of the street, a seasonal ice cream parlor, she decided that the full-time residents were...almost too good to be true.

Not perfect, no. How boring would that be? They varied in age and ambition, with vocations that spanned the imagination. Most of the businesses were clustered here on the main street, but others were spread out through the town.

None, however, were near her new home and The Love Shack, the amazing animal shelter she now ran. Privacy, that was what she had. Peaceful, wonderful privacy.

As if he'd read her thoughts, Hero gazed up at her, his tongue lolling out one side of his mouth, and his muscular body moving in time with her long strides. The brindle pit bull–boxer mix loved these walks as much as she did.

Berkley smiled down at him. "It's nice being a stranger, isn't it?"

Hero licked his chops and then sniffed the air, either smelling a squirrel in one of the mature trees that provided blessed shade everywhere, or perhaps picking up the scent of barbecue that permeated the air from a not-too-distant restaurant.

A vacationer walked by with two kids in tow, no doubt headed for the large recreational lake. As the girl, who looked to be around six, reached out for Hero, the woman asked with caution, "Is he friendly?"

Berkley stopped. "The friendliest." With his tail wagging, Hero snuffled against the kid and made her laugh. The girl's shier brother came forward and gave Hero a hug, then the mom knelt and gave him a few pets, too. As always, the dog loved the attention.

After the woman wished her a good day and corralled her kids along, Berkley resumed her walk.

The vacationers were the easiest for her to deal with because they had only a passing interest in her.

The residents, though, they had reason to want to know more about her. Most of them were caring, involved, determined— with a few quirks thrown in. Several were nosy, others liked to gossip, and of course there were often assumptions.

So far, their assumptions about her hadn't come anywhere near the truth. No one here knew her history, her infamy.

If she could help it, no one ever would.

She no sooner had that thought than she saw Hero go on the alert. Berkley followed the direction of the dog's stare and encountered a very fine male behind.

Maybe if the guy hadn't been leaning into what looked like a well in front of a shop, things would have gone differently. But there he was, legs braced with a muscular tush on display in board shorts, his head and part of his shoulders hidden inside the well. She and Hero weren't the only ones to notice, either. Berkley saw several women taking in the view.

It was her distraction with the other women, as well as the packages she carried, that made her lose hold of the leash when Hero launched forward, already on a mission. She shouted, "Hero, no!" But of course, it was too late.

Hearing her, the man straightened too quickly and smacked his head on the roof frame of the well. Before he could complain, Hero had him by the seat of his shorts, determinedly tugging him a foot away to "safety," which made the guy lose his footing on the gravel lot. He fell forward with a barely subdued curse.

Filled with dread, Berkley sprinted forward, dropped her flowers and pastry box, and grabbed for Hero's leash. "He's fine, bud. I swear. Hero, *drop him.*"

Obediently, the dog released his grip on the shorts, then wagged his tail, very proud of himself. And damn, she was pretty proud of him, too. He'd gotten much better at following commands. "Good boy."

Grumbling, the guy pushed to his feet, dusted off his knees and stared down at her.

Holy crap. *I know him.*

Lawson Salder, in the flesh. She hadn't seen him in nearly a decade, and honestly, that wasn't long enough to suit her. She would have been happy to never again set eyes on anyone from her old neighborhood, her old life—anyone who knew of the god-awful scandal that had overtaken her existence.

Why had no one told her he lived in Cemetery, Indiana?

It wasn't like anyone in the area wouldn't know Lawson. The man was testosterone on a stick. A walking ad for sex appeal. Windblown blond hair, light brown eyes, drool-worthy shoulders and a "don't care" attitude that had drawn admiration from all the girls on their street, as well as many of the guys.

Back then, most had struggled in the run-down town, but Lawson had gone about his business as if he owned it all.

Eight years had not only made him older, but also better-looking, with more of an edge—and damn him, he'd always been edgy enough.

How unfair was that?

His thick brows came together in a severe frown. "Your dog is a menace."

Since she was holding her breath, waiting to see if he'd recognize her, it took a second to actually comprehend his insult.

Then she got annoyed.

"He was trying to save you. You're welcome."

"Save me from *what*?"

She gestured at the well. "He probably thought you were falling in."

"When it's only decorative?"

His continued antagonism had her teeth locking. "Well, I'll be sure to explain the difference to him." She turned to Hero, who stared back with his intelligent brown eyes alert. "Sweetheart, the mean man wants you to know that the well isn't real."

With a disgruntled huff, Lawson muttered, "I am not mean." Then to the dog, he said, "You almost ripped my shorts, bud."

The way they hung loose around his lean hips, it was a wonder Hero hadn't pulled them right off him—and no, *no no no*, she did not need that image in her head. Small town, anonymity, fresh start—that was her focus. Not a blast from the past in the form of a hot guy with a gruff attitude.

She inhaled a slow breath and said precisely, "Hero is a rescue dog, and he's sensitive."

"Odd, doesn't seem like I've hurt his feelings. You're the only one who's pissed off."

New umbrage filled her lungs and she took an aggressive step toward him. "Don't curse in front of my dog." Yup, those ridiculous words actually left her mouth. But now with them out there, she copped an attitude and stood by them.

Lawson let Hero smell his hand, then he stroked the dog's neck while saying in a gentle, affectionate tone, "Does cursing offend you, Hero? She is pissed off, isn't she? You see it, don't you, buddy? I only spoke the truth."

Of course the dog wagged his tail adoringly, shuffling nearer to Lawson.

"When you say it like that," Berkley complained, "he doesn't know you're still cursing."

Wearing a smirk, Lawson gave his attention to her. "So you adopted him?"

"I did, yeah, but that's not what I meant by a rescue dog. Hero rescues people. All the time."

"Whether they need rescuing or not?"

Don't look at him. Don't look at him. Hearing the smile in his tone did something funny to her and she absolutely, positively, could not get drawn in by him. "It's when they appear to need help." Suddenly aware of others standing around, attempting to listen in, Berkley decided it was time to go. The last thing she wanted to do was attract attention.

While picking up her flowers, which were a little crushed, and her pastry, which thankfully was unharmed, she asked, "Do I owe you anything?"

He didn't reply.

Unable to help herself, she glanced at him—and yup, she got snagged. *Oh, the power of those eyes...*

His gaze searched hers. "You look familiar."

Hoping to slide past any memories, she said fast, "I run The Love Shack, the new animal shelter. We opened late spring, so you've probably seen me around." She hesitated. "Your shorts are okay?"

"They're old, so no worries." He continued to study her. "Wait a minute."

"Nope. Gotta roll." Arms loaded with her packages and the leash firmly in hand, she got Hero moving, but she was a second too late.

"Berkley Carr."

The way he said her name, with equal parts recognition and disbelief, made her want to bolt. To simply walk away—from him and the town and the promise of a new start. She could keep going as if the ugly memories of her younger days had never happened. Then this awkward, stomach-churning moment wouldn't exist.

And the man now staring intently at her would have no interest in her at all.

But she had a shelter full of animals relying on her. Her cat was probably getting up to no good. The people in the town had welcomed her.

And she'd already decided this place was home.

A breeze blew over her face, reminding her of the scents of summer she'd appreciated minutes ago. Someone laughed. A child raced past.

Life went on all around her. Her life would go on, too.

Repressing the burn of humiliation that tried to shrivel her, she stiffened her spine and managed to make her lips lift in the semblance of a smile. "Yes, that's me." And now he'd bring up the past, the scorn, the disgrace. He'd have questions, because everyone always had questions once they knew who she was.

Frowning in what looked like concern, he stepped closer.

For a second there, she was the old Berkley, downtrodden and ashamed, and she retreated a step. *Damn it.* To cover that reaction, she planted her feet and stared up at him.

He stalled—and then his expression cleared and he gave her a carefully neutral look. "The wishing well will be finished by the end of the week. It was a great idea."

Her clenched muscles went slack, proving she'd been braced for the worst. Grateful that he'd let their association go and hoping to avoid the mention of it again, Berkley peered at the well as if she'd never seen one before. Her thoughts scrambled, but he'd given her an out, and by God, she'd take it. "An idea for…what?"

"Betty didn't tell you?"

Awed that he sounded merely friendly, his recognition hidden, she breathed a little easier. "Betty Cemetery? She's always up to something. I lose track of her shenanigans." The town matriarch—and a descendant of the town founder, which was how Cemetery, Indiana, got its name—seemed to get busier with age. At eighty-seven, she should have been slowing down, and instead she'd found renewed purpose in the hometown she loved.

"Agreed. It amazes me everything she does."

"All good things," Berkley said in defense of the elder. She'd heard enough whispers to know that some considered Betty a bully, a powerful woman who used her prestige to coerce others into her way of thinking.

And maybe she did.

But to Berkley, she'd been nothing but amazing. A lover of pets. A generous benefactor to the shelter. Accepting and encouraging. She owed Betty for this new start.

"Many good things," Lawson countered. "But not all." He gave her a brief, teasing smile. "The wishing well directly assists the shelter, though, so I assumed you knew all about it.

See, the plan is for people to toss in change, make a wish, take a photo if they want, and then the money will be collected monthly for the shelter."

"Huh." Great idea. "Betty didn't tell me anything about it, but The Love Shack can always use the funds." Edging closer to the well, which made Hero whine, she peeked inside.

"Unique name for the place."

She shot him a warning glance. "Betty chose it."

Without asking, Lawson took the leash from her, and said to the dog, "Come here, bud." He patted the top of the well wall. "Come on, now. It's okay." Cautiously, Hero obeyed, peeking in and darting back, then, after realizing what he'd seen, peeking in again. "Damn, you really are a smart one, aren't you?"

"You're cursing again."

Rolling his eyes, he said, "You'll survive." He patted Hero. "His coloring is unusual."

"Gorgeous, right? He's a brindle pit bull–boxer mix. Super-smart, overall well-behaved—"

"But he has that thing about rescuing."

The tension in her neck loosened. Talking about animals always put her at ease. "He was a companion to a senior who used a wheelchair, so he'd already gained a tendency to help. When his owner passed away, Hero was lost."

"Lost?" Lawson asked softly.

Emotion thickened her throat. She understood being lost, and that was why she'd fallen so madly in love with Hero. "Shelter life was hard on him. He was so obviously sad and alone, even with the other animals around him. I figured out that he needed a purpose, but after two tries at finding his forever home, he was brought back."

"He wanted to rescue someone."

Despite herself, the corner of her mouth lifted. "Yeah, and he gave it his all. Over and over again."

Lawson knelt to stroke the dog, giving him a little extra affection, and Hero ate it up.

Funny how that made her feel, to see badass Lawson Salder being so tender with the dog. "Hero needed someone who understood him." And she'd badly needed a friend. "So we're family now."

Lawson looked up at her, and wow, it froze her to the spot. "You're not going to cry, are you?"

Of all the... "Of course not! Why would you think that?"

His gaze assessed her. "I think you have a very soft heart when it comes to this good boy."

"I love him, but I won't cry about it." Not here and not now. In the past, before Hero—and maybe a few times since adopting him—tears had gotten the better of her. It always made her feel worse. Stuffy-headed and weary. Weak.

To change the subject yet again, Berkley asked, "How will you get the money from the well?" The structure wasn't deep, maybe three or four feet, but the interior of the well was like a funnel, so any change dropped in would roll into a center hole.

Lawson stood again, all six-feet-plus of him as he contemplated the well while still idly stroking Hero's ears. "Once I finish and turn on the water, it'll be a fountain, with the water circulating." After a silly, furtive look around, he leaned in close and whispered, "There's a secret door built in the base. I use a key to unlock it, withdraw a basket and collect the change."

"Ingenious." This time, since he wasn't in the process of remembering her and the mortifying shame of her past, his nearness didn't bother her. Not much, anyway. "And this was Betty's idea?"

"We came up with the plan together." He lifted his hand to the tidy shop front behind him, where numerous T-shirts, sweatshirts, spirit wear, backpacks and more could be seen through a spotlessly clean window. "It seemed like good business marketing, so I offered to build it in front of my place. You know, get people here taking pics, hanging around, and maybe they'll see something they like. Betty was able to push the idea through with the town council because the money collected will be put to good use."

"It's a great idea, really."

He eyed the well. "When I finish with it, it'll be a beauty. We'll add a *Cemetery, Indiana* town sign on one side of it, so people have a great reason to pose there. Dropping in money will be optional, but obviously suggested."

"You're like a marketing guru." Of all the things she'd known about him, the art of subtle promotion didn't seem to fit. A bouncer at a bar, sure. Coach for a football team, probably. But custom printing? "Do you own the shop alone or do you have partners?"

"It's mine."

She didn't exactly mean to be nosy, but the words slipped out. "What about your wife?"

"Not married. You?"

God, no. She would *never* marry. Even thinking it caused her to take a step back.

Sorry that she'd brought it up, she shook her head. "No. It's just me—well, and several wonderful volunteers who'll help at the shelter. Right now there aren't that many animals to deal with, but we're taking some overflow from other shelters, so I'll be getting a few new dogs and cats soon."

"You've been settled here for a while now?"

"Still new," she said. "The shelter was just completed in the spring, and then I needed to get moved in. You?"

"I've been here since last summer. I was renting for a while, but just bought a house."

So he was here to stay.

And she was here to stay.

Where, then, did that leave them? With her trying to avoid him, most likely.

★ ★ ★

Watching as Berkley made a hasty escape, Lawson felt a dozen things, none of them expected. Overall, he tended to avoid any reminders from the "old neighborhood." Once he'd gotten out of there, he'd put the place to rest. Buried it and stuck a tombstone on the grave—at least in his mind. That plan hadn't always gone as he'd hoped because sometimes the past crept in, bringing unpleasant reminders of a time he wished he could forget.

His work around the world had been productive, and he'd learned a lot, but it had shown him more tragedy and despair.

He was here now in Cemetery, with a business he loved, one that also made him proud and gave him independence. It was a happy place, nearly devoid of crime, where the people pulled together, and the overall atmosphere was fun and optimistic. A perfect balm to his past. A way to put down roots and move forward, leaving all the darkness behind him. Repeatedly, he told himself that it didn't matter where he'd started, only where he ended up.

Overall, he was content.

Or at least, he had been. At the moment, as Berkley rounded a bend and disappeared from sight, a subtle uneasiness stirred inside him. Recognizing him had unsettled her.

Had unsettled him, too.

Way back, when they'd both been trapped in the ugly circumstances of poverty, neglect and the unending threat of danger, he hadn't known her that well. He'd been twenty to her seventeen, old enough to feel sympathy but too determined on his own course to get involved.

She'd changed up her look a lot. Gone was the plain, quiet girl in clothes that didn't fit, dull hair and a gaze that was never direct. The corner of his mouth hitched as he considered the way she'd given him hell.

For cursing in front of her dog.

A dog that had managed to catch the seat of his shorts without biting him, or even causing a pinch. Clever mutt.

Clever woman, too. With her bleached hair and hot-pink tips, eye makeup that accentuated the blue of her irises, and multiple earrings in only one ear, Berkley Carr was a standout. The point, though, seemed to be that few who knew her as an awkward teen accused of stealing a local celebrity's husband would recognize her now. The transformation made him curious. Her new confidence deserved applause, but he doubted she wanted any.

His thoughts circled around to fate. What were the odds of two young people escaping one of the worst neighborhoods in Kentucky, only to land in the same small town in Indiana? Slim, he assumed, yet here they were.

Wondering about the shelter she ran and where exactly she lived, he turned—and drew up short at the sight of a mannequin, sightlessly staring right at him, positioned near the well. His entire body tensed.

Kathleen, they called her, as if she was a beloved member of Cemetery. He'd seen her all over town, posed in different scenarios like a celebrity mascot. It was some truly twisted shit.

Almost everything about the town appealed to him—except Kathleen.

Damn, but mannequins gave him the creeps.

A few women standing nearby laughed, no doubt over his dumbstruck expression. Dredging up a smile, he turned to them. "One of you guilty of putting that thing in my way?"

"Don't call her a *thing*," the tallest woman said with a giggle. "You'll hurt Kathleen's feelings."

Flirting? He couldn't tell for sure, and didn't want to find out. "Fiberglass doesn't have feelings."

Another woman pressed forward between the others, dark hair softly framing her face, her slate-gray eyes understanding.

"She takes a little getting used to, right?" Holding out a delicate hand, she said, "I'm Lark Penny, a new stylist at the salon."

"Lawson Salder." Her sudden appearance and introduction saved him from more conversation with the others. And since this woman seemed reasonable, he appealed to her before releasing her hand. "Hopefully you're here for an order." His low voice wouldn't carry. "I'd rather escape this situation if possible."

In an equally soft whisper, she asked, "Would that situation be your fan club, or Kathleen?"

"Both, honestly."

With a big grin, she said louder, "Mr. Salder, I believe you have freshly printed smocks for us." She gestured to the shop. "I hate to interrupt, but I'm in a bit of a rush. Would you mind?"

"Not at all." Impressed with how quickly she'd adapted, he walked around Kathleen, avoiding the dummy's dead stare, and picked up his tools on the way in. When he opened his door, a bell chimed.

William, his part-time help, glanced up from his seat behind the counter. "Got the well done already?"

"Not yet. I'll finish it up tomorrow." Then they'd only need to add the sign, which a local artist was creating as part of her contribution to support the shelter. He did love how the town pulled together to assist one another. To Lark, he said, "Give me just a second to find your order."

As he went to the back room, he heard Lark introduce herself. William was a great kid, mature for a nineteen-year-old, but given how Lark looked—like an ad for feminine sweetness—he wasn't surprised that William croaked a little in his reply. Pretty women with big smiles and engaging attitudes could be kryptonite to many young men.

After he found the package, he stepped back out and noticed that William's color was high, his expression a little glazed while Lark continued to talk to him.

Tempering his grin, Lawson said, "Here you go." At the counter, he set down the package and pulled out one of the smocks so she could inspect it. "What do you think?"

"Ohhh, love them. They'll be a big hit, I'm sure." She ran her fingertips over the stylized logo on the front center pocket. "The gold on black looks amazing. Was that your idea?"

Over the years, he'd found he had a good eye for color, first in painting houses, then in customized printing. "I guided the decision a little, but I also have plenty of samples around to show customers how things will look."

While refolding the smock, she sent him another smile. "I'm fairly new here, but so far I'm really impressed with how pretty everything is. The whole town seems to take a lot of pride in presentation."

William said, "Probably not Dad's hardware store." He grinned. "Hard to pretty up tools."

"Your dad is Daniel?"

Obviously, William wasn't expecting her to know that. "Yeah. I'm his youngest son."

"I had to go by there to get a few things for my apartment, plus I'm trying to familiarize myself with the people who live here. I plan to stay, you know. I think so far I've visited half the shops in the town proper. Your dad was super nice, and the store was so organized. Tools might not be pretty, but he had some great displays."

"Er…thanks. I'll tell him you said so."

"I already did." She turned back to Lawson. "I should get going, but it was terrific to meet you."

As he walked her to the door, he said, "Thanks for the rescue. I appreciate it."

After glancing out the door, she faced him and leaned a little closer. "If no one is looking, want me to move Kathleen?"

The genuineness of her offer took him by surprise. She didn't tease him about it, didn't even question him. If he wasn't committed to staying uninvolved, he'd be tempted to see if Lark, with her friendly manner and easy smiles, was interested in more. "It's fine. Harmless fun."

"Ah, so it was more the fan club than the mannequin." With a sage nod of understanding, she said, "No worries. I totally get it. A guy like you probably draws a lot of attention."

"A guy like me?" No one had referred to him that way in years, and his shoulders automatically stiffened.

Dark, slim brows lifted. "Big, good-looking." The brows tweaked together. "Rugged, too, I guess. That's all I meant. This is a vacation town, after all, and there are always hordes of women hanging around. Pretty sure those were vacationers teasing you before I interrupted. I mean, they've been in bikinis all day. Do the locals do that?"

His mouth twitched. "Not that I've seen." But then, he hadn't even noticed that the woman taunting him with Kathleen was in a bathing suit.

Leaning back on the door frame, Lark confided, "I had two women come in to have their hair styled, and they were both wearing bikinis."

"I take it that's not usual?"

She snorted. "One of the other stylists told me that with our walk-in policy, it happens a lot during the summer." She fluffed her own hair. "Guess if you get windblown on the beach, but a date works out, it's quickest just to drop in."

Lawson wondered if Berkley got her hair done in the local beauty shop. For some reason, he doubted it. She seemed like the type to do her own hair—if that was even possible with the intricacy of her color choices.

Straightening again, Lark said "Here" and handed the order back to him, then took her purse off her shoulder, opened it and peered inside. She rummaged around a moment and produced a card. "This is me. If you ever want to stop in, I do guys' hair, too."

"Suggesting I need a little work?" He took the card and then pocketed it.

"Not really." Still wearing a smile, she took back the package and opened the door. "The natural look suits you."

As he said his goodbyes to Lark, he found himself wondering about Berkley again. Did *she* think his look worked?

And damn it, since when did he even have a "look"?

2

A little more than a week later, at exactly 7:00 a.m. on a Sunday, Berkley had just finished hosing down the dog runs when the sound of a loud power tool suddenly had all the dogs howling. Six of them. Well, seven counting Hero.

"What in the world?" She'd thought surely she was the only one up and working so early on a weekend. Of course, weekend or weekday, it didn't matter when there were animals who needed tending.

Each and every one of her days, rain or shine, hot or cold, started at 5:00 a.m. Before Betty had hired her to run this shelter, she'd worked at another location where the regular director was often missing. She hadn't minded too much because he had never done things the way she'd preferred. When she'd made the decision to relocate to Cemetery, she'd first found a wonderful replacement for herself—and she'd ensured the director was removed.

Now *she* was in charge, and she absolutely loved it. Everything would be under her guidance, which meant the animals would always get the very best care. That included rising early to get them fed and give them fresh water. She spent a little time playing with each of the dogs so they wouldn't feel too lonely, then they were let outside in their individually contained areas while she hosed down their spaces and prepped fresh bedding.

And of course, fresh bedding meant laundry to do, but she had a volunteer who helped with that three times a week as long as there were no big messes. Another volunteer came by every other day to take a turn walking the dogs and brushing the cats. Her two part-time workers assisted with everything else, including the paperwork to show that each animal had been vaccinated and treated for worms and parasites. There were also the records for intakes and, hopefully soon, adoptions.

For a new shelter, it was a busy place, but the cacophony of dogs yapping and cats meowing was music to her ears. It was only the whines of fear—or worse, pain—that could destroy her. Her heart ached to even think of the numerous times she'd dealt with that.

Some people didn't deserve animals.

When the noisy power tool roared again, Hero gave a hearty bark, a sound she chose to mean curiosity. "I know," she said. "It's odd to hear when we should be relatively alone." Odd, and slightly alarming. Pulling off a glove, she bit at a thumb nail and considered what to do. No one else was around right now. A glance up showed that sunrise had painted the sky in tangerine hues that would soon lighten to gold before giving way to the brightest blue.

Berkley loved it here, the isolation of her small house and the brand-spanking-new shelter surrounded by trees. Somewhere in the distance, the lake curved into a cove. She couldn't see it, but the scents of the water sometimes carried through the woods.

Hero waited expectantly, so she said, "It's probably a county worker taking care of a phone line or cable or something. Let me finish up here and then we'll investigate."

She and Hero often liked to romp around the woods, exploring interesting things like mushrooms and tiny wildflowers, frogs, snails and skinks.

The noise continued as she completed her morning chores. Hunger tried to divert her—she hadn't yet had breakfast—but seeing how anxious Hero had become, she washed her hands, hooked the leash to the dog and set out. She'd be back in a few minutes and then she'd get a bowl of cereal or something.

Without makeup or her usual array of earrings, her hair stuffed into a ball cap, she ventured into the woods. Morning dew left the ground damp while the rising sun filtered through the trees, providing shadows that shifted around her.

Hero didn't do his usual investigation of every weed, rock and leaf. Instead, the muscular dog made a beeline for the sound that grew louder with every few feet they traveled.

Since getting settled into her house, she hadn't ventured off quite this far and now she had second thoughts. That was, until the tree line opened onto a cleared property and she saw a man, shirtless, shorts drooping over trim hips, using a chain saw on a downed tree.

A funny thing happened to her. She *admired* him.

That tall, honed body, the flex of biceps as he handled the heavy saw, the firm set of his jaw...

"Lawson?" She'd barely breathed his name, a mere whisper of surprise, so it was unfortunate that he'd released the chain saw trigger at the same time.

Suddenly aware that he was no longer alone, he turned his head.

From the distance of twenty feet or so, they stared at each other. At first she saw confusion, and then recognition.

"Berkley?" He straightened, inadvertently showing off that powerful body as if it were nothing. A light dusting of brown hair covered his chest, sweat-damp in places despite the mild temps of the morning air.

Her breath shuddered in, but good God, the man was half-naked. For years now, she'd made a deliberate effort to avoid situations like this, and here she'd just blundered into one. "Hi." Pathetic. She supposed the weak greeting was better than Hero's effusive welcome. The dog's entire body jiggled with the need to run to his new friend.

After glancing around, like maybe he thought she'd brought others along, Lawson zeroed in on her again. He set the chain saw aside, ran a forearm over his face and asked, "What are you doing here?"

His question galvanized her. Shaking off her aberrant admiration, she came forward with a lot of attitude. "That should be my question to you."

With obvious confusion, he shook his head. "I live here."

Abruptly stopping, she almost tripped over her own feet. Hero continued on, and that meant she got dragged reluctantly forward so that the dog could greet Lawson with eagerness bordering on adoration.

"You can't *live* here." Absurd. That would put him right behind the shelter...and her own house. How could she avoid him if he was so close?

Smiling, he knelt to welcome Hero with a few rousing pets and even a hug. "Good to see you, too, bud." Then in a loud whisper, he asked, "What's she pissed about this time?"

Berkley started to reply, but then it dawned on her that she was a wreck. Worse than a wreck. Without her makeup and jewelry, her usual hairstyle, she felt exposed. Raw. Like that same young girl from years ago.

She wasn't even wearing a bra.

The urge to fold her arms over her chest nearly overwhelmed her. Automatically, her hand tightened on the leash and she blinked once, twice, three times, trying to gather her wits.

"Hey." Lawson stood again. "You okay?"

Her audible swallow seemed to echo over the placid surface of the lake behind him. "I'm fine." But she wasn't. "Why wouldn't I be?" No one saw her like this. Not since...

She abruptly turned away, then stopped again, stumped as to where to go, or even how to leave when she had a dog still worshipping at Lawson's feet. Dragging the dog away would be unkind. Bracing herself, she tried to think of her next step.

"Want a drink?"

Aware of Lawson moving in the opposite direction, she peeked over her shoulder. Yup, that was him heading toward a building.

Or...a house? Overgrown shrubs and trees nearly hid it, so she hadn't noticed it right off the bat.

Hero whined. Obviously, the dog wanted to follow him. "What is this?" she asked, taking a tentative step forward.

"I told you, I live here. I know it's not much right now, but I got it for a steal and I'm fixing it up." Bounding up to a wooden deck, he turned. "Want to come take a look around? I'll pour some tea, or water, or I might still have a cola in the fridge."

"You don't know?" Curiosity had her trailing after him. It helped that he hadn't even seemed to notice her near panic, or the fact that she was pared down to her old, insecure self.

Maybe his thoughts hadn't made the same mental leap. Maybe, to him, she was still just boring Berkley, a girl hardly worth noticing—then or now.

The idea relieved her.

And oddly, it caused a stirring of resentment. She'd changed a lot, in every...okay, *most*...ways possible. To prove it to herself, she hitched her chin. "How can you not know what drinks you have?"

"I have other things on my mind." Standing aside, he stretched out one muscular arm to hold open the wooden door.

Um, yeah. That long reach did interesting things to his chest and shoulders.

His gaze was on her, patiently waiting for her verdict.

It felt like a test, so screw it. She sidled past with Hero. Accidentally, *on purpose*, she inhaled the scent of warm, sweat-damp man mingled with the fresh outdoors. *Intoxicating*. That was, *if* she could be intoxicated…but she couldn't, because for real, she didn't care about men in *that* way anymore.

He brushed past her as he came in, leading the way through an empty living room that was definitely under construction, into a kitchen that appeared functional.

"So you worked on the kitchen first?"

"Enough to make it usable." He grabbed a black T-shirt off the back of a chair and pulled it on.

Shame. Or maybe it was good. She'd done enough ogling this morning.

He opened a big white fridge and began rummaging around past numerous food bags.

"What is all that?"

"The bags? I get my dinner from Saul's restaurant."

"Wow. Looks like you really worked up an appetite." His fridge was crammed full.

After a short laugh, he explained, "I buy enough to cover the whole week. Between the T-shirt shop and working here, I don't have much time to cook. I buy seven entrées from Saul, along with a bunch of sides, then all I have to do is choose what I want and nuke my meal."

Amazing. "What about breakfast and lunch?"

He found two waters, a Coke and a bottle of iced tea. After setting them all on the table, he said, "There's a smaller fridge at the shop in town. I keep lunch meat and bread there. Break-fast is usually coffee and a protein bar."

Okay, so that was how he stayed so ripped. He deprived himself of food while working all day. "Balanced meals are important."

"I get by." He nodded at the drinks. "Here are your choices. What do you think?"

She thought she didn't want to take a single thing from him, given that'd leave him with less.

"Berkley," he said, dragging out her name like a complaint. "You won't leave me short on supplies. I have to be at the shop tomorrow morning and I'll grab more drinks on my way home."

Refusing him now would be rude, so she smiled and reached for a bottle of water. "Thanks." Coffee would have been even better, but his carafe was empty. She tipped her bottle at the bare walls on one side of the kitchen "So what's going on here?"

"Do you have a good imagination?"

Once, years ago, she'd imagined herself recovered from pub-lic scorn, a functioning, happy person, even when that dream had seemed far, far out of reach. Now, living here, that dream was reality. "Sure. Great imagination. Lay it on me."

The curve of his mouth showed admiration. "The upper part of this wall, from here and including that small corner, will be white subway tiles, with the oven and stovetop here, a few cabinets and a dishwasher below. The sink will be in that corner. I'm taking out the rest of that wall and replacing it with sliders that'll open to the side yard. The counter will be stained concrete."

"Sweet. What color stain?"

"Dark brown, to reflect the window trim and wood floor-ing."

She looked down and found rustic wood beneath her feet. "Huh. Original?"

He nodded. "I'll replace a board or two, sand out the rough spots, then give it a fresh coat of stain, finished with polyurethane. Overall, the floor is in great shape."

Getting into his description, she asked, "Stainless steel appliances?"

"The kitchen is small, so I figured white. They'll blend with the cabinets and subway tile to make it feel bigger."

"Love it. What else?"

"This old beat-up table." He smoothed his hand over the marred surface. "It'll be replaced with a bar and some stools to free up floor space and give a little more prep area."

"Do you ever cook?"

"Not much. You?"

She was actually a great cook, and she enjoyed it, but for years she'd only had herself to care for. "Not often." That should have been the end of her statement, but somehow more words tumbled out. "I can cook." *Damn it.* "Not bragging, just saying." *Double damn.* Defensively, she lifted her chin. "I'm actually good at it." *Just shut up.* She clamped her lips together, determined to keep any further thoughts private.

"Maybe when my house is done, you can help me celebrate, like a housewarming gift or something, by fixing dinner here. Sort of break in the place."

Appalled by the invitation, she opened her mouth, but she had no idea how to decline.

He saved her by moving on with a quick smile. "How about I show you around? It's coming together, but you're the first person to see it."

He seriously didn't seem to notice that she was a mess today, or that she was babbling about things she'd rather not discuss.

She dredged up a shrug. "Sure, as long as you don't mind Hero snooping around, too."

"Not at all." Lawson paused. "He doesn't mark his territory or anything, does he?"

Fighting a grin, she replied, "Only outside."

"Yeah, well, he can piddle on all the trees and rocks he wants. Maybe it'll keep the raccoons away." He went down a hallway, then stopped at a door. "Guest bath."

She peered around him. "Wow, it's bigger than I expected."

"I hear that a lot."

It took her a second, but the double entendre sank in, and when she glanced at him—standing far too close as they both crowded into the bathroom doorway—she saw his mischievous grin and the humor in his light brown eyes.

Huffing a laugh, she said, "Men! You're all braggarts." *Dear God. Did I just make a joke about male anatomy?* Unheard of. In her experience, men weren't funny. Absurd, maybe. Often obnoxious.

Sometimes total heartless dicks.

A rush of heat poured through her system, making her skin burn and her throat tighten.

Smoothly, Lawson said, "I got rid of the tub to make the room feel bigger. The white tiled shower and glass door help with the illusion."

Doing her best to recover—*again*—she said, "You must be a neat freak to be able to keep all this white clean."

Looking her in the eyes, he said, "I grew up in the same place you did, Berkley. Maybe the inside of your house was a little nicer, but in ours, nothing was ever white, or even clean for that matter. The way my folks smoked, nicotine layered everything we owned. On humid days, it dripped from the ceiling. When I left, I decided I'd never live like that again."

The words, said dispassionately, still carried an emotional punch. He'd always been so confident that even as a high school boy he'd stood out. There'd been the people like her, those just trying to survive. Pitiful and sometimes desperate. The many addicted to drugs and alcohol. And the bullies and thugs, taking advantage of others. The abusers.

And there'd been Lawson Salder...in a league all his own.

In some indefinable way, he'd boldly owned his space, unbothered by the threats around him, neither joining the gangs nor inflicting cruelty on the vulnerable.

He'd seemed so above it all, she'd never considered how their shared beginning might have affected him—which was maybe selfish of her, because he was right. The street they'd lived on had been filthy, in ways beyond the aesthetics.

"I'm sorry."

He nodded his acceptance. "I'm not fanatical about being clean," he said, "and when you see the bedroom, you'll know I'm messier than some."

See his bedroom?

"I like organization. I like things to be bright." His gaze met hers. "I shook off the grime and stench of the past long ago."

She'd tried to do the same, damn it, but for her, that big scandal had left an indelible mark, a jagged scar—whether he could see it or not.

As if she weren't standing there ruminating about the past, he walked on. "Down here are two other bedrooms, although they're empty right now and will probably stay that way until everything else is done. Not like I have overnight guests."

Was he, like her, without family now? The things they had in common were starting to add up. Yet, the ways in which they differed were vast.

"These stairs lead to my bedroom and a much smaller private bathroom. Those are already done." Watching her intently, he asked, "Want to go up?"

Hero hurried forward. Clearly, the dog was all for more exploring, yet she held back. She shouldn't want to see the rest of his house, but she did.

It disconcerted her how Lawson made talking about the past seem so easy, just tossing it out there like a grocery list or the weather from last week. She'd never been able to do that. For her, any mention of the past, even thinking of it, still caused her pain. Avoidance had been her way of coping.

Bury it, plant a tree on top, move on.

Only now, with Lawson here in Cemetery, it appeared that option had been snatched away.

Hero paused by the stairs and looked at her, probably unsure why they were standing in the hallway. Lawson waited calmly while she stood as motionless as a rabbit just sighted—before it bolted away.

Only she didn't want to bolt. Not this time.

Something about Lawson's approach to life, his "let's just move on without making a thing of it," helped to blunt the edge of her uneasiness. For the first time since arriving and finding him as a neighbor, she drew a full, deep breath.

When she released it, she said, "Lead the way."

Damn, she impressed him.

Like a movie playing before him, Berkley's thoughts had flitted over her face with picture-perfect clarity. She'd been tense since discovering him. Her expressive features were easy to read, but there were other clues as well, especially the rigid way she held her shoulders, as if bracing herself for negativity.

He still didn't know what she'd been doing in the woods, and her obvious wariness pained him.

But he sure liked the look of her this morning.

Fresh, a little messy, her face clean of makeup and her cheeks flushed from her walk. Sometimes she seemed bold and confident, but then there were moments when she reminded him of the young girl she used to be, stuck in a horrid situation with a dying mother and public humiliation hanging over her head.

Acutely aware of her and Hero trailing behind him, Lawson reached the top of the open stairs and stepped aside. This room, along with the connecting bath, was the first he'd finished. He could deal with the construction mess below, tackling it day by day, envisioning how it'd look in the end.

But he'd never again sleep in a cramped, dingy space, with scratchy sheets that stunk of smoke and sweat.

"It's not white," she teased as she stepped into the room and looked around with awe. "You're like a designer or something. Everything looks amazing."

He ran a hand over the back of his neck, mildly uncomfortable with showing her his private dwelling. In fact, he wouldn't have, except that he'd needed to do something to remove the shadows of sadness in her eyes. Why the hell had he taken offense at her "neat freak" comment? Dredging up the past hadn't been his intent, and yet the words were out there before he could censor them. He didn't discuss those days with anyone. Ever.

So why did it feel so natural with Berkley? Maybe because he knew she'd understand.

She meandered to the custom wall of windows and gazed out. "Such an incredible view." Glancing back at him, she asked, "This is all new?"

He nodded. "The two standard windows didn't cut it for me." Now custom windows, cut to fit together, filled the entire wall all the way up to the peak of the cathedral ceiling. This space, more than any other, was strictly for him. His comfort, his retreat. It was all geared to match his personal preferences and habits.

"It's like you've framed the lake."

Exactly how he'd envisioned it. Smiling, he said, "At night I can see the stars."

"And in the morning the sun blinds you?"

Teasing again? He did like seeing her in this mood, less defensive, more relaxed. "I've always been an early riser, so I don't mind."

"You're awfully handy. You worked in construction?"

"Carpentry, but I'm a licensed electrician and plumber, too."

"Holy smokes. Talent."

He shrugged. Basically, he had experience with anything and everything he needed to know to restore a crumbling house.

"So why a T-shirt shop?" she asked, still strolling around the room with Hero close on her heels.

It was amusing that the dog seemed to show interest in anything that interested her. He really was a smart pooch.

"I've traveled a lot. All over the country and to different places around the world."

She shot him a look. "No kidding?"

It wasn't all it was cracked up to be, but he wouldn't say that to her now, not with her opening up and honestly engaging. "That was the out for me. From where we both started, I mean."

The second he mentioned it, her enthusiasm dimmed. Undaunted, he explained, "I signed on for some heavy construction, basically traveling wherever the company went. A lot of it was cleanup work after disasters, so from coast to coast." He'd seen awful things. Death. Destruction. Desperation. Focusing on a better future had been his salvation, his way of coping with the day-to-day hardships.

Cautiously, she remarked, "Sounds like an adventure."

Maybe to someone who liked to romanticize things. "The lodging wasn't the best, but I kept to myself, got in as much work as I could and socked away a fair amount of money. Guess I caught on quick, because more opportunities kept pouring in." He paused, thinking back over the years. "There are a lot of good people in the world. I don't know about you, but I hadn't really considered that." He'd set out on his own carrying a massive chip on his shoulder and determined to do whatever was necessary to be different.

Different from his parents. From his hometown. From his upbringing and environment.

"Good men were patient with me, teaching me and…" Often praising him.

Honest to God, he'd liked how that felt. Before then, he hadn't had much praise in his life.

Emotion twisted in his guts, but he tamped it down real fast.

Glancing around, trying to see the room through her eyes, he wondered what she really thought. "I wanted to soften it a little, you know? The white is great in other areas, but not here." The pale gray rug nearly covered the entire hardwood floor, and his striped gray-and-tan comforter went with the rattan chair and gray bookcase. "A sterile setting didn't seem right for sleeping."

"I see your point." She meandered over to his books. "You do a lot of reading?"

"More so than TV. It's a great way to unwind in the evening."

Picking up one heavy book, she quirked a brow in doubt and read the title aloud. "*It Comes for You*?"

"Edge-of-your-seat reading. Imagine an evil spirit that methodically terrorizes you, then feeds off your fear, growing stronger until he can devour you."

She tucked in her chin. "I'd rather not." Quickly, she put the book back in place. "I'd never be able to sleep if I read something like that."

It struck him that her past and what she'd gone through were similar to the dark threat in the book. He'd found a way to move on, but was the same true for Berkley? He didn't think so. Not entirely. "Fictional monsters don't scare me." Wishing he could get closer to her, that he could offer some comfort, he said quietly, "It's the things real people can do that's disturbing."

She shot him a glance. "Yeah, well."

The opening was there. She could talk about it with him, if only she would.

Her lips curled—and she dodged the opportunity. "Living alone in the woods hadn't bothered me, but now I might be imagining all kinds of things."

Living in the woods? So that's how she'd showed up at his door? She had a place nearby?

Propping a shoulder on the wall, Lawson said, "I showed you mine. Will you show me yours?"

Those lively blue eyes, free of the dramatic makeup, flared wide.

"The shelter?" he clarified, while fighting a grin. She was so easy to bait. "Where you live?"

"Oh." She touched a hand to her hat, adjusted it and nodded. "Sorry, I'm not at my best right now. With my outfit or my wits, apparently. My days start so early that I basically wash my face, brush my teeth and get to work." She lifted the water bottle. "Would've been better if this was coffee, but I appreciate it all the same."

"I started with the dawn, but didn't think the noise would disturb anyone, since I didn't know anyone else was around."

"The shelter is on the other side of the woods, with my house next to it." She walked over to look through the window facing his side yard. He knew she'd see his clothesline there, along with the laundry he'd hung out last night. "I'd been just about finished with chores and anxious for some breakfast when we heard your chain saw. Now I need sustenance to think clearly."

He'd offer her something, but he wasn't even sure what he had in the way of breakfast food.

"Finding you here…" She hesitated, then finally faced him, her manner once again guarded. "I mean, both of us being in Cemetery is shock enough. But neighbors? That seems like a really sucky twist of fate, don't you think?"

3

Berkley hated feeling guilty, but for an entire week, the awful emotion had gnawed at her.

What she'd said to Lawson had most definitely sounded like an insult. *Sucky twist of fate.* Yeah, how else was he supposed to take it?

She hadn't meant it to be mean, but after she'd made a fast exit with the excuse that she needed to get back to work—which hadn't been a lie—and without even thanking him for the tour of his house, she could only imagine what he thought of her.

Since then, she'd avoided seeing him.

Thinking about him? That she couldn't avoid. It was worse at night when she could hear a million crickets chirping in the woods behind her house, when stars covered the sky and the scent of the lake filled the air.

She knew Lawson was experiencing all those same things. Probably enjoying them just as much, too.

What would it be like to share?

No. Giving her a head a shake, she reminded herself that she'd been down that stupid road once before and was permanently marred because of it.

Never again.

Midday, one of her two part-time workers, Whitley Teeter, a bubbly, sweet twenty-two-year-old woman who loved animals and possessed infinite patience, arrived to exercise the dogs. Earlier in the week, she and Whitley had cautiously introduced the newly arrived animals to each other to ensure there wouldn't be any conflicts. Most got along great with zero issues, but there seemed to be some natural pairings taking place. Like friends choosing besties.

Using a few of the enclosed runs out back, they allowed the dogs a chance to frolic in the grass and chase balls and bark happily at each other. Berkley was overseeing that when Betty showed up.

She would never get used to seeing little Betty Cemetery, a spry eighty-seven-year-old, climbing from her car. That seemed to be the woman's most difficult part of driving—getting in and out. Perhaps her legs weren't as flexible as they'd once been, but otherwise she did great.

Wearing a loose, flowery dress and carrying a clutch purse, Betty smiled at the animals as she made her way over to Berkley. "Oh, how I love seeing this. Indeed I do. Such a grand idea to get our own shelter. Someday we may need to expand it, even. Every dog and cat should have a loving temporary home until they find their family."

See? That was why Berkley adored the woman. "My mother would have cheered you on. She loved animals, too." On impulse, she embraced Betty, giving the elder a snug but careful hug that left her flustered.

"Yes. Your mother." She smoothed her short, gray hair even though not a single strand was out of place. "Sounds like a lovely woman."

"She was." Why had she mentioned her mother now, though? Perhaps that visit a week ago with Lawson was still dredging up memories. "She was ill for a lot of years." Too many. "But we had an older dog who remained her companion right up to the end. They were practically inseparable."

Betty's gaze softened. "When did she pass away?"

"I was not quite nineteen." Berkley often wondered if the stress she had inadvertently caused her mother was the final straw. Drawing a breath, she looked out at Whitley as she ran along with the dogs, playing. "Our rooms were close together. Her dog, Baby, scratched at my door, and of course I knew." She could still recall being jerked awake, her heart drumming in dread, and then discovering that the inevitable had finally happened.

Her mother had suffered as she'd faded, but Berkley had selfishly prayed anyway, prayed as she'd stumbled from the bed, as she'd run with Baby to her mother's room. Prayed as she'd tried to revive her mother...

Tears burned her throat, and it infuriated her. She shouldn't still be this weepy about it.

"Anyway," Berkley said, ignoring the scratch in her voice. "Baby lived for another year, but he grieved, maybe as much as I did. We consoled each other, and I'll always be grateful that my mother had him."

"And that you had him."

Berkley nodded. That little dog had saved her from sinking into despair. "Caring for him had kept me going." Even when she'd wanted to give up. "After he passed away, I knew what I wanted to do."

"Continue caring for animals," Betty said with quiet conviction.

"They deserve it." And Berkley liked to think that she deserved the love they returned so freely.

A perfect example was the way Hero plopped down and leaned against her, almost making her stumble into Betty.

They were quietly laughing when a flash of black sped past them.

"What in the world?" Betty exclaimed.

"Cheese!" Berkley saw her sometimes-feral pet cat, Cheese, leap onto Betty's car and stop on the roof with something black, like clothing or a towel, caught in her teeth.

Thankfully, it wasn't a critter. Cheese still considered herself a mighty hunter, and with the woods all around, she had her pick of things to torment.

"I'm sorry," she said to Betty. "You'll now have paw prints all over your car."

Uncaring about that, Betty asked, "What does she have?"

"No idea, but Cheese is a terrible thief, so it could be anything."

A second later, Lawson burst from the woods, then drew up short, seeing that he'd come onto the shelter property.

With a deep warning bark, Hero had lurched in front of Berkley, but now that he saw it was Lawson, he started a jubilant jiggling dance on his way to greet him.

It was obvious Lawson had been running, probably trying to catch her klepto cat. Although his forehead looked a little damp and his hair was more disheveled than usual, he wasn't all that winded.

Once again shirtless, he faced Berkley and Betty with a frown. Even though he was clearly irate, he still dropped a hand to idly stroke Hero's head and neck.

"My, my," Betty said low. "Are the men getting better looking or is my eyesight deceiving me?"

"I don't know about all men," Berkley muttered, "but this

one is put together fine." Even as she said it, she tried to take the words back. She blinked at Betty. "I mean…"

Betty's grin creased the fragile skin of her face. "I was young once. Believe me, I understand."

It was a potent mixture, Berkley decided. Lawson inspiring newfound admiration, and Betty being so easy to talk to. Combined, she didn't stand a chance, so she tried to clamp her lips together and stay silent.

Straightening one long arm to point at Cheese, Lawson growled, "That cat stole my boxers."

Huh. So it was underwear that Cheese had?

"Do tell," Betty said. "So you're…what do the young people call it?" she asked Berkley. "Commando?"

Hearing that from Betty almost made her laugh, but then she wondered, *Is he?* It took a lot of effort to keep her gaze on his face and off his shorts.

"The cat didn't steal them *off* me." Lawson rolled his eyes. "I was collecting my laundry from the line, and the little thief grabbed them and ran off."

Berkley confided to Betty, "He hangs his laundry out to dry."

"No dryer, dear?"

Aggrieved, Lawson said, "Not yet, but I'll get one soon."

"He's remodeling his house," Berkley explained. "It looks incredible, but I'm guessing with working full-time at the T-shirt shop, he's had to prioritize."

"Exactly." After glaring at the cat, Lawson inhaled and released a deep breath, becoming marginally more relaxed. "I only take my stuff to the laundromat once a week. In between, I hand-wash."

Berkley folded her arms. "Proprietor, salesman, builder and launderer. A man of many talents."

He narrowed his eyes at her, but it didn't feel hostile as much as…intense.

"Ran out of undies, did you?" Betty asked.

His mouth twitched. "Men do not wear *undies*, Betty. They wear boxers or briefs."

"And you're a boxer kind of man, I take it?"

He put his nose in the air in a comical way. "I like variety."

Unable to hold her standoffish manner, Berkley cracked a grin. "They're black, though, not white." In an aside to Betty, she said, "He has a preference for white."

With his gaze holding hers, he walked closer. "Variety, remember? Black, gray, navy blue, white…"

"Red?" Betty asked, as if there'd be a test. "Green?" She brightened. "Oh, I know. Purple." She turned to Berkley. "Wouldn't he look striking in purple?"

Her grin widened. "I dunno." She pretended to mull it over. "I'm thinking sunny yellow."

Instead of being embarrassed by their teasing, Lawson stopped right in front of her and said, "You're imagining me in my boxers."

He stated it as a fact, causing her face to go hot as she sputtered denials.

Betty quipped, "Well, I am, certainly. What do you expect when your underwear is being tossed around Cemetery?"

"I didn't *toss* anything," Lawson grumbled. "That cat is a crook."

They all turned to see Cheese now curled up comfortably on the boxers, using them as a bed—on Betty's car—and watching them with her large yellow eyes.

"Aww," Betty said. "I think you should let her keep them."

"Are we talking Berkley or Cheese?"

Berkley choked, and without thinking better of it, she gave Lawson a shove. Or tried to, anyway. The man was rock-solid and didn't budge. All she managed was to get Lawson and Betty both laughing. Betty even braced a hand on Lawson's forearm, as if she needed help staying upright in her hilarity.

Many people in the town considered the matriarch stuffy and strict, and they always seemed to be extra proper and mannered around her.

Berkley didn't know how to be proper and mannered, and besides, around the shelter, Betty was always more relaxed, open and friendly, and the elder had a wicked sense of humor.

Animals did that for people, bringing joy in unexpected ways.

Winding down on her laughter, Betty wiped her eyes, patted Lawson and smiled at Berkley. "I came today to help walk the dogs. You don't mind, do you?"

Thrilled for a different focus, Berkley said, "Of course not. You're wonderful with them. Just let Whitley know and she can make sure you don't get one of the more rambunctious animals." She didn't want Betty dragged or tripped. Some of the dogs were still learning manners.

Hero came to attention, his tail swinging. Betty bent to pat the dog's head. "Is it okay for him to go along, too?"

"Sure. Hero is great with the new animals. He's not leashed here because he doesn't stray off, and in fact, he helps to keep the others corralled."

"Perfect. Come on, then, Hero. Let's go visit."

Once Betty and the dog walked off, the air around her and Lawson grew remarkably warmer, making it more difficult to breathe.

"Is it always so chaotic around here?"

Understanding his meaning, she, too, glanced at the scene, with dogs barking, and chatting people coming and going, her workers busy supervising. Birds sang overhead from the trees. From somewhere inside the shelter, she could hear cats meowing. "Yes," she said. "It is. Not at all the order and neatness you seem to prefer."

"Oh, I don't know. This is an enjoyable kind of chaos."

Because his gaze rested on her, Berkley felt herself tensing.

"You do that a lot, you know."

She turned up her face to meet his eyes. Lawson was so blasted tall. Not that she was a short woman, but next to him… "Do what?"

He cupped her left shoulder, his fingers lightly massaging while his thumb pressed. "You tense up, like you're bracing for impact. Am I so scary?"

Working up a very real frown, she said, "You don't scare me at all." *Such a lie.* In many ways, he terrified her.

"The memories do, then."

Her lungs compressed, and she gasped for air. *How dare he say such a thing?*

"Relax. I can feel how your muscles are knotted." He had the audacity to step behind her so he could rub both shoulders.

Oh God, it felt like heaven—but at the same time, she was ready to jump out of her skin from unfamiliar sensations. "This is obscene," she whispered.

"Do you want me to stop?"

He'd asked that way too close to her ear, and now her ear was tingling, too. Very distracting.

"Should I take your silence to mean you're at a loss for words?"

It was better than her saying a lot of things she didn't want to say. "Maybe."

"How does it feel?"

Like I'm going to melt. "Good."

"There ya go."

She heard the smile in his tone, as if she'd pleased him with the admission. It took a lot of effort not to let her head drop back. "I'm sorry Cheese stole your shorts."

"Where did you get the name Cheese?"

She mulled that over, then decided, *Why not?* "So, I have a super-susceptible appetite." An understatement, actually. "Someone mentions food, or I see a snack in an ad, maybe on a commercial, and I want it." Not entirely accurate. "I *crave* it."

"Pretty sure that's the point of advertisements."

Definitely for people like her. "On the day I found Cheese, I'd seen a commercial with a ham-and-cheese sandwich." Good grief, the man had magic fingers. For a second there, she forgot what she was saying while she concentrated on holding back a groan.

"So you wanted a sandwich?"

Right. She had to keep up her end of this convo or he'd probably stop. "I had ham, bread, lettuce, mayo, even a tomato."

He leaned down near her ear again. "But no cheese?"

Okay, yeah, time to call a halt before he seduced her just by breathing in her ear. Reluctantly, she stepped away, then turned to face him, trying to act like none of it had happened, or at least that she hadn't reacted quite so strongly to his hands. "I had to make a grocery run, but on the way, it started raining. Not a soft, drizzly rain, but a raging downpour. Buckets of rain, you know? The kind where the wipers can't keep up."

"I know what you mean." Hands on his hips, he listened, appearing engrossed in the story.

Shirtless.

He looked engrossed *shirtless*, and it should be illegal for a man to look like him, especially in front of a woman like her, meaning a woman who did not want to notice a man's body.

"So," she said, trying to regroup and not stare at his chest. Or his pecs. Or that downy line of hair on his abdomen… Oh crap. She was looking!

She snapped her attention up so fast, her eyes ached. "I had to slow down, right?" Saying it quickly helped to distract her, so she zoomed through the rest of the story. "Then I pulled over to the side of the road. I figured I'd wait it out. A lot of other cars were doing the same. I was just sitting there, listening to the rain pound on the hood and wondering if I was nuts for still wanting that damn cheese, when bam! A cat landed against the windshield."

Lawson straightened with a scowl. "What do you mean, she landed?"

"It almost startled a scream out of me! One second I was lost in the fury of the storm, and then—cat! Not just any cat, either. No, Cheese was a pushy little thing. She stared in at me and I saw her mouth constantly opening with really demanding meows. I couldn't hear her, not with all the other noise, but I rolled down my window, and do you know what she did?"

Shaking his head, Lawson asked, "What?"

"She jumped off the hood, and before I could open the door to try to get her, she jumped in the window. Into my lap. *Soaking* wet. For real, her fur was like a sponge. And the stinker just kept rubbing against me. All over me. I thought maybe she was cold, but I didn't have anything to wrap her in."

Lawson searched her face, then said, "You were wearing clothes."

She winced. "Yeah, clothes that were mostly drenched with rainwater and cat fur. A nasty mix."

A slow smile appeared on his handsome face. "You took off your shirt anyway, didn't you, Berkley?"

Flushing, she wondered how he could possibly know her so well. "Um…"

"You did, and then you wrapped up the cat to keep her warm, and since you couldn't go topless to the grocery store for cheese—"

"I was wearing a bra," she argued.

"—you named the cat Cheese."

Yup, he knew her. "I got Cheese," she said, "just not the kind I could put on a sandwich. Instead, I ate ham and mustard, which was okay, because at least Cheese wasn't still out in the storm." They both looked over at the cat, who was now dozing…on Lawson's boxers. "Poor little thing was half-starved and covered in fleas. I fed her in the laundry room, then immediately gave her a flea bath. Let me tell you, Cheese was not a fan. She's never entirely given up her feral ways." She gave Lawson the side-eye. "And she's always been a thief."

"Meaning I can expect more things to go missing?"

"Probably." She added in another rush, "I'm sorry, but it's just her way."

Lawson smiled. "At least now if I can't find something, I'll have a reason to check in here. And that, Berkley Carr, means you might be seeing me more often." With that, he sauntered over, boldly lifted the cat into his arms and took back his boxers.

Did he not know that cats had murder mitts? Cheese certainly wasn't declawed—such a thing was inhumane—and she'd just explained that the cat was still feral in many ways.

For most, Cheese was more of a "pet me with your eyes" kind of cat. She didn't like strangers to touch her.

With Lawson, she appeared too surprised to react, and the man wasn't even wearing a shirt!

Yet something about the confident, gentle way he handled Cheese must have done the trick, because the cat was on her best behavior.

He returned and handed Cheese to her. "I like that story, especially how it turned out."

"Me with a thieving cat?"

"You caring enough to save her." He gave Cheese a stroke, smiled at Berkley and walked away, back into the woods.

Berkley looked at Cheese, who looked back, both of them nonplussed over what had just happened. "Thank you for not shredding that very nice chest. You showed great restraint."

Too bad she couldn't claim the same.

Now she wondered if she could convince Cheese to steal something else.

The past eight hours had been the longest of her life. Lark Penny couldn't remember another time where she'd had to deal with such flighty customers. Actually, *flighty* was putting it mildly. Vain, verbose and vacuous. A trifecta of *V*'s, that was what the beachgoers had been. No amount of hairstyling or complimenting had appeased the ridiculous women. Literally, her ears hurt from listening to their complaints, often topped by outrageous laughter.

Usually she liked everyone, man and woman alike. Kids and old people. Introverts and extroverts. Today she'd had to deal with some weird variation of women on the hunt…or something. In between demands, they'd very inappropriately commented on men they'd seen at the lake. Conquests would take place, Lark had no doubt about that.

Thinking to stroll along the sandy beach and clear her head, she drove to the lake instead of heading home, and found a parking spot. The air was clean, early evening was a little cooler, and the sights were incredible. Then she spotted the *V*'s—the very trio of beach beauties who had tried her patience—still on the prowl. Lark had to admit, they looked great with the backdrop of the early evening sunlight reflecting off the lake.

Maybe if she looked like that, she'd live in a bikini, too… No. With her fair skin, she'd need a bucket of sunscreen. Nothing sexy in that.

Changing her mind on her destination, she left her sporty little car and headed in the opposite direction, away from the body of water.

Being somewhat new to town didn't slow her down. She'd made a point of finding all the different businesses—a girl liked to be prepared—and had even introduced herself to as many proprietors as possible.

Good Lord, she was the queen of alliteration today.

Smiling to herself, she headed for the barbecue restaurant. Apparently, this was a day for indulgence.

In minutes, she stepped through the door and was greeted by air-conditioning and the laughter of a busy crowd. She didn't see any empty tables, so she headed to the bar, where she spotted an empty stool. To the right of the seat was an obvious couple, angled toward each other and in close conversation.

To the left was a dark-haired man sitting alone. Broad shoulders strained the fine fabric of his blue button-up shirt worn over faded jeans. He had the sleeves rolled up over hair-dusted forearms. Keeping his concentration on a plate of food before him, he didn't notice her approach.

Lark cleared her throat.

Nothing. It was as if the rest of the busy restaurant didn't exist.

Lightly, she touched his shoulder. "Excuse me."

His neck stiffened, then his head jerked around. Through black-rimmed glasses, he stared at her hand in surprise. Older than her, judging by the faint touch of silver at his temples, but definitely not *old*. Midthirties, maybe.

Intense. That was the first description to imprint on her brain. So very, very intense.

"I'm sorry to interrupt your meal," she said while removing her hand.

Dark eyes stared at her in question.

Oh, he wouldn't be an easy one to win over. Did she want to win him over? Yes, maybe she did. "Is this stool taken? If you're saving it for someone—"

"Feel free." He turned back to his food.

Lark barely tempered her smile at his deliberate dismissal. "Is that good?"

His disbelieving gaze swung back to her.

"The food, I mean. I haven't eaten here yet, but it's been a rough day, so I need something totally decadent, usually forbidden and terrible for me. If I was a drinker, I'd order a whiskey, but I can't go that far, so it'll have to be something fried, even greasy, with a lot of flavor and calories."

It took the man three whole seconds to react. Casually, he lifted a napkin and wiped his mouth, then turned slightly to face her, a forearm braced on the bar. "It's my first time here, too, and I had a similar plan in mind." Wearing a slight frown, he adjusted his glasses. "They don't serve whiskey."

Lips twitching, Lark asked, "You tried?"

"No, not really. I researched the place. The whole town, actually."

"Really? That's wonderful. When I relocated here a month ago, I made a point of doing the same. I even went around and met as many business proprietors as I could, just to familiarize myself. Not enough people do that. It's important to know a place, don't you think?"

He looked at her as if unsure what to make of her.

Yes, she had gotten a little too perky and chatty there. It was like meeting a kindred spirit. She instantly wanted to bond, maybe compare notes on outlooks. It was especially refreshing after her trying day at the salon.

A very handsome young man approached and said, "Hey there. I'm Wheeler and I'll be serving you."

She held out a hand. "I'm Lark Penny, new at the salon. Nice to meet you, Wheeler."

His very engaging smile brightened a few watts. "Nice to meet you, Lark." His voice was now a degree deeper, and a little smoother. "What can I get you? Or do you need a menu?"

She turned back to her stool neighbor. "The food?"

Blankly, her Clark Kent look-alike glanced at his half-eaten meal. "The loaded burger is great. They have some kind of special sauce that adds a little zest. Fries are perfectly browned."

"Awesome. I'll have what he's having, with a Coke, light ice." She leaned toward Wheeler. "I need all the caffeine I can get, and ice waters it down."

"You've got it. I'll be right back."

She watched him saunter away to the kitchen. Wheeler was

closer to her age, blond and had dark brown eyes like the man next to her, though the two of them couldn't be more different. Where Wheeler was athletic in build, the other dude was thicker, more solid.

And very appealing.

She shifted around to face him. In this position, her knees almost touched his thigh, a fact that her entire body seemed to note. "Now I've met Wheeler, and most everyone else in the area." Holding out her hand, she said, "And you know my name, so you are…?"

His level brows tweaked together once again. "Oliver Roth." He took her hand in his, and holy smokes, the man had big hands.

The thought darted through her mind that he could easily crush someone with his size, and yet he was so gentle, clasping her fingers only briefly.

"Do you live here, Oliver, or are you just visiting?"

Pensive, he lifted his drink, then took a draw off the straw, possibly giving himself a moment to think. "I've rented a place."

"A home?" she pressed. "Or a business?" Like a quintessential grumpy Gus, his frown increased. "Not to be nosy," she added with a smile. "Just curious."

"Both, actually. That is, I'm renting an apartment, and I've bought a building." He held up a hand, no doubt anticipating more interrogation from her. "I'm opening a fitness spa."

With his overly serious demeanor and lumberjack physique, that didn't really fit. Drill sergeant would work. Construction worker, maybe. But a spa? Before she could grill him further, Wheeler returned with her order and, heaven, it looked and smelled delicious. "Thank you *so* much. I'm ravenous."

Wheeler gave her a crooked grin full of appreciation. At least he wasn't grumpy. "If you need anything else, let me know."

Another customer signaled him, and off he went.

She'd just taken a big bite of her burger, which caused a

hum of appreciation, when a warm body sidled in next to her. She looked up, and there was Lawson. *My, my, my.* Hotties all around.

She savored her burger—and the testosterone in the air.

4

Oliver had seen many women work their wiles, but he had to admit, Lark was so open and friendly about it, most guys wouldn't see it coming. Take Wheeler, for instance. The guy would probably ask her out before she finished her meal.

And now here was another man crowding in next to her. That disgruntled him enough that he returned his attention to his food and the massive task of winning over the town matriarch.

Betty Cemetery did not have wiles. She had picky standards and the determination of a mule. She was no soft granny. More like an iron ruler who wanted things her way, no exceptions.

He heard Lark say, "Lawson, hi."

So yeah, out of the corner of his eye, Oliver watched the scene play out between the two of them. He'd do so until he finished his food, which should be in the next ten minutes as long as he didn't linger.

The man next to her glanced down in surprise. Yeah right. Like he hadn't noticed Lark? Get real. With her big smiles and friendly manner, no man would not notice her…except that Oliver hadn't at first. But then, he had a lot on his mind.

"Lark? Sorry. I don't mean to crowd you. Just trying to get Wheeler's attention so I can pick up my order."

Wheeler noticed him then, gave him a thumbs-up and disappeared into the kitchen.

"No problem," Lark said. "It's busy here, so crowding is expected." Then she turned back to him. "Oliver, have you met Lawson Salder? He owns the custom print shop with the new, beautiful wishing well out front. I can personally vouch for the quality of his products and the excellent service."

"Appreciate the endorsement," Lawson said to her.

Oliver stood and held out a hand. "Oliver Roth. Nice to meet you."

"You, too," Lawson said. "New to town?"

"I was around all spring, choosing property, working out the details, ordering equipment, all that. But I just officially moved here a week ago."

"I've got a year on you, then." Lawson smiled. "Welcome to Cemetery. It's a great place. What business are you in?"

"I'm opening a fitness studio in a week—that is, it'll open if I can get Betty Cemetery and the town council to agree on a few things."

Leaning back on the bar and folding his arms, Lawson advised, "Don't let Betty bulldoze you. She means well, but her love of the town can sometimes turn her into a dictator. In the end she's usually reasonable."

"I must have missed that side of her so far."

They both laughed.

Tilting back to see them, Lark raised her brows in surprise.

"So for Lawson, you just offered all that up. For me, it was like prying out state secrets or something."

Lawson grinned at her. "Were you doing a little bulldozing of your own, Lark?"

She flashed the guy a smile. "Just being my usual friendly self."

Wheeler returned with a few massive, loaded bags of food. "Here you go, Lawson. You're all set."

"Thanks."

"Good heavens," Lark said. "Are you feeding an army?"

Still amused, Lawson shook his head. "This is my dinner for a week. Until I'm done renovating my place, it's a lot easier to microwave a meal."

"A masterful plan," she declared.

The two of them conversed for a minute more, teasing back and forth while Oliver did his best to finish up. He wanted to retreat, to work out his arguments with Betty so he'd be prepared when next he spoke to her.

Naturally, he couldn't concentrate with little Miss Sunshine sitting beside him, bubbling over with effusive charm. How old was she, anyway? Nineteen, twenty? With him being thirty-four, she was far too young for him to be noticing her.

Never mind that the girl had incredibly flawless skin, smooth and pale with the faintest rose hue on her cheeks. Her thick, nearly black hair framing her face offered a pretty contrast, as did those storm-colored eyes framed by dark lashes.

Sinking his teeth into his burger, Oliver tried to banish all the poetic BS from his brain. He didn't care about her skin and hair, her gray eyes or that sweet smile...

Breaking into his thoughts, Lawson said, "I'm at the shop most weekdays." He gathered up his bags. "If you find the time, stop by to chat. I can give you the ins and outs of the town council."

Nice guy. Friendly, welcoming. Oliver nodded. "I appreciate that. Thanks."

Lawson put a hand on Lark's shoulder. "This one could give you a rundown of the vacationers. She's had some unique experiences."

"True that," she said, as if they shared a secret.

What the hell did that even mean? Oliver eyed her, but didn't ask. He wouldn't ask. Instead he nodded at Lawson and then ate two more fries.

Suddenly Lawson glanced out the big front window, went alert at whatever he saw and quickly gave his goodbyes, leaving in a bit of a rush.

After watching him a moment, Lark dug back into her food with gusto.

Silence reigned. Not a companionable silence, either. More like the kind that throbbed with impatience, the kind that built tension until one of them broke.

He had no intention of starting another conversation, and made it clear by putting all his focus on his food.

Of course, that didn't deter Miss Sunshine. After only a few minutes, she sighed. Loudly. "You know you're curious."

He gave her the side-eye and asked with believable confusion, "Are you talking to me?"

Laughing as if delighted by his act, she swiveled around on her stool to face him again. Her shiny hair, just long enough to drift across her shoulders, swung with her movement.

His fingers twitched—and he knew why. He wanted to touch her hair, touch *her*. Feel the softness of both. The warmth.

Didn't matter that he'd been flying solo a little too long, or that she was boldly flirting. Becoming involved with her was not happening. He had priorities, and getting drawn into a dead-end relationship wasn't one of them.

A bubbly, attractive, engaging young woman did not factor into his long-term plans.

"Stylists," she said, while holding a pickle, "are a lot like bartenders. We hear everything, from everyone. Lawson is right. I have a feel for the town already."

"Stylist, as in you do hair?"

"I do hair," she confirmed, "and so much more." Adding a lofty note to her voice, she claimed, "I create beauty, accentuate looks, give complete makeovers and make people feel good about themselves."

And maybe she was a little full of herself, too. "Clearly your endless talents are wasted in Cemetery. Shouldn't you be in Chicago, LA or maybe New York?"

Pink lips curled in a smile that could sway the most cynical of men. "I'm a small-town girl at heart."

Something in her tone, in the way her eyes shifted away from his, told him there was more at play. This time, the silence got to him. "Okay, I'll bite. What wise insights have you learned?"

"None," she said, and now her smile didn't quite reach her eyes. "Lawson and I were just joking."

Not buying it, Oliver said, "You started this," by way of challenge.

"I didn't start anything."

Oliver snorted.

The rude sound caused her mouth to twitch. "Okay, so maybe I did, just a little."

Glad that she was back to teasing, he tipped his drink at her and said, "So let's hear it."

She ate another fry first. "Much as Betty would deny it, a lot of hookups happen on the beach. That means I get plenty of bikini-clad walk-ins wanting their hair quickly styled so they can get back to the beach for an evening stroll."

Dubious, he sipped his drink. She made *evening stroll* sound like a euphemism. "So despite being in and out of the lake, the wind and sun—"

"That stuff can be brutal to hair, and that's all fine when a group is enjoying the water during the day. But for evenings..."

She shrugged. "Seems everyone has given up the joy of a neat ponytail, braid or messy bun, which are all acceptable and casual styles."

His gaze moved over her perfect hair. "Somehow I can't picture you with messy hair."

"It happens, but a really good cut makes it easier to repair."

It was off their original topic, but he asked, "Do you cut your own hair?"

"That's almost impossible to do. I have a friend who used to do it, but now that I'm here…" Her shoulders lifted. "I'll need to see if one of the other stylists at the salon can do it the way I like."

By the second, his curiosity about her, about her life before moving here, expanded. "Your friend is too far away to visit?"

"Yup." She didn't explain. "So anyway, when these women come in, often in their bathing suits, they talk a lot. Who's hot, who's available, who to avoid—that kind of thing." She leaned in to confide, "I didn't tell him, but Lawson is considered prime material." Her gaze slanted to the bar, and she added, "Now that I've met him, I'm guessing Wheeler is, too. See, I've heard mention of the guy working at the restaurant, but wasn't sure who they meant."

He had less than zero interest in "hot guys."

As if she'd read his thoughts, she said, "Know what you should do? Get Lawson to make you up some promotional T-shirts, and get the finest guys to wear them. Guaranteed a lot of women would notice."

Genius advertising. But what really struck him was the way she said it, as if *she* wouldn't be all that interested in either Lawson or Wheeler, and for some damned bizarre reason, he was glad.

Resting a forearm on the bar, he asked, "How old are you, Lark Penny?"

Her brows lifted. "Twenty-four, why?"

A decade younger than him, but not really *too* young. Ignoring her question, he asked, "What size do you wear?"

Her brows went even higher, followed by a light laugh. "I think I need to know why you're asking before I answer."

Finding his first real grin in a week, Oliver said, "So I can make sure your promotional T-shirt fits. Why else?"

Lawson could barely see Berkley by the time he got out of the restaurant. Wearing a wide-brimmed white hat, and with Hero on a leash, she bypassed the beach and headed to the rockier shore of the lake, where vegetation grew in thick grasses, skinny trees and weeds.

Maybe dogs weren't allowed on the sandy beach—or maybe she just wanted to walk alone. He should respect that.

But what if the opposite was true? What if she was lonely?

What if the past still plagued her...?

He didn't like the idea of kind, bighearted Berkley—a woman who loved and protected animals—lying awake at night with foul memories hounding her sleep.

Didn't like it, but understood it.

He stood there hesitating for so long, he nearly lost sight of her. "Screw it." Jogging, he went to his truck, loaded the food into the oversize cooler he'd bought for just this reason, then locked it up and took off in a sprint.

Why did it feel like he needed to catch up to her? She was clearly fine, out walking on a beautiful day. She couldn't be lonely, or she'd have visited again.

He definitely wasn't lonely—and yet, he ran fast enough to catch up to her, past people who gaped at him, dodging around two kids, jumping over a rough-edged rock. In jeans and work boots.

No wonder people stared.

When he finally got near enough to call out to her, he noticed that she'd taken off her sandals, removed her shirt and shorts, and was now wearing a red two-piece bathing suit.

His heart punched hard against his ribs. Naturally, his gaze devoured her. Now, seeing her like this, he was glad she'd sought privacy. In many ways, Berkley felt like his own personal...what? Fantasy? Regret? A combo of both?

She looks amazing.

Body toned from all the work she did around the shelter, yet still curved in the right places, she had a body to draw attention. Standing ankle-deep in the lake, she stared out at the horizon. Lost in thought, or maybe musing over the future.

When her head dropped forward, his heart twisted in actual pain and he automatically got moving again.

Hero heard his noisy approach, turned with a warning bark and nearly jerked her off her feet. She flailed, lost her footing and landed with a splash on her rump.

He should feel guilty, he thought, and instead he grinned as Hero's warning turned into a happy woof, his body wiggling with excitement. And yeah, Berkley's scowling face. Her awkward posture in the lake. Now doused in lake water.

When he was near enough, he slowed to a walk until he could greet Hero properly. "Dude, you are a menace. First you jerk me off my feet by my shorts, and now you've dunked Berkley in the lake." He rubbed the dog's ears and scruff, then patted his sides.

"*He's* not the menace." The leash slapped into Lawson's chest and Berkley snarled, "Hang on to that."

He quickly got hold, but it wasn't an issue. Hero wasn't going anywhere. The dog was far happier to see him than Berkley was. As she sat in the water fuming, he strode closer and smiled as she jammed her now wet hat back onto her head. "Do you need a hand up?"

From beneath the brim, she shot dagger-eyes at him. *While wearing a little red suit.*

You'd think he'd never seen a woman before, given the way he struggled to keep his attention on her angry face. Fact was, though, he'd never seen Berkley like this, showing so much skin.

And what beautiful skin it was.

"Why in the world did you charge us like that?"

"I didn't. I was just…" Jogging? Again, jeans and work boots. He'd sound like an idiot if he said that, so instead he knelt down and asked, "What's wrong?"

The antagonism left her, replaced with disbelief. She slapped the water with an open hand. "What makes you think anything is wrong?"

"I don't know." He felt it, though. Years ago, when he'd see her out and about, her expression had often been firmly neutral. He'd understood that. In the neighborhood where they'd lived, a wrong look could set off a dozen bad reactions. Someone would feel challenged. *What? What the fuck are you looking at?* Or they'd get ideas. *Where you going, baby? Come and play.* The worst was if they felt targeted, because that always resulted in violence.

It was best to be invisible when possible. And when that didn't work, stay utterly blank.

That was how she'd usually been, so neutral that she nearly disappeared—until the scandal.

Seeing the stiffness in her shoulders, he tried a smile. "Come on." He caught her upper arm and helped heft her to her feet. From her waist down, water dripped along her body. "Careful." Tiny waves lapped at his boots, but he didn't care.

Stepping away from him, she irritably slogged through the moss-filled water and over to a flat rock, where she sat with an audible plop.

Hero was at her side in an instant, laying his block-shaped head over her thighs and staring at her in worry.

"I'm okay, bud." She bent over, pressing her face to him and effectively hiding.

The curve of her spine intrigued him, rising from those minuscule briefs, past her narrower waist and up to her drooping shoulders.

Lawson was starting to feel like a dick. Without being invited, he scrunched onto the limited space beside her. He shouldn't—he'd already overstepped enough—but his palm touched her sun-warmed back before he made the conscious decision to do it, and since it was already done, he stroked her. Lightly, gently, a touch of commiseration before he removed his hand. "Rough day?"

Seconds ticked by before she nodded. "The worst."

The crack in her voice sharpened his awareness even more. "Want to talk about it?" The *worst* had to be pretty bad, considering how and where they both used to live.

"No." She drew a slow breath and straightened, her gaze aimed out at the lake. "But I need to get it together because Hero worries."

"Yeah, somehow he's transformed his furry face into grandmotherly concern or something." When her lips quirked, it felt like a gift.

She stroked a hand over the dog's head. "He has the most amazingly expressive face."

Looking at her did awful but incredible things to him, things he didn't want to experience, so Lawson gave his attention to the lake. Mid-June shouldn't be this warm, but the humidity added a degree of misery to the sunshine. "I thought it would smell better here."

Berkley actually laughed, then nudged her shoulder playfully against his side. "Pretty sure there's a dead fish somewhere, probably half-eaten by a gull or something." She wrinkled her nose. "It's especially strong if *someone* causes you to fall into the lake." The look she slanted his way left no doubt where she put the blame for that.

Repetitive lapping of water over rocks, mixed with the chirp of insects and the occasional trill of birds, lent a sort of peace to the day. "It's still peaceful here."

She turned her head to look at him. "You live on the lake. You can enjoy it anytime you want."

You're welcome to enjoy it with me. No, he wouldn't say that. Right now he was slammed with work, both at the shop and on his house. Added to that were the complicated aspects of their history. The unpleasantness. So instead, he said, "Feel free to enjoy it anytime you want."

"That's what I'm doing."

"No, I meant…" What the hell did he mean? If he said, *You can visit it from my property, but without my participation,* he'd just sound like a giant ass. He did some quick editing in his head, and came up with a more pleasant invitation. "You're just a short walk through the woods, right? Be forewarned, though, I don't have a sandy shoreline like this. Mine is all water weeds and the occasional snake or snapping turtle."

She wrinkled her nose. "As enticing as that sounds, I think I'll pass."

He grinned with her. "Eventually I'll add a dock, and maybe get a paddleboat or a fishing boat—something with oars."

"Do you fish?"

"Not so far."

"You've had other things to do." She wiggled her wet toes, stared down the shoreline for the longest time before she said softly, "A dog died today." Subtly, she swiped at her face.

It leveled him that she might be wiping away a tear, but when he glanced at her, her cheeks were dry. Didn't matter, when all that sadness showed in her pretty blue eyes. It nearly shredded his composure.

Instinctively he knew that if he touched her again, she'd lose it, and that would upset her even more. Instead he asked, "One that you're housing?"

She shook her head. "No. I do everything I can to make sure they're healthy, and that they're getting any care they need. Other shelters are overrun, though. So many people ditch their pets, as if they're not important."

He'd witnessed it, here in the States, and around the world. Sadly, sometimes kids and elders were ditched, too.

When she spoke again, her voice was steadier. "A driver saw a dog get hit on a busy road. No one stopped except him."

"Not even the person who hit the dog?"

She shook her head. "The dog was still alive, but badly hurt, so he was afraid to move it. He called a sister shelter in a panic, asking what to do."

"Were they able to help?"

"The Love Shack is closer, so they contacted me..." She took a few uneven breaths, and her voice lowered. "I went as fast as I could, but the dog had passed away before I got there."

Damn. Lawson let his shoulder brush hers. Just that, nothing else. There were times when human contact could make a real difference because it proved you weren't alone—no matter how it sometimes felt. Occasionally it had worked for him, even when the contact came from a stranger.

She didn't move away, so he took that for encouragement.

"The guy who found him said he hadn't suffered. He'd sat with him, talking softly, stroking his side...and then the dog faded away." She blinked twice. "He was upset, but I told him that he'd done the right thing."

So she'd not only had to face that situation, she'd had to comfort someone else. Her strength and compassion amazed him. "That was kind of you."

"I was glad he'd stayed with the dog. He took one of my cards." She cleared her throat. "He also offered to bury the dog. He was...irritated that the driver hadn't stopped."

"You mean pissed off." For only a second, Lawson leaned a little closer. "There's a difference."

She gave a half smile. "Yeah. He was pretty pissed off. It looked as if the dog had been on his own for a while. I'm glad he had company at the end."

"Me, too." Maintaining their slight physical connection, they sat in silence. Even through his T-shirt, he could feel the warmth of her skin, and the sunshine amplified her scent, that of sweet musk. Of woman.

Of this one particular woman.

Hero still fretted, watching Berkley, while she leisurely stroked the dog's neck.

Knowing she must see some awful things in her line of work, he wondered how she handled it, and at the same time, he was glad the animals had her.

She was so different from what he'd imagined when he knew her as a kid. Different, too, from the persona she now projected to the world. Her personal style exuded bold confidence. Edgy jewelry. Fun hair.

A killer red bikini.

Yet in her daily life, she was overall reserved and private. Fascinating conflicts that made him want to know more. About her, her thoughts. Future plans.

He didn't doubt that her direct manner made her more than capable of dealing with people who dropped off unwanted pets. She'd be brisk but polite, and deep down she'd be glad to have the animals so she could care for them properly.

She'd do equally well with people anxious to adopt a new furry friend, probably researching them to ensure the dog or cat would be safe, loved and included.

When the silence stretched out, he asked, "Do sad things like that happen very often?" How many times had she been called to an impossible situation?

She used her hat to fan her face. "There's always something."

When she said nothing more, he got the message: she didn't want to elaborate. Nothing made a guy feel more helpless than wanting, *needing*, to make things better, but not knowing how.

The sun sank lower in the sky, glinting on the metallic hoops in her ear. A light breeze, scented by the lake—and the dead fish—stirred the pink tips of her hair. She was all color, shine and sadness, rolled together.

He should be getting as far away from her as he could. In some indefinable way, she was a threat to his peace of mind, to the new life he wanted here in this odd little town where gossip and a creepy mannequin were the biggest problems. He had a load of work to do yet tonight. The coolers in his truck would only protect the food for so long. It was getting late.

None of that seemed to matter right now. "Is there anything I can do to help?"

She let out a sigh. "Honestly, you already did it."

Didn't that just make him feel ten feet tall? Glad that he hadn't budged, he studied her profile, the line of her small nose and the curve of her rosy cheek. Those lips that had softened...

The urge was there to put his arm around her, to ask more questions, but instead, he remained still, afraid that anything at all might spoil the moment.

She turned his way and gave him a small smile.

Yeah, pretty sure he just fell into her gaze. Smack-dab into all that blue. "I'm glad I spotted you, chased you down, accidently caused you to fall in the lake and didn't let your grumpy face scare me off."

That earned him a grin, which had Hero flagging his whip of a tail hard enough to leave marks.

"Damn, ease up, boy."

"Don't cuss in front of my dog," she reminded him, then added, "And yeah, that tail is almost a weapon, but then his block head is, too." She cuddled the dog closer. "He's left a few bruises on me. Once when I was going in for a kiss, he turned his head and nearly broke my nose." She cupped the dog's face, saying sweetly, "Sometimes, Hero's love hurts."

That concerned Lawson, because although Berkley stood five feet five inches, and wasn't a delicate woman, more like compact, it wouldn't take much for a dog Hero's size to knock her over.

He could see that Hero was a big lover-mutt and never meant any harm. Unfortunately, the dog sometimes had the awkwardness of a puppy and, as Lawson had already pointed out, the fretfulness of a grandma. He also had the heart of a rescuer, so overall, the dog was pretty awesome.

"You have a way with awkward pets."

"Just Hero," she said.

"I disagree. Your thief of a cat has been visiting me."

Her brows lifted. "Oh?"

Right. Look at her playing innocent with her little *Oh?* like she didn't know how sneaky that cat could be. "I've busted her twice trying to steal my things. When she's not doing that, she has her butt in my face."

Expression comical, Berkley said, "Should I ask?"

He gave her a mock frown. "I was squatted down, working on some plumbing, and somehow she got in the house. One minute I was under the kitchen sink facing a drainpipe, and then suddenly a cat tail swiped across my nose. It startled me so badly, I clunked my head on the cabinet and then fell on my ass."

She fought a grin to say with a measure of seriousness, "But you didn't land in the lake, so you can't complain too much."

"Good point." Her skin was now dry, and her nose was turning pink from the sunshine. He liked seeing her like this. Friendlier. More open.

His food might all spoil before he got it home, but at the moment he didn't really care. Helping Berkley lift some of her worries seemed like the most important thing he might do this week. "I looked around, but I couldn't figure out how she got in."

"I'm not surprised. I spent months trying to make her a house cat, just so she'd be protected from predators and accidents, and I worried that she'd leave or get lost." Heaving a sigh, she said, "It was terrible. She screeched like I was mistreating her!"

He cracked a grin. "Poor Berkley. Trying to do the right thing but I guess the cat didn't appreciate having her freedom curtailed?"

"She hated it, and it didn't matter anyway. Cheese kept finding a way out."

"And you worried every time?"

"At first, but then she always came back, so I stopped torturing us both and just let her do her thing while I watched to figure out her pattern. Only once or twice have I had to let her in, and that was in the winter. In the summer, if there's a screen in a window, she'll wiggle in around it somehow. If it's a screen door, she'll open it."

"I have a sliding door, but the screen was closed when I checked."

Berkley tilted toward him and confessed, "I've seen her open *and close* doors that aren't latched. Finding it closed only shows how polite she is."

"No way," he said, just to keep her talking. Every time he was around her, he saw a new facet of her. Antagonistic, vulnerable, proud, determined. And now teasing and happy—probably because pets were her favorite subject. It worked for him.

She put a hand on her heart as if swearing an oath.

All it did was draw his eyes to her chest, to plump breasts cupped in red material.

"One hundred percent true."

Her words shot his gaze back to her face, to a smile that was pure sunshine, and he hadn't known that he liked sunshine so much. He'd lived and labored in countries that were hotter than

Hades, where the sun could roast you, especially while doing heavy construction. To him, a cloudy day meant cooler conditions to accomplish whatever he had on his agenda.

Here in Cemetery it was a little different. A pleasant day brought out the vacationers, which added to his print shop sales, but he was typically indoors until the early evening.

When he was working on his renovations after work, the lowering sun meant a respite from the blistering heat, mosquitoes galore and the extra humidity from the lake.

Sitting here with Berkley, the sun reflecting off the lake seemed nice. Peaceful.

Even the stench of the dead fish didn't bother him.

Taking his silence for interest, she continued. "Totally shocked me the first time Cheese did it. She nudged the door open with one little paw, came in, then nudged at it until she got it closed again."

"You realize how unbelievable that sounds, right?"

As if to convince him, she said, "One time I was soaking in the tub. I was at home alone—I mean, I'm always alone, you know?"

That was a double whammy right there. First putting that particular image in his head, and then squeezing his heart with the easy acceptance of her isolation. He nodded.

"When the bathroom door opened, I almost died of fright—until Cheese stepped in, casual as you please, and then closed the door again."

Okay, yeah, so he was still back there with her soaking in the tub. The visual of that, complete with steam, played out in his mind. Didn't take much imagination to remove the swimsuit from the picture of her now. He could see her with her pink-tipped hair pinned up, all the camouflage of her makeup removed.

And alone. Far too often alone.

Had she ever had a meaningful romantic relationship? He

opened his mouth to ask, changed his mind and affected a look of surprise instead.

Smiling, she shook her head. "The little thief even curled up on my towel."

Lawson rubbed the bridge of his nose, then his mouth. The image remained, blunted only by the casual way she'd stated her relationship status. *I was at home alone—I mean, I'm always alone, you know?* That had to be by choice, and now he wondered if she'd said it like a warning, so he wouldn't get any ideas.

Probably too late.

But the reality was, she'd been incredibly sad over losing an animal, and now she was smiling. He refused to ruin the shift in her mood by turning into a typical "sex on the brain" kind of guy. It was an effort, but he came up with a bland but suitable comment. "Wonder where she learned to do that."

"I wish I knew. Cats are adaptable, and smarter than most people realize."

He'd never really thought about the intelligence of cats one way or the other. "I've never had a pet."

"Never?" she asked with disbelief, like he'd claimed to never bathe or sleep.

"Growing up..." He shook his head, glossing over it as best he could because she'd made it clear she didn't want to reminisce. "I felt bad for the roaches that had to scrounge around our place." Not a lie. His folks were not the domestic type. "I wouldn't have left an actual pet alone with either of my parents while I was at school and work." And he'd worked a lot, going straight from school to various part-time jobs. For him, any credible excuse to stay away from the house was a blessing.

And he'd needed the money. Saving up for an escape had become his obsession early on.

When she averted her face, he verbally pivoted to say, "Once I moved out on my own, I definitely wasn't home often enough to care for a dog or cat, and then I started traveling..."

They sat quietly a moment, each of them snagged on that long-ago time and how utterly miserable it had been.

"I didn't know I wanted pets," she finally said. "Not until my mom passed away and I took over caring for her dog, Baby."

His heart tripped at her softly spoken words. It was a connection, and it was trust. Until that moment, she hadn't even hinted at their roots. Given where they'd come from, he'd understood.

Tentatively, he inched into the conversation with her. "I kind of remember that pooch. Bristly gray fur, like a schnauzer or something, right? I saw you out on the front lawn with him a few times."

"I didn't know you saw me. You never seemed to see anyone."

He took that one on the chin, because yeah, he'd been deliberately aloof, his way of dealing with his circumstances. He didn't do small talk, didn't wave to neighbors.

Overall, he pitied or detested them. The only two emotions he'd allowed himself to feel back then.

Keeping it light, he said, "You'd be hard to miss with the way that dog yapped at everyone."

Again she smiled. "I was probably letting him do his business. My mom…she got to where she couldn't get out of bed." A beat of silence passed, then another.

Lawson felt regret welling inside him. How hard was this for her? What could he do to make it easier?

Emotions shifted over her features, and her voice softened. "When I was away from the house too long, the stinker would go in the corner. I couldn't blame him, since there was no one there to let him out, and he was getting older. Then I discovered piddle papers, these plastic-lined pads for dogs that had accidents, and he was pretty good about using them. I just had to remember to throw the old one away when I got home, and put a clean one out each morning."

Meaning that turned into one more thing for her to do. Get

to school, care for her mother and the house, do the shopping and cooking, and clean up after the dog. "Sounds like a lot of responsibility."

"When you love someone, taking care of them is nothing at all. I was glad to do it."

Were they talking about the dog—or her mother? Lawson couldn't quite read her face, especially since she gave all her attention to Hero, who remained relaxed beside her.

So if the dog wasn't worried, maybe she wasn't too upset discussing this particular topic. He really needed to get his food home, but he couldn't seem to force himself to stand. "I think I'd already moved away before you lost your mother."

She pressed her forearm to her middle, as if she had a stomachache. "You were there for the headline news, right?"

Another shocker: she'd just brought up the scandal.

After a slow exhale, Berkley rolled her eyes. "Don't expire on me."

"No, I…" He what? "I got the feeling you didn't want to talk about it."

"There isn't much to say, is there?" Her jaw worked, her lips compressed. When she spoke, he barely heard her. "It was so freaking awful."

Because she'd had the bad luck to have an affair with a married man.

And not just any married man, but Chad Durkinson, husband to a local news anchor, a hometown girl who'd made it big and was considered a real success story.

"It's the elephant in the room, right?" She smirked at him. "I know you know. You know I don't want to talk about it. So there it sits, taking up space and sometimes making things awkward."

Sometimes… But not always. Mostly, his time with Berkley was interesting, refreshing and in some ways addictive. The more he saw her, the more he wanted to see her. The more she shared, the more he wanted to know.

With barely muted defiance, and a touch of hope, she met his gaze. "Not that it matters anymore, but I thought he was single. That's what he'd told me. If I'd known Chad was married, none of it ever would have happened."

So the hope was for him to believe her? Lawson didn't have a single doubt. "He was a lying bastard."

For once, she didn't chide him for swearing. Relief widened her eyes a little, and then she nodded. "He was that and more, but I didn't see it until it all blew up in my face."

An apt description for the way the story had been sensationalized. "Durkinson was a complete coward, too. He let you take all the heat."

Tipping her head back, she stared up at the sky. "That's not how the public saw it. Chad was the poor victim, don't you know, somehow bewitched by the dog-faced nobody who wanted to use him...for something." Her gaze slanted his way. "No one ever really specified what I was supposedly after."

He nearly flinched at the moniker—*dog-faced nobody*. Obviously, she'd heard—or read—all the insults thrown her way. "You've always been attractive, Berkley. Whoever started that name was probably jealous."

"Jealous of *me*? Hardly." Then she muttered, "The name sure caught on, though."

Only because Durkinson's wife had used her access to local media to trash Berkley far and wide. What dirty work she couldn't accomplish herself—like the absurd name-calling—her loyal fan base was happy to handle for her. There were a few social media defenders for Berkley, just not enough to counter the group taunts. Even online news sites and local commentators had something to say about it.

Berkley huffed. "I never quite got why everyone painted him as such a catch. I mean, I liked him because he liked me and..."

And her life had been a giant cyclone of sadness. An older guy who treated her kindly, who gave her reprieves from the poverty and treated her dying mother with respect, would have felt like a gift. "The dude was doughy," he grumbled. "A thirty-year-old man-baby with a receding hairline."

Snickering, she said, "That's mean."

"But true—and don't you dare defend him."

"Wouldn't dream of it. Especially since it wasn't his looks that won me over." She turned thoughtful for a moment. "Chad was just an outlet, you know? A way to forget about things for a little while. Seeing him was separate from everything else that was falling apart."

"I get it." For Berkley, the asshole had probably seemed like a knight in shining armor.

"When I couldn't go out, Chad would come to the house and bring my mom flowers. When he took me to dinner, he'd insist on getting food for her, too. He seemed so considerate, to both of us." Her mouth twisted. "My mom always worried about me, but she told me once that she was glad I'd found someone. She didn't like the idea of me being alone after she...was gone."

No doubt Berkley's dying mom had also been looking for a light in the darkness. A polite, older man to help care for her teenage daughter so she wouldn't be left alone in the world. It had to have been hell for her. For both of them.

Lawson wished he'd been a better person back then, some-one they both could have turned to.

Not that he'd been in a position to offer any real help. He'd been fighting his own battles and because of that, he'd been a powder keg of rage waiting to detonate. He'd avoided com-mitments, but he'd definitely felt pity.

Pretty sure Berkley would hate it if she knew.

Since she'd been brave enough to bring it up, to own it, maybe he should own his part in it, too. "I'm the one."

"The one?" she asked, confused.

Yeah, probably didn't make any sense to her. "The one who got her to end her reign of terror on you." He'd threatened

Chad against ever using Berkley again. She wasn't a plaything for him, and Lawson told him to stay away—or else. Then he'd flat-out told the wife the truth of things. Actually, in a way, he'd threatened her, as well.

Yet until this moment, he'd never admitted it to anyone, because he hadn't wanted to be involved. Hadn't wanted to be drawn in.

Hadn't wanted to *care*, because caring would only make it harder to get away.

Now, here with Berkley so many years later...maybe that was changing.

5

"Okay," she said, tilting away from him with a dark frown. "Back up. What do you mean you got her to end her reign of terror against me?"

Incredibly aware that she wore only a swimsuit while he was fully clothed in a shirt, jeans and boots, his gaze dipped over her. *Not* looking at her body became harder by the second. "I told her that I saw her creepy husband repeatedly coming on to you, and I saw you repeatedly tell him to get lost."

Berkley blinked. "You did?"

Back then, he hadn't missed much. He'd felt like his survival depended on him being aware, and that was true as far as it went—yet with Berkley, he'd always noticed her a bit more than anyone else.

There'd been certain "types" in their neighborhood. Those

who needed something, those who'd take what they wanted and those who were utterly lost. Berkley had stood out as something else. Quiet but not cowed, determined but not ruthless. Dedicated to her mother and that yappy little dog in a way he hadn't seen before.

Look at her now. She'd spent her childhood helping to care for her mom, and as an adult, she cared for animals. Yet she kept to herself as much as she could, not cold and standoffish, just very private—not asking anything of others.

Her uniqueness was something that couldn't be ignored.

"I saw what you were going through," he said, and didn't elaborate further.

Her expression softened. "A spectacle like that would have been hard to miss."

"I'm sure for you, being in the middle of it, it felt that way. But think about it. People sold themselves on the corner. Others OD'd on their front steps. There were street races, brawls and shoot-outs monthly." Talking about it put him back there, to where he could almost smell the tar on the street, hear the shouts and curses, and feel the threat of too many eyes watching him. "The gangs were always trolling for recruits." Outside...and in his home.

It sickened him to recall that his parents hadn't offered any safety. No, they'd often been complicit with a gang and different dealers. A son? They saw him as a ball and chain, and often his dad accused him of thinking he was too good to carry his own weight.

By helping with their illegal activities.

Tension seeped into his neck and tightened his jaw, a bead of sweat rolled down his temple, and then suddenly, Hero was there in front of him, watching him with a whine, catching the hem of his shirt and giving it a tug.

"He's saving you," Berkley murmured. "You might want to let him know you're okay."

Lawson regrouped.

Subtly, through his nose, he inhaled a cleansing breath. As if he hadn't just been dragged back from the hell of his youth, he idly reached out to scratch Hero's ear. His fur was soft, almost velvety there, and it felt soothing to touch him.

Releasing him, Hero sat back on his haunches and closed his eyes in pleasure.

Berkley didn't say anything else, but he knew she was aware of his struggle. Not about to mention the relief Hero had just given him, Lawson got back to his point. "A high school girl having a fling with an older guy was tame in comparison to what we regularly saw."

She hesitated, then nodded her agreement. "I guess, but you're right. It hadn't felt that way to me."

"That's because Sabrina Durkinson pushed it." He shifted, which put Hero on alert again. "Relax, buddy. It's all good."

Hero tipped his head, snuffled against him, then sprawled out on the rough ground with a sigh of relaxation. He looked content with his bed of sand and rocks and weeds.

"He's astute" was all Berkley said.

No kidding. It made Lawson wonder if Hero was trained be-yond being a companion dog. He'd have to remember to stay chill so the dog wouldn't fret. "I noticed when the jerk showed up at your place a few times, and when you argued with him on your porch." Now, looking back, Lawson wished he'd taken the guy apart. "I also saw *her* show up at your house." Durkin-son's wife. Sabrina had been no more than a female version of Chad, both of them cruel.

Covering her face, Berkley gave a long, aggrieved groan that ended with a rough laugh. "God, that was such a horren-dous day." She dropped her hands and then used her bare toes to rub Hero's hip. Probably her way of letting the dog know she was fine.

"Want to tell me about it?"

"Why not? We're doing all this confessing stuff, right? But you first." She nodded at him. "Let's hear it. What did you do?"

Yeah, he should probably get it over with, especially since he didn't know how she'd react. "The newscaster lady came tearing out of your house in a fury, all dressed up like she was ready to go on the air but with steam coming out her ears." He especially remembered that because she'd stood out so badly. She might as well have been waving red meat in front of a pack of hungry jackals. Sure, people knew her roots and generally cheered for her, but that wouldn't have stopped one of them from taking what they wanted, like her jewelry, clothes, car—or *her*. A lot of brutality happened in their neighborhood, sometimes in the middle of the day. Those who saw it pretended they didn't; it was safer for them that way.

Luck was on the news lady's side, though, because other than appearing red-faced with anger, she'd reached her car at the curb without anyone approaching her.

Anyone other than him.

Lawson rubbed the back of his neck, but he was careful not to let the memories grip him. With Berkley's foot rhythmically rubbing Hero's hip, the dog slept peacefully. "It didn't take a genius to know the princess had just caused an ugly scene. I figured I might as well use the opportunity to…dissuade her from giving you more trouble."

"Oh, boy. Now my curiosity is curdling."

He half smiled at that expression. "I reached her right before she got in her car and told her if she didn't let up, I'd share the photos I'd taken of good old Chad *begging* you for forgiveness, of him trying to kiss you with you shoving him away. I told her I had a dozen photos of him sniveling around your door."

Berkley snorted. "He wasn't at my house a dozen times."

Lifting a shoulder, Lawson dismissed that little fact as irrelevant. "She didn't know that, though. Telling her that I'd do my own press conference to set the record straight, that I'd talk to anyone who would listen—including any online news people—convinced her that she'd end up looking like a loser. She called me some choice names, got in her fancy little red car and burned rubber in her rush to leave."

Berkley's wide eyes stared at him in fascination.

He wasn't done yet. "I also told good old Chad that if I saw him back in our neighborhood, I'd tell everyone he was a narc, and he'd never make it out again." With all the drug dealers nearby, it was a convincing threat.

"Lawson!" She sounded both incredulous and amused.

It didn't matter how many times he'd told himself not to get involved, that the important thing was for him to get away, as fast and far as possible before he ended up like the lost souls surrounding him, he couldn't turn a blind eye to her.

The nastiness had been relentless, and the way he'd seen it, a seventeen-year-old girl with a dying mother in a shit hometown was a victim, not a husband stealer. It was the married man who should have been held accountable for taking advantage of her, and cheating on his wife.

So he'd done his own minuscule part, and it had worked.

"Well." Berkley blinked twice, tugged at a few of the earrings hanging from one ear and then grinned. "I always wondered why she finally stopped trashing me. All this time, I thought it was because of something I did."

He really wanted to know what she'd done, but she pushed to her feet, making it clear that their visit had ended. "Thank you, Lawson." She set her hat on the rock, picked up her shirt, shook the sand and dirt from it, then tugged it over her head.

An eye-boggling experience, watching Berkley dress.

"Back then, I hadn't known that anyone was on my side." Pulling on her shorts over the bathing suit bottoms, she said, "Finding out now... It's nice." She zipped and snapped as if his fascinated gaze didn't track the movement, and then stepped into her sandals and replaced her hat.

Damp air from the lake had added messy waves to her hair. Her nose and cheeks were rosy. And that hat... Everything about her appealed to him.

She held out her hand. "Thank you."

He should have told her sooner. And he wanted her to share what she'd done, but the second she'd stood, Hero had jumped up to join her, and they both appeared ready to call it a night.

He couldn't shake her hand. Literally couldn't. Instead he gently squeezed her fingers. "My pleasure." The sun was sinking, the air finally cooling a little. "I parked near the beach. You?"

She nodded.

Shifting his hand to the small of her back, he said, "I'll walk with you, then."

She didn't agree, but she didn't disagree, either. Better still, a small smile stayed on her mouth.

The hot sun turned into an orange ball, spilling color over the lake. As they neared the beach, the scents changed to sunscreen, sand and earth, and barbecue. A few people sent them friendly waves. Kids laughed. Gulls swooped overhead.

Cemetery really was an awesome place.

And overall, it had turned into a pretty special night.

She seemed to be on a weekly schedule with Lawson. Every time she saw him, she learned something new, and then they'd both get busy and another six or seven days would pass before they visited again.

Did that mean she'd see him again soon? She waffled between hope that she would and determination to steer clear of him. Odd how running into someone from her past had started out causing her dread, but now felt somewhat comforting.

She wasn't alone.

Despite how busy her week had been, he'd plagued her thoughts far too often.

So long ago, he'd backed her up.

Her mother hadn't been able to, and no one else had tried. Her world had felt so *empty*. But now she knew that Lawson had, and as ridiculous as it seemed, it softened the memories of her past.

He suffered his own harsh recollections of their youth. On the beach, the way he'd coiled tighter and tighter—she'd felt it, and so had Hero. She could only imagine how much worse daily life would have been for him. A tall, good-looking, strong young man—no doubt he'd been expected to do many things, by many people.

Despite what he'd said, she'd been a homely girl, so most of the local boys had left her alone with her awkwardness. Oh, she'd been propositioned a few times, but not overly. Her stammering, red-faced replies had usually sufficed.

"You're smiling, dear."

Berkley turned to Betty with a start. Somehow she'd forgotten all about her. Heck, she'd forgotten that she was outside, that she'd been cleaning a dog kennel and that other people were around. How long had she been standing there lost in thought?

Bustling now, she began rewinding her hose while saying to Betty "So are you." She liked seeing the town matriarch like this. Betty, who was always impeccably dressed, her short gray hair permed into an enduring style, looked so happy whenever she visited The Love Shack. Animals did that for a person.

"Care to share your thoughts?" Betty asked. She took a seat on a bench, and the dog she'd been walking tried to jump up, too, but couldn't quite manage it with her short legs and stocky body. "Oh, sweetie." When Betty started to reach for the insistent pooch, Berkley hurried forward.

"Let me." She gently scooped up Gladys and placed her beside Betty.

Elder and dog both seemed content.

"So," Betty said. "These thoughts of yours?"

How was it that Betty always saw right through her? It had

been like that from the start. Odd that a twenty-six-year-old and a woman nearing ninety could become instant friends, but they had.

"Remember I told you about that scandal I went through?"

Betty's brows lifted. "About the cheating man-whore who abused you? Yes, I remember."

"Er...not exactly how I put it."

"I'm too old to play word games. I speak the truth. It saves me time, and as you know, at my age, time is limited."

"Betty!" No, Berkley did not want to hear her talk like that. "You're an energetic, sharp-witted woman with plenty of years ahead of you."

"Baloney. My hips hurt, my feet hurt, I can't get in or out of the tub, so it's only showers for me—and I *loved* long baths. There are certain things that come with age, and one of those is the right not to sugarcoat things. The man was a reprehensible pig. I hope his selfish, shortsighted wife has made him miserable."

After biting her lip to hold back a laugh, Berkley said, "Actually, I think they're divorced now."

"Good. She might be a better person without him. So what's the problem?"

"Lawson lived in my neighborhood. He recognized me."

With no reaction at all, Betty waited.

"Don't you see? I had hoped to never..." She trailed off, unsure what to say. The past was there, and it wouldn't magically go away.

"Never what?" Betty softly demanded. "Remember the hard times? You'll have more, believe me. Some worse, some not as bad. All are worth remembering for the lessons we learned, or the trials we overcame. You know how strong you are because you got through it and you're still a wonderful person."

Wow, that heartfelt speech humbled Berkley.

Betty wasn't through, though. "If you forget the bad times,

then you forget the good times that were woven around them, like your mother and how much you loved each other. How dedicated you were to her and how she worried about you."

"Yes," Berkley whispered, thinking those things right now. Right up to the end, her mother had loved her the best that she could. Disease had weakened her, and even then, she'd smile at Berkley in a way that made her feel whole. "I still miss my mom." Pretty sure she'd miss her every single day for the rest of her life.

"I wish I could have met her," Betty quietly replied.

That made her smile, because her mother and Betty were as different as night and day. "Mom was such a gentle person to go through so much." And Berkley knew she had added to her worries.

"Well," Betty said, turning all brisk and businesslike. "We can't pick and choose the parts of our past that look the prettiest to our memories. We can move on from them. We can get over the rough times and celebrate the good times. But forgetting them completely is never the way. Take it from someone who's lived a long time. I've made mistakes, and I have regrets, but oh, it's been a wonderful life and I wouldn't trade a single moment that led me to this point because I'm enjoying my life so much." She patted Berkley's hand. "Especially with you as a friend."

"I feel the same about you." She glanced around with satisfaction. This shelter was hers to run, set up with her requests in mind, and she took so much pride in it. Her life, with the various twists and turns, had gotten her here. "You're right, I know that. It's just that thinking about those days, all the humiliation, it makes me sick to my stomach." Even though no one else could hear them, she lowered her voice. "You can't know how vile some people got, the things they said about me. The names they called me."

"Small-minded fools. You have my permission to forget

them." Betty waved a hand as if making them disappear. "Now, if you tell me Lawson was unkind, I'll march over there right now and set him straight. I won't allow him to say or do anything to upset you." Betty tipped her chin and chided gently, "You're not alone anymore."

From the moment she'd met Betty, they'd connected in fun and meaningful ways, so Berkley felt free to tease her now. "But your hips hurt. Your feet hurt. How in the world will you march?"

"Ha!" Betty swatted at her, grinning. "Don't get cheeky with me. Anger is a powerful motivator. If the man needs his butt chewed, I'll chew it."

They looked at each other—and Berkley cracked first. But once she started to laugh, Betty did, too, and soon they were roaring with it, disturbing poor Gladys, who wanted to sleep, and even drawing Hero from his nap in the sunshine.

When the two dogs joined in, howling and yapping, things really got out of hand.

By the time they could draw breath, Betty's face was red, her eyes watering, and the two volunteers nearby smiled at them in curiosity.

"Shh, hush," Betty said, gasping for breath and fanning her face. "This isn't at all dignified."

"You're the one who said it, not me."

Betty snickered. "It came out all wrong, and if you ever repeat it, I'll deny it."

Still chuckling, Berkley crossed her heart. "Never."

"You understood my meaning, though. I'll stop on my way home and give him a piece of my mind."

"Thank you." Wow, she could get used to having backup. For the longest time, she'd faced every issue, resolved every difficulty, completely on her own. Now she knew Lawson had defended her, and Betty was ready to do so right now. "It means a lot to me that you'd offer, but it's not necessary. Talking to Lawson about it…" She couldn't quite find the right words for how it had affected her, so she settled on saying, "It was nice. *He* was nice."

New interest showed in Betty's raised brows. "So you two discussed it?"

She shrugged. "It was the oddest thing, but we were sitting at a secluded section of the lake, away from the beach crowd, and it just sort of happened."

Turning to face her, Betty demanded, "What? What happened?"

Realizing what she thought brought a rush of heat to Berkley's cheeks. "Not *that*. Nothing like *that*."

"Like what?"

She opened her mouth, caught Betty's grin and laughed. "When you decide to cut loose, you go all out. Does the rest of the town know about this wild streak of yours?"

"Heavens, no. They think I'm a dragon, and that works for me. A gal has to have her rep."

Berkley chuckled. "A rep, huh?" She thought everyone should know about Betty's warm, humorous side, but she'd respect her wishes. Besides, if Betty kept up like this, everyone would find out eventually.

"Don't change the subject. We're talking about you and Lawson."

"Fine, but don't make more of it than it is. We're just…"

"Friends?" Betty supplied.

"Not even that, really. More like distant acquaintances from long ago who are now being friendly, but we're not tight or anything."

Making a circular motion with her finger, Betty tried to hurry her along. "You were alone on the beach…?"

As briefly as possible, Berkley explained how she'd needed some fresh air and time to think, and how Lawson had chased her down, and then they'd started talking. "I don't know how it happened, but suddenly it felt right to clear the air. With him, I mean. We're both living here and it was like this giant wall of awkwardness between us." Sitting there on a rock, with the foul stench of fish and the too-hot sun, her bikini bottoms wet from the lake, had felt remarkably natural. Enjoyable. And then the words had just tumbled out. "I brought it up, and we talked about it."

"And?" Betty gently prompted.

"It doesn't feel so heavy anymore." She'd carried that shame for so long, as well as guilt for what her mother had gone through with her, and now... Now it didn't feel quite so awful. "I'm glad I did, because I found out that he'd defended me." She shared Lawson's good deed with her friend, giving her all the details.

"My, that young man just keeps looking better and better," Betty mused.

Berkley quickly gave her attention to the volunteers, who were finishing up.

"I didn't mean physically, though that's true, as well."

"I should probably help the volunteers get the dogs squared away."

Betty caught her arm. "You've been working all day. They can handle it." When she relented by sinking back into her seat, Betty said, "Don't try to tell me you haven't noticed how handsome Lawson is."

She'd noticed all right, but tried to play it off. "He was always attractive like that. Always stood out, too, because he didn't bully anyone, and he wasn't intimidated by those who tried to bully him." To Berkley, his character had meant more than his physique and handsome face.

"What is it the young people say? That he's the whole package?"

She grinned. "Sounds legit." Especially when applied to Lawson.

"It's not every day that you meet someone who looks like

him, but is also a hard worker, pleasant to customers and generous, too. You know he volunteered to build the well, and the money is already adding up."

"It's a clever idea, Betty. Thank you."

"I couldn't have done it without Lawson's help. His only issue is how often people pose Kathleen there."

"He has a problem with the mannequin?" Kathleen was like a town mascot. Everyone loved Kathleen.

"It's his only flaw," Betty said, giving her a sly side-eye. "Obviously he's a keeper."

That outrageous comment made her forget all about Kathleen. "Planning to make him a pet?"

After another un-Betty-like laugh, the older woman turned stern. "Not me, *you*."

Shaking her head, Berkley said, "I already have Hero and Cheese."

Betty stared her in the eyes. "Not a pet. A companion."

"They are companions."

Her brows drew together. "A human companion. A *man*."

Betty said *man* with a lot of innuendo. "No way. I told you, I've sworn off men."

"Yes, yes, and it made sense when you said it." Betty waved it off dismissively. "But that was before Lawson."

The last thing she needed was Betty playing matchmaker. "It's forever."

"Because one loser treated you poorly? That's on him, not you."

She was about to debate it further with Betty when the volunteers finished and started toward them. Using it as the perfect excuse to end the discussion, Berkley stood and called out "All done?" She excused herself to Betty. "Sorry, but I need to go over a few things with them. And we should probably get Gladys back to her bed." The older dog was sound asleep, mouth open, tongue lolling out, her head against Betty's hip.

Actually, Betty looked tired as well and it filled Berkley with concern. She had less than a fifteen-minute drive, but at her age, she'd probably prefer to be at home with her feet up. Not that Berkley would say that to her. She'd never met anyone with more pride and backbone than Betty Cemetery.

Stifling a yawn, Betty stood, which prompted Gladys to rise, as well. The dog had less trouble hopping down from the bench.

Together, they thanked the volunteers, who both promised to return at the same time next week. Nearly every day someone came out to help walk the dogs, to play with them in the yard, exercise them and give them attention. In so many ways, the town and the people in it were magical.

She, Gladys and Hero walked with Betty to her car. Berkley opened the door for her and watched as Betty took a moment to get seated, start the air-conditioning and then adjust her seat belt.

In such a short time, this woman had become so precious to her. A friend, a confidant, but also family. On impulse, Berkley leaned down and put a kiss to her cheek. "Drive safely, okay?"

For a second, Betty looked flustered, then she smiled, patted Berkley's arm and said, "Take good care of my Gladys."

Her Gladys? Smiling, Berkley said, "I'll give her an extra treat tonight."

Both dogs resoundingly agreed with that plan.

The weekend brought drizzling rain that made everyone miserable, most especially Lawson.

Kathleen was out in the rain, and damn it, he felt guilty about it. Someone had decked out the mannequin in a swimsuit, wide-brimmed hat and sunglasses.

They should have put an umbrella in her hand instead.

Her wig, probably some kind of synthetic hair, would be ruined soon.

Behind his counter, Lawson shifted so he couldn't see the

mannequin so easily through the front window. At least it wasn't looking at him.

A jokester—though he had no idea who—had at one point positioned the thing so it was staring in at him. Ha, ha. Very funny. Not.

He'd kept busy in the back room for a few hours, and when he came back out, Will had repositioned her. That was yesterday, and she was still here.

Weren't the townspeople supposed to move her around or something? He'd heard all these stories of Kathleen showing up everywhere, but lately she spent most of her time in front of his shop. Pretty sure people did it just to annoy him, but he wouldn't give them the satisfaction of complaining.

Today there weren't that many customers around. Without foot traffic to the beach, everything had slowed to a near standstill. He'd already taken care of inventory, cleaned, eaten, cleaned again… In the idleness, he spent his time noticing the mannequin.

If only he hadn't let Will take off, but the young man had a date and there wasn't enough work to require them both.

When a sunny yellow umbrella came past the window, Lawson stared, but he couldn't see who carried it. Whoever it was, they struggled to hold the umbrella—while trying to take Kathleen.

He'd be glad to help with that.

Quickly, he pulled on his rain slicker and opened the door. "Need a hand?"

Lark jumped, nearly losing her umbrella. She tried to juggle both, and lost.

Kathleen landed on the gravel lot, and the umbrella nearly went flying with a fast wind.

He darted out and caught it, and then heard Lark laughing. When he turned, she sat beside Kathleen, both of them soaked. Quickly going to her, he asked, "You okay?"

When she reached up, he took her hand and hauled her to her feet. "I thought you'd left for the day, so I was trying to save you. Figured I'd move Kathleen somewhere else so you wouldn't have to deal with her tomorrow."

"And instead I startled you." He held the umbrella over her head, but already her face was wet, tendrils of hair sticking to her cheeks. "Sorry about that."

Kathleen still laid on the ground, all stiff arms and legs, her expression somehow stoic.

"Oh," Lark said, as if she'd just had the same realization. "Poor Kathleen!" Leaving him with the umbrella, she bent to collect the mannequin, but it wasn't easy. Her plastic body was now wet and slippery.

Lawson looked at her with distaste, but he couldn't stand by—holding a bright yellow umbrella—while Lark struggled.

"Here." He caught her arm again, urging her up and to the side, then he gave her the umbrella. "Where do you want her?"

"My car?"

Her car? Definitely said with a question, because no way would Kathleen fit. He gave Lark an incredulous look.

"Yes, see, I thought I'd let her legs stick out the window or something."

While they discussed it, he was oddly aware of holding the mannequin upright. What was it about her that creeped him out so much? "Where were you going to take her?"

"Oh, the restaurant. It's so nearby, and Saul, the owner— Have you met Saul?"

"Yeah. Nice guy."

She nodded. "He said he wouldn't mind letting her dry off at his place. Kathleen is a regular there, you know."

See, that was the creepy part. Everyone talked about the dummy as if she were a real person. Feeling as stiff-armed as Kathleen, he carried the mannequin to his truck and put her in the back.

"Um, Lawson?"

"Let me lock up and I'll meet you at the restaurant. I'll get her inside for you, then you and Saul and everyone else can figure out what to do with her."

A smile teased her mouth. "Aren't you the gallant one? Why, the stories will spread far and wide across Cemetery of how you saved Kathleen—"

He jerked around to face her, and realized she was teasing him. Suppressing a grin, he pointed at her. "Not a word about it."

Playfully, she pretended to zip her lips.

Knowing women as he did, he distracted her by saying, "Makeup is running down your cheeks."

Her eyes widened. "Mascara!" Quickly, still standing in the rain, she ran her fingers under her eyes.

"Making it worse," he informed her, then he went to the door to hold it open. "Come on in. You can clean up while I shut things down and get my keys. We can leave together."

"So very gallant," she teased again as she sashayed past him with raccoon eyes and rain dripping off her nose.

"I'll grab you a towel first. Be right back."

In less than five minutes, Lark had removed her ruined makeup, he'd closed down the shop, and they were each in their own separate vehicles, headed to the restaurant. He was starkly aware of Kathleen tucked into the bed of his truck. It almost felt like he'd stowed a body there or something. *Made of fiberglass*, he reminded himself.

Fortunately, he had a cover over the bed so the worsening rain didn't damage her—*it*—more than it already had.

At the restaurant, Lark quickly parked, hopped out of her car and darted for the restaurant, meaning he was supposed to bring in Kathleen? Apparently, given how she smiled at him while holding open the door.

He liked Lark. She was light and funny, in contrast to Berkley's intensity. She freely teased while Berkley usually sent out off-limits vibes. Lark chatted up everyone, and Berkley largely kept to herself.

Yet it was Berkley he couldn't get off his mind. It wasn't just the pull of a shared past, or the knowledge of a painful memory. It was more than that, something he'd felt nearly a decade ago. It had never really faded away, and now that she was close again, the sense of fate had intensified.

As he pulled up the hood of his slicker and left his truck, he wondered what Berkley was doing right now. Probably curled up in a chair with Hero and Cheese, reading or watching TV, not thinking about him, so he needed to stop thinking about her.

The second he stepped into the restaurant, Kathleen's rigid body in his arms, applause broke out. It startled him enough that he damn near dropped the dummy.

One woman said "Oops!" and darted forward to adjust Kathleen's bikini top.

Good God, both plastic breasts had been exposed!

With heat creeping up his neck, he stuck Kathleen in the corner and scowled at everyone. Which only made them clap louder.

Lark leaned into him, using his shoulder for leverage as she went on tiptoes to say near his ear, "You're egging them on. Smile, take a bow, present Kathleen safe and sound, and I promise they'll let up."

He didn't want to, but he also didn't want to remain the center of attention, so he pointed at Lark, saying loudly, "The real hero," and then raised her arm like the winner of a prize fight.

The cheers doubled, especially when he grinned, and together he and Lark bowed. When he came up, that was when he saw Berkley, and he immediately lost focus on everything else.

6

Berkley sipped her cola while watching Lawson and the woman from her small table at the back of the busy restaurant. What a cute couple they'd make.

The woman was all bubbly, laughing and teasing, and Lawson kept glancing at Kathleen in disgust. The poor mannequin was half-naked. Good thing her body parts weren't in any detail.

If Betty was here, she'd be having a fit. Thinking that made Berkley smile, but the smile didn't last, not when Lawson raised the woman's hand and then took a dramatic bow with her.

Maybe they were already a couple and she just hadn't heard the news yet.

He looked happy, and that was important, right? A guy like him deserved...everything.

When he straightened again, his attention snagged on her.

Berkley didn't know if she should wave, look away, or maybe just leave the remainder of her dinner and get back to the shelter.

Before she could decide, he said something to the woman, who shook her head, and then with his hand at the small of her back, he guided her through the restaurant.

Toward Berkley.

For real, she didn't need an introduction to his date. She grabbed a fry, ready to stuff it into her mouth so she'd have an excuse to ignore them, but it was already too late.

"Berkley, I'm surprised to see you here."

Yeah, right. Because, what? She avoided humans? Okay, so she did. "Hi." Oh, good going. So warm. So carefree. Berkley pinned on a smile. "It's after-hours for the shelter, so I figured I'd grab some dinner." It wasn't easy, but she managed not to stare at the woman standing beside him. With any luck, the two of them would mosey on.

"Oh, you're Berkley Carr," the woman suddenly gushed and, uninvited, pulled out the chair across from her to join her table. She stuck out her hand. "It's great to finally meet you in person."

Um… Berkley took her hand. "Hello." Was this another person from her past, someone she didn't remember? The thought sent a river of ice through her veins.

Worse, what if Lawson had told her—

Since there were no other chairs, Lawson crouched down beside Berkley. "Let me do the introductions. Berkley, this is Lark Penny. She recently moved to Cemetery and she's made it her mission to meet all the business owners and as many neighbors as she can."

Lark squeezed her hand before releasing her. "Everyone talks about you and the newly built shelter you're running. I've heard so many wonderful stories about The Love Shack, and your way with animals."

Relief settled in, but the ice was slow to melt. "We can thank Betty for that. It was all her idea."

"And she's been the force behind it," Lark said. "I know." Then with a grin, she added, "She's told me all about it."

"You know Betty?"

"Of course. She was one of the first people I met." Lark leaned in and added in a whisper, "She's giving Oliver fits, but I have my money on Betty."

"Oliver?" she asked. Did this woman already know everyone?

"He's opening a fitness place and I guess he and Betty are conflicting on a few things. Oh! I just had a wonderful idea."

Did this woman never slow down? All the while she spoke, Lawson remained there, near Berkley's chair, crouched as if his strong thighs didn't mind in the least.

Well, she minded. "Just a second." Standing, she looked around, saw an empty seat and hurried over to it. When she started hauling it across the floor, Lawson caught on and took it from her.

"I've got it."

"I figured if you're both going to stay…"

"Thank you, Berkley. I'd love to join you."

She hadn't really invited him to do that, but neither did she mind.

Lark, having overheard him, laughed. "I could have given you my seat. I'm not staying. I just wanted to save Kathleen."

"And me," he said as he sat and pulled the chair closer until his knee bumped Berkley's. He tilted toward her and confided, "I'm not a fan of the mannequin. This is twice now that Lark's lent me a hand with the ridiculous thing."

They all looked up then to see people fussing around the mannequin. She now wore a colorful T-shirt with a beach towel wrapped around her hips, and another around her head. Two women worked on her sodden wig, one holding it while another dried it. Through it all, Kathleen leaned against the bar, a drink at her elbow.

It was comical how the town treated the doll. Comical, and apparently disturbing to poor Lawson.

"Look at how she's getting pampered." When Lawson rolled his eyes, Lark aimed her smile at him. "You should have put one of your T-shirts on her. That would have been great marketing."

He looked struck. "You're right. Next time I'll try to remember that."

"Was that your wonderful idea?" Berkley asked. Now that she was starting to relax, she was actually enjoying Lark's energetic, upbeat vibe.

"No, I was thinking of Oliver. That seems to be my new favorite pastime."

Now Berkley wanted to meet the mysterious Oliver. Maybe Lark had the right idea about meeting everyone. She should give it a try.

"What's your idea?" Lawson asked.

"Okay, what do you think of this?" Gesturing grandly, Lark announced, "Cat yoga."

She and Lawson stared at Lark.

Frowning, Lark asked, "You do have cats, right?"

Berkley nodded.

"Oliver wants to draw people into his new fitness studio, but apparently Betty has an issue with him. But," she stressed, "Betty loves animals. You have animals. So… Cat yoga!"

"How does a cat do yoga?"

Lark laughed. "All cats are great at difficult poses, right? But cat yoga is the new fitness trend. If you have room at the shelter, you and Oliver could work together to set up a weekly or monthly visit—whatever fits with your schedules—and then those people signed up with his studio would come out and have a special yoga program with the cats interacting. Who knows, someone might want to adopt a cat."

Berkley drew back. "I can't let a vacationer take a cat. I have to research them. I need to know—"

"Oh, see, I knew I'd like you. I agree one hundred percent. But it won't just be vacationers, right? Locals will want to do the fitness classes, too, and especially the cat yoga. I bet Betty would embrace it. Wonder if I could convince her to get some yoga pants."

Berkley choked, which prompted Lawson to pat her back... and then his hand stayed there, resting on the top edge of her chair. Even though Berkley was acutely aware of his touch, Lark didn't seem to notice.

"Yardley and Mimi would be on board—you know them, right? They're terrific. And Emily, Saul's wife." She paused for air. "Anyway, there are so many fun people in Cemetery. Plus I imagine Oliver might get clients from the neighboring counties. You could research them easily. They're close." She held out her arms. "And the cats would have company. People to love on them and show them affection."

It was absolutely impossible not to like Lark. "It's a brilliant idea." Berkley turned to Lawson and caught his warm gaze on her, his mouth tipped in a small smile. For a second, she forgot everything. "What do you think?"

"I think it could be fun."

Lark gave a sly grin. "Will you do yoga, too?"

He shook his head. "No."

"What if I promise Kathleen won't be there?"

He started to say something, but then Saul, the owner of the restaurant, stopped by. "Sorry for the delay. You two want drinks?"

Immediately, Lark popped up. "Oh, I'm not staying. I was just..." Her gaze went past Saul and then locked on someone. Her voice dropped to a purring rumble. "Speaking of fine ideas."

She, Lawson and Saul all twisted around, and there was a

tall, dark man wearing glasses and searching for a seat in the packed restaurant.

Lawson grinned. "Go get 'em, Lark."

Without a reply, she darted away.

"Interesting," Saul said.

"With those two? Definitely. Lark isn't the type to hide her thoughts."

"Noticed that," Saul said. "So how about you? Are you sticking around for a meal?"

Deferring to Berkley, he asked, "Would you mind?"

Like she'd rudely say if she did? She'd probably finish before he ever got his food. Or maybe she'd order dessert. Either way, she was enjoying his company, especially now that she knew he wasn't "with" Lark. "Of course not. Feel free."

He switched seats, taking the one Lark had vacated so that he sat across from her. His knees bumped hers again, but the man did have very long legs. "What are you having?"

"BLT, light on the L, with french fries and cola."

"Sounds perfect." To Saul, he said, "I'll take the same."

"You've got it." Saul dropped the order off, then started circulating the restaurant to offer drink refills or hand over checks.

Lawson sat back in his seat. "Thanks for letting me join you. My original plan was to cut out early and microwave something at home." His gaze moved over her face. "This is better."

She offered him a french fry, which he accepted. "As one of my volunteers was leaving today, she said she was coming by here to eat a BLT."

He grinned. "So here you are."

"Me and my susceptible mind." It was nice to share these little parts of herself, things most people didn't know since she kept to herself. "I had everything at home except the tomato. At first I was just planning a grocery run, but the rain wasn't letting up. It had all the animals sleepy, including Hero and Cheese, and honestly, I was getting sleepy, too. I decided a little people-watching might wake me up." She sipped her cola, then tipped it toward him in a mock toast. "Didn't expect entertainment with the meal."

"You mean Lark?"

"I mean you waltzing in from the rain carrying a mostly naked Kathleen."

With a theatrical wince, he grumbled, "Don't remind me." Then lower, he added, "I didn't know she'd lost her top. The way people carried on, you'd think she was real."

"Real enough to them." She nodded at the crowd of people taking photos with the mannequin, doting on her and still decorating her. She now wore someone's sunglasses, and a kid hung a sand pail from her hand.

Lawson didn't look, choosing to ignore Kathleen instead. "Someone keeps returning her to the well. If she's not there when I get to work, she shows up before I leave."

"Did Lark really rescue you?"

Sitting back in his seat with a smile, he said, "She's a whirlwind, isn't she? It's hard not to like her when she's so happy about everything." He shook his head as if the woman amazed him. "When I first met her, yeah, she rescued me, but mostly from some flirting vacationers." He gave it a moment's thought. "And Kathleen, I guess." He proceeded to explain how they'd met.

Huh. She hadn't realized Lark was a stylist, but then, her hair was soaked from the rain and her makeup mostly washed away.

"Today," Lawson continued, "she was mostly trying to rescue Kathleen since she was left out in the storm."

"Still in front of your shop?" At his nod, she asked, "You didn't want to bring her in?"

"Not particularly." He stole another of her fries. "The comedians around here think it's funny to turn her head so that she's staring in at me." He watched her a second, then murmured, "You're trying so hard not to laugh. It's okay, you know." He popped the fry into his mouth. "I don't mind. I know it's ridiculous."

She *did* snicker, but only a little. Taking another bite of her sandwich helped to temper her humor. By the time she swallowed and took a drink, she was back to her mostly serious self. "It's not ridiculous. I'm afraid of spiders. Doesn't matter if it's an itty-bitty spider, I still freak out if it gets near me. The really absurd part is that I don't want them hurt. I just want them relocated. Try explaining that to someone who comes to the rescue."

He smiled. "I like that you don't want them hurt. It's a very Berkley-like attitude."

Rather than get off track talking about her bug phobias, Berkley asked, "So you and Lark haven't known each other long?"

"We've only spoken a few times, but I like her. She's..." He searched for a word and came up with "Natural. Authentic. Seems she has a thing for Oliver, but even around him, she's still herself. It's like she doesn't know any other way to be, which is admirable."

Very true. Genuine people were rare. Chad certainly hadn't been genuine. He'd lied to her from the start. And his wife? She'd always seemed one way on TV, but in person, her personality was the total opposite.

"If you're thinking of him, don't."

Startled, Berkley looked at him. How had he read her mind?

"Few people are as two-faced as him. He doesn't deserve your thoughts."

"You're right, he doesn't." If only it was that easy. "Lark is certainly upbeat and outgoing." Did that type of personality appeal to Lawson? Seemed so.

"Check out her and Oliver now. He doesn't know what hit him."

Berkley glanced around the restaurant and caught sight of

Lark seated with the newcomer. Lark was busy chatting and the man appeared bemused. "He's the new guy to town?"

Lawson nodded. "I'm making up some promo shirts for him—something Lark suggested. He used to be a physical therapist but now he'll be running his own fitness place."

"That seems to be a trend, people giving up one career to have their own business here."

"Think it'll change Cemetery?"

"Not as long as Betty is around." The second she said the words, it hit her that at Betty's age, any day could be her last.

Lawson reached across the table and took her hand. "Hey. What's wrong?"

She hadn't realized how she'd frozen until Lawson's warm fingers closed around hers. It felt good. So good that she didn't draw away.

And neither did he.

He frowned. "You're not thinking of that dumbass again, are you?"

She nearly laughed. "No, so don't bring him up. Actually, it's just that I've gotten close to Betty. I don't like to think about her age, but it's a reality."

He stroked his thumb over her knuckles. "A few years back, when I was working in Haiti, I met a guy who was one hundred and two. He spoke Haitian Creole, French and English. Sharp as a tack and he liked to debate everything—sometimes in all three languages." Lawson smiled. "My own mother died shortly after she turned forty-five. Hard living, drugs, alcohol, who knows. I hadn't seen her in years and then I got a notice that she was gone." His hand slid from hers as he sat back again. "Betty's still driving, and apparently she's giving Oliver hell. No one would call her frail."

Amazing. He'd just revealed all that like it was nothing. To Berkley, each bit of information, the sharing of his life, felt like a gift. The kind she never received, not since her mother had passed away.

She had dozens of questions, and a lot of sympathy to share, but she didn't want him to regret confiding in her. "Anything could happen at Betty's age."

"To anyone, at any age, really. I don't think you need to worry about losing her yet."

Saul returned to the table with Lawson's food. "Sorry for the wait. With the rain closing the beach, we're swamped, even with all hands on deck." He'd brought a fresh glass of cola for Berkley and also set out a dessert menu. "I'll check back in a bit to see if you need anything else." Snagging the chair they were no longer using, he then disappeared into the crowd.

Lawson picked up his sandwich. "Do you need to get back to the shelter soon?"

"Not unless the rain turns into a storm. A lot of animals get panicky with thunder and lightning. I'd want to be there for them."

"Then how about coffee and dessert when we finish this?"

Her conversation with Betty stuck in her mind. If he was a keeper, did she dare extend her time with him? She didn't want a keeper. Men were forever off her to-do list. Yes, she knew that made her seem shallow, judging all men by one bad experience.

But it had been really bad.

And yes, it also made her a coward. She didn't care. Going through that shame, suffering the vile verbal attacks, the hatred, while also watching her mother's life fade away... It was a nightmare she'd never be able to forget.

Betty had the right idea. Focus on the positive times. Look to the future.

Maybe have a little fun.

"Should I retract my offer?" His gaze was solemn, sincere. "I didn't mean to put you on the spot."

With a crooked smile, she shook her head. "You didn't. I just have the bad habit of overanalyzing everything."

"Meaning us?"

Especially anything that had to do with him, but she shook her head and said, "Life in general. But yes, if the weather holds, I'd enjoy dessert and coffee."

Concern remained in his eyes, but he accepted her answer. "Then I'm glad I asked."

Now that she'd committed, she was glad, too. This was a much better way to spend a dark, rainy evening than sitting home alone, dwelling on things she couldn't change. Looked like this would be the second time Lawson had made her evening better.

If she wasn't careful, it might become a habit.

Lark ordered her own meal once she'd decided to intrude on Oliver. Belatedly, it struck her that he might have been meeting someone else. She watched him as the waiter set out their food, grilled chicken and vegetables for him, soup and a salad for her. They were each enjoying iced tea.

"So," she said, hoping she hadn't done the unthinkable. "Did you have a date?"

He paused with a bite of chicken halfway to his mouth. "A date?"

"Yes, you know. A social activity between two people who are attracted to each other."

He went perfectly still. "Lark, this is not a date."

Her lips wanted so badly to lift in a smile, but she managed to suppress the urge. Barely. "I didn't mean *me*, so mellow out already. I'm pushy, but I'm not that bad."

He didn't appear to agree.

"By the way, it's a little insulting for you to look so appalled by the idea of a date with me." The humor got the better of her and she grinned. "Look, I know I'm a mess right now, and

I don't generally come on strong when I'm interested. I'm just friendly."

One of his brows lifted, but otherwise his gaze stayed serious behind his glasses.

Oh, he wouldn't be an easy one, but then, she enjoyed a challenge. "I'm asking if I messed up your plans with someone else."

After giving her a long look, he said simply, "No."

She went on as if he hadn't spoken. "Because if so, I can get my food to go."

Two seconds passed in condemning silence.

Never let it be said that she couldn't take a hint—especially when she was hit over the head with it. "In fact, if that's what you prefer..." This time she didn't allow an uncomfortable silence. She quickly shook her head and corrected her words with a laugh. "Obviously, it's what you prefer. I'm sorry I crowded you." His clear annoyance left her feeling equal parts insulted and downcast. Ready for an escape, she searched the restaurant to flag down a waiter. "Let me just find someone and I'll get out of your hair."

"You don't have to leave."

"No, it's fine. There aren't any other seats for me to move to, and besides, I'm soaked through to the skin. I wouldn't mind changing into dry clothes." Her slicker was cute, and for a dash through the rain it would have been fine. Lingering with Kathleen, though, had done her in. Her hair was sodden. Her makeup was mostly removed...with some smudges remaining.

She hadn't cared until now. Before realizing that her company was unwanted, she'd been having fun, enjoying the wet rescue of the town mannequin and seeing it as an adventure. She'd been lighthearted, something she hadn't genuinely felt in too long.

Now, though, well, she refused to analyze the uncomfortable feelings plaguing her.

"Blast. Everyone is so busy. I'll go to the bar and ask for a take-home container." She half stood while saying, "Give me just a second—"

"Lark." He reached out, his hand catching hers and halting her retreat. "I'm sorry."

"No, really, it's fine." Her butt remained off the chair, caught between standing and sitting. She wasn't sure what to do. Maybe if his hand wasn't so big and warm, and his touch wasn't so gentle, almost careful, she'd have found the backbone to tug it away and continue on with her plan of escape.

"It's not," he insisted. "I had a hectic day and I'm taking it out on you."

"Wouldn't have happened if I hadn't forced myself on you." Her eyes almost crossed as the words left her mouth. *Her*, force herself on *him*? The man was twice her size.

"You didn't…" He coughed to cover a laugh, then gently tugged to urge her back into her seat. "How about we start over?"

Giving in, she sat. Unlike him, she wasn't into fitness and her thighs hadn't been at all keen on the awkward pose. "Fine." She freed her hand and relaxed back in her chair. "From what point? Where I nearly ran you down, where I hauled you to an empty table, or where I joined you and then ordered food?"

"Back to you almost running me down." He put his elbows on the table beside his plate, laced his fingers together and tapped them to his chin. "Lark. Hello. It's good to see you again."

Ha! She liked this game. Holding out her arms in enthusiastic greeting, she said, "Oliver! Hey. I wasn't planning to eat but now that you're here, and I see a table, you should grab it."

"Consider it grabbed."

She stifled her laugh to ask demurely, "Would you mind if I joined you?"

His snort was loud enough to draw attention. "That sounds *nothing* like you."

Lark put her nose in the air. "This is a do-over, if you'll re-call. Your idea. I can replay it however I choose."

"Right, okay." He cleared his throat. "Wow, you're right, it is crowded. Sure, we should definitely share a table. That is, if you're not here with anyone else?"

Her heart gave a little jump of joy at his interest, but she did her best to play it cool. "Nope. I was just helping a friend get Kathleen out of the rain, and then in you came. Oh, and that reminds me! *Cat yoga.*"

His brows twitched down in confusion. "Okay, sorry, I was keeping up just fine until that last part."

Seriously, she needed to slow down and think before speak-ing, not just blurt out whatever was in her head. Then again, he was here with her now, sharing a meal and no longer so put out with her. "Go ahead and eat and I'll tell you all about it, and then you can tell me how I'm the answer to all your problems."

"*All* my problems, huh?"

"Well, obviously I don't know every problem you have, but I suspect your bad day was tied around your fitness center and has to do with the formidable Betty Cemetery, so in this case, I think I can help."

His brows crowded closer together, but he huffed a laugh and dutifully dug into his food. "Can't wait to hear it."

Lark knew she had to pitch this right, to really sell it, and with any luck he'd start to actually like her—because already she more than liked him.

Oliver had to admit, he was impressed with Lark's pitch. She seemed to be full of creative solutions to problems. "If you ever lose interest in being a stylist, you should go into marketing."

She gave him a beautiful smile, and even with her dark hair limp from the weather, and her face a little smudged with the makeup she'd tried to remove, she looked incredible. Here, in the restaurant, the color of her eyes matched the stormy skies outside.

He asked, "Have you ever done any yoga?"

"Tiny bit," she said. "Just at home by my lonesome, not out in a class or anything. I was…" Her words trailed off, and a nearly painful expression fell over her face before she blinked it away and produced an unconvincing smile. "I had a rough patch, you know? I was trying to figure out how to get back to my happy self, and yoga sounded like it could be relaxing."

"Physically," he agreed. "Emotionally, too, if you can get into the right frame of mind and adjust your breathing with it." Oliver couldn't imagine anything dampening Lark's spirits. She was always so cheery, practically bubbling over with enthusiasm. Curiosity gnawed on him, but he wouldn't ask.

However, if she ever chose to share, he'd listen.

She changed the subject. "I have other marketing ideas, if you really wouldn't mind hearing them."

"Only if you let me pay for your dinner."

Her gaze searched his.

He said easily, "I used to pay marketing people, and you're just giving away incredible ideas. It's the least I can do."

"Oh. Well, then…"

Her uncertainty made him feel like a jackass. He'd done that to her, being so cross and cold. Hoping to repair some of the damage, he said, "I'd like us to be friends."

She said quickly, "I'd like that, too."

"Perfect. So let's continue with the do-over. You'll forget my grumpiness and accept my offer of dinner, and you'll share these brilliant ideas of yours with me, all in the name of friendship."

A smile teased her lips. "Okay, then. Thank you." With a breath, she announced, "Other ideas—although they might not apply to everyone who visits your fitness center. I assume people will be looking for different outcomes?"

"Very much so." The idea of discussing business with her appealed to him. There hadn't really been anyone, not since the death of his father. He rubbed his mouth, considering how much to say. This wasn't a date—it absolutely wasn't—but if it was, he wouldn't talk about endless, dull business stuff. So he'd hit the highlights, and if she had questions, he'd answer them.

She watched him as he considered things, then snickered. "You are always so serious."

And she was always happy. "Just trying to decide how much to share."

"Your secrets are safe with me."

Odd, but he believed her. He didn't know her that well, yet he instinctively trusted her. "Thank you, but we won't talk secrets tonight."

"Darn."

She so easily made him laugh. "I just don't want to put you to sleep."

"Plan to be boring, huh? Hey, I have trouble sleeping, so lay it on me."

His thoughts jumped around from her smile and sunny disposition, to her restless in her bed with some unsolvable worry. Both images made him too warm, and he really wouldn't mind helping her with the sleep problem... *No.* This was friendship only. He had to keep that in mind.

"All right, then. The plan is to offer just about everything, from instructor-led classes, to yoga and Pilates, to high-intensity interval training. I was a physical therapist before deciding to open the fitness center, so I'm qualified to do fitness assessments, which is one of the things Betty objects to. She seems to think I should only smile at people and tell them they're perfect, instead of helping them to reach goals."

Lark laughed. "That doesn't sound at all like Betty, because I'm not sure she thinks anyone is perfect."

"She said her girls had changed her."

"Her girls?"

He shrugged. "According to Betty, body positivity is a must and I can't be running a business where I'll make people feel bad. Didn't matter how many ways I tried to explain to her that people come to me with objectives in mind and I just help them find the best workout for achievement." He got irked all over again, and took a long swallow of his tea. "You'd think I had stormed around the town throwing insults at people or something."

"Betty doesn't actually own the town, you know. You don't have to have her approval."

"Very true. My business has been approved, and strictly speaking, she can't dictate to me how to run it. That said, the woman has clout around here and I prefer to keep things on an even keel." He wanted to take an active part in the town, not be treated as an outsider. He could help others, give them a positive outlet when stress, frustration or anger overtook their lives, as it had with his brother.

All of that would be more easily accomplished with Betty Cemetery on board.

"Tell you what," Lark said. "I'll talk to her, subtly of course, and tell her that I'd really like to tone up. It's the truth—the most exercise I get is walking around the salon chair with my arms up to cut, curl or style hair."

His gaze dipped over her. "You look in great shape to me." Incredible shape. Distracting shape. He wouldn't mind seeing more of her shape.

Her lips pursed as she struggled not to laugh. "Thank you. My arms are toned, I guess." She wrinkled her nose. "The rest of me not so much. I could use some firming up, and some slimming around the hip-and-thigh area."

"See, this—" he gestured at her body "—is exactly what

Betty was talking about. Body image is important, and you have a beautiful body."

Her eyes flared and she glanced around as if worried others might hear. "I don't," she insisted.

"You absolutely do. If you want to work on flexibility, or strength, or just general fitness, I'm happy to help." Any way at all. "But you don't need any slimming. You don't need any firming."

"You," she said, pointing a forkful of salad at him, "haven't seen that much of my body to judge."

"You wear leggings, Lark. And fitted shirts. Your shape is pretty obvious."

"It is?"

Oliver leaned closer. "You're a woman who attracts attention and there's nothing wrong with that. Body, face, style and especially your smile. You walk in a room and take over—in a good way."

She shared that stunning smile with him. "Well, you're making my day."

"I'm sincere when I say your body is perfect. Perfect proportions, perfect symmetry, perfectly appealing."

"I think I'm going to blush."

"You think?" He could see the heat in her cheeks, but damn, she even looked good flustered. "Just so you know, that isn't the usual body assessments we'll be sharing at my center."

That earned him another laugh. "You should try it on Betty. She'd love it."

"I won't lie to her, but neither would I give an unsolicited opinion. If she shared realistic goals, I'd calculate a plan based on her age and overall fitness."

"You sound like a guru."

He tapped his temple. "It's just knowledge, learned through a lot of schooling and practical application."

"And your own fitness," she said. "Because I noticed right off that you were plenty buff."

Absurd how much her comment warmed him. "I stay in shape." He took extra care with his physical and mental health after watching his brother fade to a shell of a man.

"What other knowledge do you have?"

"I've learned a lot about setting up and running a business. I have a fair understanding of security, too."

"Security?"

"For protecting a business, or a home. It's just something that always interested me. When my parents had security set up at our home, I was in my late teens and dogged the installers every step. Then at a previous job, I noticed some inadequacies in their system and suggested some upgrades."

"Thankfully," she said, "there isn't a lot of crime in Cemetery."

His frown gathered. "No one can ever be too careful, so even here, I hope you take precautions." As a woman alone, she needed to be aware of every risk imaginable.

"Sure. I look both ways before crossing the street, and I lock my apartment door at night."

Not at all what he meant, but her amused smile kept him from belaboring the point. "So let's hear the details for your marketing ideas."

"On top of handing out some T-shirts to the hot guys and women in town, and the cat yoga, of course, you could coordinate with Berkley for a weekly or monthly thing where you walk the dogs at the shelter. Maybe have a designated starting point. It'd score big with Betty, I'm sure. Kathleen the mannequin could be there, and Betty could lead it off, like a walk through the park, and around the scenic part of town."

"Almost like a parade."

"A parade! Yes, we should coordinate that, too."

Happiness looked good on her, but then, he suspected this particular woman was always appealing. "I like it."

"Sounds fun, right?"

He grinned at her. "So fun that one meal might not be repayment enough."

7

Three days of rain turned the shelter's exercise yard into a muddy mess, which made Berkley, her two part-time staff and every available volunteer put in extra hours to keep paws and kennels clean. They'd no sooner get the job done than it became muddy again. She couldn't wait for the return of super-hot, sunny days.

Thankfully, Hero was a fastidious fellow who avoided mud puddles when possible. Still, his paws had to be cleaned every time he went out, and when playing with a few of the other dogs at the shelter? It was game on. If one leaped into mud, Hero followed.

The upside to that was they were each equally exhausted at the end of the day. Dinner, a couple of hours cuddling on the couch, and they were both ready to crash.

Hero slept wherever he wanted, as did Cheese. Sometimes they were in her bed, sometimes on the floor—which meant she always had to step carefully when first awakening—and sometimes they'd go to another room.

Made her wonder if she snored, or more likely, tossed and turned too much.

Today, as she sluggishly stirred and opened her eyes, she found Cheese staring down at her intently, a clue that the cat was hungry. Berkley groaned, gave her a tickle under her furry chin, then lifted her head to locate Hero.

On the floor, curled up nose to butt, Hero snoozed on.

Smiling down at him, she then whispered, "Morning, bud."

He jerked awake with a start, legs wheeling in the air a moment before he got upright and greeted her with a wide yawn, showing sharp teeth and curling his long tongue.

Body aching and head muzzy, Berkley sat up and stretched. It didn't help. "How lucky am I to wake up with two such amazing friends?"

Cheese headbutted her once before leaping from the bed and leaving the room, no doubt heading to the kitchen for breakfast.

For only a moment, as she sat there on the side of the bed, Berkley was transported back in time to the naive age of seventeen. She'd always awakened then with a stretch, too, anxious to check on her mom, who had good days and bad. Full of love and hopes for a bright future, Berkley had found the mornings easier then. Her mother, despite her illness, had been happier, uplifted by Berkley's romance with a considerate, mature man who'd promised to help her through all the tough times. In those days, her mother had thought her only daughter had found love and she'd been upbeat.

Then the news had struck, and her name became synonymous with everything ugly in the world. She was a husband stealer, a dog-faced, pathetic loser. A few people had said it was

good her mother was dying, because that was preferable to living with Berkley.

Pain struck her anew, and her hand automatically went to
her stomach as if to soothe the queasiness churning there. Until
that awful episode of her life, she hadn't known people could
be so deliberately cruel. And she'd never expected such cruelty
to be aimed at her.

Hero whined, snapping her back to her morning and the
long list of things she had to get done.

"I'm sorry, Hero. Didn't mean to worry you."

Her soft tone did the trick, sending his whip tail swinging
wildly. "C'mon. Let's get going." She let him out to his enclosed area first thing, thankful that she didn't smell any rain
in the air. She was exhausted through and through, so it was
no wonder that it took her a few minutes to get clearheaded
enough to realize she didn't feel great.

This was not going to be a typical Monday morning.

Every muscle ached and her head hurt. Her eyes burned.
Her throat felt scratchy.

Didn't matter. Her job was the type that didn't allow for
unplanned breaks. Whether she was sick or not, those animals
depended on her, so ten minutes later she had her tangled hair
tied up, her face washed and her teeth brushed. She grabbed
a cup of coffee, hurriedly drank it while leaning against the
sink and watched the dawn lighten the dark sky. She couldn't
stop yawning.

It wasn't just the surfeit of work and a possible cold that made
her tired, though. Ever since their shared dinner, her nights
had been restless with thoughts of Lawson. How nice his no-
pressure company had been. He'd been considerate without
coming on to her, concerned without showing pity. And he'd
seemed to enjoy it as much as she had.

But that was a few evenings ago and she really wouldn't have minded a *little* interest from him. He could stop in and say hi. Or something.

Blah. She annoyed herself with her endless speculation. If she wanted his company, she could stop by—but she didn't. She could call him after work and ask him if he'd like to share another meal.

She wouldn't.

Instead, she rinsed her cup, jammed a hat on her head, stuffed a few tissues into her pocket, and trudged out to greet her adoring fan club of dogs and cats. As she allowed them out into their private grassy areas, she once again gave heartfelt thanks to Betty and the town council, as well as every person residing in Cemetery, for the generous accommodations supplied to the animals. For a small town, they'd really pulled together to set up a fantastic shelter. Right now, they had plenty of room, but she knew that would eventually change. There'd be times when they were so crowded, they'd need help fostering pets.

But for now, even while feeling crappy, she enjoyed the extra care she could give each animal. Hero joined her out in the yard, though she kept him contained on a long lead. That was another perk of her job. She didn't need to leave her pets.

At eight o'clock, Whitley showed up and greeted her with the explanation "You looked tuckered out yesterday, so I thought I'd get here earlier today and give you a hand."

Leaning on the broom handle, Berkley said, "You're a welcome sight. Thank you. I was just about to feed the hungry hoard, so—"

"I'll do it." Whitley gave her a long look. "Maybe you should take a break."

"I'm fine." Or she would be, as soon as she found her pep. She'd lost it somewhere, and her sneakers seemed to be made of lead.

Unconvinced, Whitley said, "Okay, but don't overdo it. This

place couldn't run without you. You're the heart here, you know."

What a wonderful way to put it. "Thanks. Maybe I'll go grab a protein bar, but I won't be long."

Saying it was easier than doing it. For some reason, even the bland snack made her stomach flinch. After consuming half the bar, she opted for another cup of coffee, again standing at the sink. If she sat down, she wasn't sure she'd get back up. In fact… She forced herself to get moving.

Two hours later, she was just about finished with her morning chores when her phone vibrated with an incoming call. Pulling it from her pocket, she checked the screen and automatically smiled when she saw it was Betty.

It was as good of an excuse to sit down as any, so as she answered, she went to a bench and dropped—literally dropped—onto it. "Good morning."

"Morning, sunshine," Betty said. "I'm coming out to see you. Do you need anything?"

Confused, Berkley checked the time. "It's only ten."

"So? You've been up and working for five hours now."

True. She and Betty talked often enough that Betty knew her schedule. "You don't usually make it here until noon or later." New worry bloomed, despite the reassurances Lawson had given her. "Are you okay?"

Betty made a sound of frustration. "Are you calling me old, Berkley?"

"Well…no. But…" She *was* old. "I, um…"

"You think I sleep my days away?"

"Of course not!" Few people got as much accomplished as the town matriarch. "No one would call you a slug, Betty, so stop trying to pick an argument with me."

Betty laughed. "Oh, I do enjoy how you stand up to me. I'm leaving now, so no more arguments. How about I bring some Danish?"

Her stomach couldn't decide if that sounded good or revolting, so she said, "Sure, but nothing too heavy for me."

Pouncing on that, Betty asked, "Why? Are you unwell?"

With her gaze seeking out Whitley, who studiously brushed a cat with her face averted, Berkley asked, "Did someone say I was unwell?"

The entirely fake laugh wouldn't fool anyone. "I'm on my way," Betty sang.

Sang. It was absurd. To many, Betty was a dragon. The woman did *not* sing. "You're up to something."

"Visiting a friend, so sue me."

"Fine." Berkley was only wasting energy debating it on the phone. "Drive safely." As soon as she disconnected, she approached Whitley, but before she could say a word or question her, Erin, her other part-time worker, pulled up.

That made two who'd come in early.

"Morning, all," Erin called. "With all the rain we've had, I figured I could lend a hand here before I get started on the paperwork for the week. Fortunately, the ten-day forecast shows only clear skies, so we'll be past this little crisis in no time."

Honestly, Berkley was glad for the help. No one hustled like Erin. "Two of the dogs need baths." That particular word caused some of the dogs to howl, while Hero leaped in hopeful joy. He did love his baths. "Make that three dogs."

They'd just gotten set up and were starting when Betty arrived.

She emerged from her car with a lot of fanfare—while shining some light on this morning's mysteries. "Oh good, you're both here."

Whitley and Erin winced with guilt.

See? Berkley knew something was afoot.

"Berkley, you need to go sit down before you fall down. We'll take Hero in with us, and would you mind fetching Gladys? I always enjoy visiting with her."

Betty and the older dog, Gladys, had gotten very friendly over the last few weeks. "I don't think—"

Her protest got cut short when Betty removed two bags from her back seat. "These pastries are for you to share," she said to Whitley and Erin. "My small way of thanking you for your help today."

Erin and Whitley looked at each other, then grinned. Usually they were wary of Betty, and with good reason.

Berkley, however, was used to Betty's kinder side. She waved a hand. "Go on, you two. Take a break and enjoy the snack."

"You're not mad?" Erin asked her.

"About the organized interference?" She wondered who had instigated it, but she'd put her money on Betty. "Of course not. I appreciate the thoughtfulness."

"You really do look kaput," Whitley said.

"I'll take care of her," Betty announced. "Now, where's Gladys?"

With a grin, Whitley said, "Go on in. I'll bring her to you."

A few minutes later, in Berkley's home with fresh coffee and a half-eaten cake donut in front of her, she accepted defeat. She really was kaput.

The second Gladys had come in, she'd greeted Betty with pure joy and hadn't quite settled down yet. The dog was a chunky thing, a mutt with short yellow fur, a thick body, small head and stubby legs that didn't match her length.

She seemed to want Betty to hold her, and kept hopping as if trying to get into Betty's lap. Betty finally said, "Oh, sweetheart. We don't have the right body types for jumping."

Berkley snorted a surprised laugh. When Betty frowned at her, she laughed even more. Exhaustion and hilarity did not go well together. She kept seeing Gladys and Betty as comparable body types and it'd set her off again. She was near tears by the time she wound down, and couldn't catch her breath without coughing. Poor Hero began to fret.

"Do you allow him on the furniture?"

"Of course," Berkley said. "This is Hero's home, too."

"Then let's go to the living room and get comfortable so these poor dogs can relax."

Berkley considered that a great idea, especially since she could barely stay upright in the straight-backed chair.

Before she dropped into a seat, Berkley helped Gladys up onto the couch, and Betty settled beside her. Hero hopped up, so Berkley took the opposite end of the couch, then propped her feet on the coffee table and put her head back.

To keep from falling asleep, she said, "Gladys has really gotten attached to you."

Betty cleared her throat. "I've been thinking of adopting her."

That got her attention. "Oh?" She turned her head and found both hope and expectation in Betty's expression—as if Berkley could deny her anything. Cautiously, she said, "That sounds wonderful."

"Gladys is old and slow, like me. She's settled, not a rambunctious puppy that would trip me up and want me to play fetch for hours. We like each other."

"All true." Gladys had already curled up beside Betty with her head in her lap. "Maturity can also mean bladder problems."

"Don't I know it," Betty muttered.

That nearly set her off in another fit of giggles, but Berkley managed to keep it together. "Arthritis, too, hip dysplasia."

"You're preaching to the choir." Betty stubbornly insisted, "I want Gladys. We'll be good company for each other."

"And when it rains and Gladys gets muddy paws? Or when she leaves messes on the floor?"

"I'll hire someone to help."

Berkley reached across the couch, palm up. Surprised, Betty reached back, and they clasped hands. "I'd love nothing more than for you and Gladys to be together. I just want to make sure that you're not overdoing it." Her throat got tight, but she didn't hesitate. "You're important to me, Betty. The most important person I've had in my life since losing my mother."

Betty's entire face pinched, her eyes going liquid and her mouth quivering. "Oh, you!" She squeezed Berkley's fingers, then swiped at her eyes. "Don't you dare make me cry. I'm such an ugly crier. It's my worst failing." She sniffled, alarming Hero, who sat at attention.

Since she loved them both, Berkley let them be themselves. If Betty wanted to cry, then she could cry. If Hero wanted to comfort her, she didn't think Betty would mind.

They were both wonderful.

Swallowing heavily, and then giving another sniff, Betty composed herself. "Thank you. I honestly never knew how nice it was to be needed." Her mouth twitched into a crooked smile. "Or how much I wanted that. I'd been alone and independent so long, and I kept assuring myself that I was living my best life."

"You are," Berkley said. "You have a wonderful life. The entire town honors you."

"Honors me, sometimes fears me and often avoids me." She sighed. "I've made friends with many young women lately. They're kind and they include me, and they're each special to me. But with you it's different."

Berkley smiled. "Because I need you."

"Maybe you do for now, but that'll change. You, too, are independent and strong—like me. You're also young, so you have time to choose a different path, if you want it."

"If you're talking about Lawson—"

"I'm talking about embracing the town and everyone in it, including Lawson. I know you're busy here, and you certainly need some time to recover from whatever bug you have now, but you should join us at the town council. We meet the second and last Thursday of every month at six. Plus we have a tea club now. That's the first and third Monday of every month."

Berkley laughed. "That's a busy schedule you keep."

"You can find your place here, Berkley. Not just on the periphery, staying out here alone with the shelter animals. In the town, with the people. Good people and annoying people, fun and bossy."

Berkley tipped her head.

"Okay, yes, I'm the bossy one."

They shared a soft laugh.

"I'm just saying, you might find people as interesting as animals."

"And then you think I won't need you?"

Betty stroked Gladys's fur. "I won't be around forever. I want to know that you'll be okay."

Her throat tightened more. "My mother said the same words to me." Right before the scandal turned their lives upside down.

Betty went right past that. "What won't ever change is our mutual love for animals. You give them the care I can't. If I didn't already love you, that'd do it right here."

Gladys began to snore, which prompted Hero to get comfortable again, too.

"Thank you," Berkley whispered. "For making this shelter possible, for being my friend and for loving me."

Heaving a deep breath and closing her eyes, Betty said, "You're most welcome."

It was the last thing said, and the last thing Berkley remembered before she dozed off.

Lawson glared at Kathleen, who was in front of his shop and now holding a sign that said *Why don't you like me?* Not funny.

He didn't know who'd put her there, but she wasn't around when he'd arrived earlier, or when he'd changed out the front window display. Lark had given him a great idea, one of many, and now, instead of just showing a variety of his products, he featured actual jobs he'd gotten.

The salon's apron was visible for all to see, as well as a T-shirt advertising Saul's restaurant. Next to that was a sleeveless shirt promoting Oliver's new gym. His favorite, though, was a T-shirt for the shelter that said *The Love Shack* in bold print, and beneath it: *Rescue, Save, Love.*

Today had been busy with a lot of people coming and going, some picking up commissioned work, others requesting special print jobs, some browsing the many designs for lake life and some specifically for Cemetery.

The town name really was catchy.

Through it all, he'd been distracted, so he had no idea when the mannequin was placed there.

Again, he looked at the clock. He had hours to go before closing tonight, but he couldn't help thinking about Berkley. In a small town, word traveled fast, so he knew she wasn't feeling well. Apparently, Betty had wrangled some extra workers for her throughout the day so she wouldn't be so busy. According to Will, Betty herself had gone out to the shelter to ensure Berkley got some rest.

Would Berkley listen, though? She adored Betty, but she also felt a huge responsibility to every single pet at the shelter. Berkley didn't just ensure they had food and a clean place to sleep. She gave them love, attention, exercise, the room to feel free while also being a part of a family.

As a customer left, Will said, "You should take your break while you can."

"What about you?" Their morning had been so busy, neither of them had gotten a break.

"I brought my lunch with me, so no worries." He gave Lawson a critical perusal and said, "Man, you should go check on her."

"Who?" If Will meant Kathleen, he could forget it. Lawson wasn't going anywhere near the mannequin.

"The woman working at the shelter. That's who you're worrying about, right?"

"Who says I'm worrying?"

Will grinned. "I don't know, dude, but you've been watching the clock ever since Wheeler stopped by and said Betty was recruiting people to work out there in shifts. Seriously, I've got this covered."

He was so damned tempted, but… "It's too much work for one person."

"Nah. We don't have any more orders going out today, and I can eat my lunch here at the counter in between customers. It's just a sandwich. Go. Take an hour if you want. I'm good."

God bless energetic nineteen-year-olds. "If you're sure you don't mind…"

"I got you. No sweat."

Lawson clapped him on the shoulder. "Remind me to give you a raise." Fortunately, he'd parked in back, so he was able to avoid Kathleen completely as he went out and got in his truck. The shelter was away from the center part of town, but Lawson cut back on the drive by going to his own house and walking through the woods. He wasn't surprised to see Whitley and Erin, since they both worked for Berkley, but Yardley and Mimi, women he'd met a few times, were also there, as well as Wheeler, who was apparently spending his day off from the restaurant by walking dogs.

When the town all pulled together like this, how could he not love it? They didn't just welcome people, they embraced them.

Whitley hurried over to him. "Lawson, what are you doing here? I thought you'd be at your shop."

"Using my lunch break to check on things."

Whitley gestured over to the fenced area for the shelter.

"We've got it covered. I don't think we've ever had this many volunteers at one time. Between me and Wheeler, the dogs are loving it, and Yardley and Mimi are keeping the cats entertained. Emily is coming tomorrow. She adopted her pets—a bonded cat and dog—from Berkley, before Berkley moved here and took over The Love Shack."

"I wasn't aware." But he liked hearing it. Keeping all the names straight had been a challenge at first, but now he knew Yardley and Mimi were best friends. "Yardley is the wedding planner, right?"

"Yup. And Emily is the flower lady."

He nodded.

"Erin's been keeping track of everything so we can give Berkley a report whenever she emerges."

"Emerges?" What did that mean?

"Yeah, see, she and Betty went inside a few hours ago and haven't come back out." She bit her lip and glanced at the door to the house, which wasn't that far from the shelter. "I hope that doesn't mean Berkley is really sick. She looked pale when I got here, like she could sit down and nod off— Where are you going?"

Already on his way, Lawson said, "I'll just check on her and see what's up." Everything Whitley had said only added to his concern. He didn't like it.

In so many ways, Berkley had an indomitable spirit. She was a fighter, thank God, given what she'd been put through. She'd been used by a cheater, viciously maligned and lost her mother, all at a young age, yet she'd come out of it with a huge heart and the drive to help animals.

Catching up to him, Whitley said, "Betty's still in there with her."

"I won't intrude," he promised. "I'll give you a full report in just a few minutes."

"Okay," she said, not looking convinced. "But if it irks Betty, tell her it was your idea."

He sent her a grin. "I'll take all the blame." Opening the door quietly, Lawson glanced around the interior. The side door he'd used, which was closest to the shelter, opened into a small laundry area and mudroom. Right beyond that was the kitchen.

It amused him, in a somewhat detached way, that although the shelter was big and modern, sleek in design with everything Berkley would need to provide the best care for the animals, her house was much more compact, clearly meant for only one person.

He wouldn't call it a tiny house, but it was definitely on the small side. A two-seater café table took up the available space between appliances and counters. Through the kitchen he could see the living room, and a hallway set at an angle that probably led to two bedrooms.

Unlike his place, her décor was purely functional. Coffee maker on the counter, cups on pegs behind it. She'd left herself almost no room for meal prep, but then, she'd already said she ate alone. As he looked around again, this time imagining her in the space, his heart gave an odd, unrecognizable thump. It was sad to think of her by herself, but it was also heartwarming to know she had the strength to face the world alone, to make her own rules about her life and how she wanted to live it.

Some people would be downhearted about living here in the woods all alone. Berkley saw it as a way to do what she loved. He didn't have a single doubt that she was grateful for this particular lifestyle—a home of her own near her beloved shelter.

Damn, he admired her.

A noise, like a low rumbling engine, drew him to the open doorway that led to the tidy living room. One small sofa, a padded chair, a couple of tables and a small TV on a stand filled the room.

He couldn't stop grinning. The women sat at either end of the sofa.

On the far side, Betty slouched in her seat as if someone had knocked her out: short legs angled out before her, arms sprawled at her sides, head tipped back and sideways, and with her mouth open while she loudly snored. A chubby yellow dog lay next to her, also snoring.

Hero, who was on the sofa, too, had come awake, but fortunately not with any alarm. He just lifted his head and watched Lawson from his position beside Berkley at the opposite end.

She was conked out, but unlike Betty, Berkley was curled in her seat with her feet resting on the edge of the coffee table. She had one arm tucked close to her body, and the other slung over Hero's neck. Her eyes were closed and her cheeks were flushed. She looked limp, messy and adorable.

As he stood there watching her, Hero seemed to smile, then he lumbered off the couch, which disturbed Berkley—but not the other dog or Betty.

They snored on.

Hero came to him for some pats while Berkley slowly blinked her eyes open. Seeing him left her disoriented for a moment, then she glanced around, spotted Betty and smiled.

What a picture she made. Soft and sleepy. Sweet. Strange things happened to his libido as he gazed at her, things that felt good in indefinable ways. All he knew was that he could have stood there watching her for hours and been content.

Lifting a finger to her lips, Berkley gave him the universal sign for quiet and gingerly left her seat, still without disturbing Betty.

When she took his hand and led him to the kitchen, he silently followed, as did Hero.

It struck him how natural it felt. It was his first time in her house, but it was as if they'd done this dozens of times. Smiled, touched, shared. Did she feel it, too?

Around the corner, nearer to the door he'd entered, she turned to face him and whispered, "I don't want to wake Betty."

Her nap hadn't done her hair any favors. She wore not a speck of makeup.

And she was still beautiful.

Slowly, in case she objected, he removed the hat from her head and set it on the counter. With his fingertips, he smoothed some of the wayward, pink-tipped locks that had escaped her updo.

Berkley didn't move. Her smile slipped away and her eyes widened a little. Blue eyes, full of questions.

It seemed the most natural thing in the world to drift his hand down until he cupped her cheek. Damn, her skin was soft.

And too warm.

Frowning a little, he put the backs of his fingers to her forehead. "I think you have a fever."

Confusion stole the dazed expression from her face, then she blinked several times and stepped back so quickly she bumped into the counter. With a wince, she rubbed her back. "I'm probably warm from sleeping. I never nap, except Betty was insistent, and we were talking, and then... I dunno."

"You're running on empty." Never would he tell her the job was too much for her. Berkley would know that better than him, but he was glad Betty had organized extra help. Instead, he nodded and said, "I should know, because it happened to me once."

"What did?"

"The weather, the job, lack of sleep—it all caught up to me. We were clearing destruction from tornados in Texas." Tension crept into his neck, just remembering. "All around us, people had lost entire homes. Some had lost family. A school was leveled."

Hero stepped up to him, bumping him with his head. When Lawson looked down at the dog, he realized Hero was looking out for him again. He didn't require a rescue, but sometimes it seemed that Hero needed to offer his services anyway.

The dog would have been a godsend on some of his trips.

So many people wounded, emotionally and physically hurt. In utter despair. Alone. In one way, it had reminded him of the place he'd escaped. Not a disaster zone, but devastated all the same.

Berkley stepped closer and put a small hand to his chest.

Talk about a touch centering someone. She brought his focus back to the present in an instant. Covering her hand with his own, he continued. "The heat was nearly unbearable, but seeing the people who searched the rubble was worse. Most of us worked sixteen hours straight. And even then, no one wanted to quit." He curled his fingers around hers. "Swear, I didn't even know I was sick until suddenly things were swirling around me, and two of the other guys caught me. It was like my legs just came out from under me."

With a small sound, Berkley stepped even closer, her slim arms going around him in a tight hug, her cheek to his chest.

His heart thundered. Until this moment, she hadn't been keen on touching, and now here she was, wrapped around him—to give him comfort.

She and Hero had a lot in common.

At first he was stiff, his arms held out to his sides, as he decided how to react. The very last thing he'd ever want to do was spook her, or take things too far too fast. But she held on, and his basic nature took over.

Gathering her closer, he pressed his mouth to the top of her head and murmured, "Hey, I was fine. Just a touch of heat exhaustion." To distract her, he said, "You're spooking the dog."

Making a gruff sound, she tilted back to see his face. Smile gentle and gaze warm, she said, "There's no such thing as a *touch* of it. Heat exhaustion is serious."

How was it that even now, while under the weather and extra

messy, she became more beautiful to him? "The guys dragged me inside and one of the women there tended me."

Her brows hitched up. "Oh? How so?"

Yeah, maybe he shouldn't have mentioned that part. Trying to skim over it, he said, "You know, cool drink, cool cloth, stuff like that."

"Uh-huh." Stepping out of his embrace and crossing her arms, she asked, "So you're standing there—"

"More like lying there. On the couch." His mouth twitched. It was kind of fun, seeing this side of Berkley. "I guess the first thing with heat exhaustion is to elevate your legs. The guys seemed to know what to do. One of them stripped off my boots and socks." His shirt, too, though he wouldn't share that…at least not yet. "She got me the wet cloth and the drink."

Tipping up her chin to eye him critically, she said, "So there you are, sweaty feet exposed, probably overflowing her couch—"

"Definitely overflowing, but it worked because my calves were on the arm of the couch, raised up some."

"—and she just hands you the cloth?"

With an exaggerated wince, he said, "Okay, so I was pretty limp, even dizzy, you know?"

New concern brought her closer again, but this time she didn't hug him.

"Louann helped me."

"By wiping you down?"

"Yeah."

"Just your face?" she asked skeptically.

She was so damn cute, Lawson couldn't help but grin. "Actually, my face, throat, chest and arms. I was sweating like a pig, my head was pounding, and I felt like I might chuck. She kept wetting the rag and using it all over me, even my stomach and then my feet. Louann said it was the best way to help, that she needed to cool my body temperature. Every so often, she had me drink more water, but she had to help me with that, too."

Still concerned, but also clearly irked, Berkley said, "I'm imagining her as a shapely, beautiful woman fawning over you."

With a laugh, Lawson gave in to impulse and leaned down to kiss her forehead. "Louann was a stout fifty-five-year-old nurse who traveled with my boss everywhere he went. They'd been life partners for over thirty years."

"Oh."

"She treated all of us like boys, bossing us around whenever she felt like it, randomly spritzing us with sunscreen or demanding we chug down a sports drink. In a lot of ways, she was the unofficial mom of the group."

"See, now I like her."

He laughed again. "She kept me down for the rest of that day and part of the next, checking my temperature and forcing me to take it easy." He remembered those days with a mix of fondness and despair. "I wanted to be out there, doing my part, but I knew she was right. Two other guys got sick, and one ended up in the hospital with heatstroke. Louann had her hands full on that trip."

"It sounds like she was an important part of the group."

"Definitely." Other partners had traveled along, and oftentimes they'd pitched in where they could, but they weren't as vital as Louann. "Nothing draws people together like a common cause, with everyone doing what they can during a tragedy. Unfortunately, there'd been too many times we couldn't help. Too many deaths, too many left homeless."

"You can't do everything," she said.

A perfect segue for him to make his point. He cupped her face in his hands and bent his knees to look her in the eyes. "Same goes for you, Berkley. You're one person. You can only do so much. This town, the people who live here, they want to help. They're proud of the shelter, and proud to have you running it. It's like an accomplishment for them. Let them do their part." He leaned in to stress his point. "Let them feel useful."

Sudden applause had them both turning. Betty sat at the side of the couch, a little more disheveled than usual, grinning widely. "Hear, hear! Perfectly said, Lawson. No one should discount such wise sentiments. I have a feeling that soon your volunteer sign-up sheets will be full, and you'll have more help than you need."

Berkley collapsed against Lawson with a laugh.

Looping his arms around her, he thought that this could become a thing…and he wouldn't mind at all.

"You're ganging up on me, so I have to give in." She didn't let him hold her long before she straightened again and smiled. "Thank you. Both of you. You make Cemetery even better, when I hadn't thought that was possible."

8

Everything seemed to change after that day. Not just the weather, which turned hot and dry over the next two weeks, but her attitude, too. About everything. Life, friends.

Men. Or rather one man.

She no longer had a need to isolate herself.

Or shy away from her growing feelings for Lawson.

No, she didn't know how he felt in return. He might only consider them friends, and if so, she'd be okay with that.

But now she was hoping for more. How much more, she didn't know. There were times when she wasn't sure how much she could do. She'd lived for years despising the idea of romance, of involvement.

Of opening herself to scorn.

Her one experience had been horrendous on every level,

starting with realizing she'd believed lies, and culminating in humiliation and loss.

She'd had no desire to give it another go. Until Lawson.

And even with him, it was only a vague possibility. A whisper of "maybe."

Around him, her instincts had seemed to take over. She'd embraced him—and how eye-opening had that been? Thoughts of Chad? Not even.

Lawson was rock-solid, and he'd felt so good. She hadn't missed his slight hesitation, and her first thought had been panic. What if she'd erred? What if he rejected her?

Then his arms, so strong but so careful, had pulled her closer and it had all felt so natural. Like the rightest thing in the world.

The story he'd told… He could have easily died from heatstroke. What if he'd pushed himself so hard, without anyone noticing, that his body had just shut down?

She didn't want to think that he was solely responsible for the changes she was going through now, the way her awful memories had shifted to the back of her brain instead of cluttering the forefront. Betty had played a role with her kindness and open but gruff affection. And Cemetery, the warmth of the small-town vibe, it was all tied in with her fresh perspective, as if the possibilities were endless.

Still, Lawson was definitely a big factor. She was twenty-six years old and she was experiencing a crush unlike anything she'd ever known.

Better late than never.

What had happened with Chad…that had been more about desperation, she knew that now. He'd been confident and an accomplished liar, and at a time when she'd felt so alone and lost in her worry for her mother, she'd allowed herself to be seduced. Sexually, yes, much to her shame, but he'd seduced her more with false consideration. His lies had been easy to accept because she'd so badly wanted them to be true.

She'd wanted something, someone, to look forward to. A light at the end of the tunnel. What a joke that had turned out to be.

Enough of that. This was the new her, a wiser woman putting regrets in the past where they belonged, while she forged into the future with courage and confidence.

Whitley joined her as she worked with a new dog that was badly in need of attention. "How's he doing?"

"Coming along." The dog, a midsize mutt with patchy tan fur, cowered at her side now that another person was near.

"Poor baby," Whitley whispered. "Sometimes I really despise people."

"Me, too." The dog was a scrawny thing, had multiple dental issues and a few scars. He'd been badly mistreated by a woman who kept him in a cage most of his life, rarely cleaning it or letting him exercise. A guy she'd brought home on a date had seen the dog and—thank God—he'd been outraged. He was the one who called animal control, and from there, the dog had ended up with Berkley. "He'll be okay, though. We'll make it so." With a lot of TLC—tender loving care.

Whitley looked near tears, even with a scowl on her face. "Well," she said softly, so she wouldn't spook the dog, "I wanted to remind you of your appointment with Oliver Roth. I can take over here if you want. We have plenty of other people working with the rest of the animals."

The smile came despite Berkley's worries for the new dog. Betty's prediction had proved correct. Over the last two weeks, Erin had signed in several new pets, including the one Whitley cooed to now, but they'd also added multiple volunteers to their roster.

"Thanks. Just keep talking gently with him, and here, I have these soft treats for him." She passed the packet to Whitley. Until the dog became acclimated, they didn't want to put him through dental surgery. The vet, Henry Upton, treated the pets for little or no payment. At sixty-three, he had passed his practice to a younger veterinarian. Now semiretired, he dedicated himself to golfing, charitable work with animals and enjoying life. "I'll go freshen up."

While carefully stroking the dog's back, Whitley asked with a sly smile, "Will Lawson be coming by tonight?"

She and Lawson had seen each other several times lately, usually at the end of the day because Cheese stole something from him. What Berkley really loved was that he never scolded the cat. He just retrieved whatever had been taken, then stuck around for a visit. "We'll see," she said, though she hoped he would. Seeing Lawson was a highlight and something she anticipated, but she wasn't ready to admit that to anyone yet.

She'd barely admitted it to herself.

Knowing she needed to repair her hair, she headed inside. She still faced her early morning chores as something of a wreck, but once that first round of duties was done, she fixed her hair and applied makeup. Not because it felt like armor. Not anymore. Now she did it because she enjoyed it. She liked her dangling earrings and how eye makeup made her feel prettier.

Soon she'd need to find a salon to freshen the color in her hair…or she might go back to her natural color. She hadn't quite decided yet.

Five minutes later, Oliver Roth arrived. His new, sleek physical fitness center was the talk of the town. Berkley wondered if they'd be discussing cat yoga, as Lark had suggested.

She greeted him with a handshake and, when he expressed an interest, she agreed to show him around the place. "I saw you at Saul's restaurant one night."

"During the endless rain?" He nodded. "Lark pointed you out to me. She suggested some ways we might work together."

"Cat yoga, I know. I thought you'd decided against the idea, since I hadn't heard from you."

"Actually, the gym has been packed from the day we opened

last week. I had hoped it would be successful, but I hadn't expected quite that much interest. Not at first, anyway."

Curious, she asked, "So you and Betty have worked out your differences?"

His brows drew together behind his lenses. "I hope so. She's formidable, and she has high expectations, but I think it stems from a protectiveness for the town."

Berkley beamed at him. "Exactly. She's a descendant of the founder, you know."

"She told me all about it. Fascinating history." As they strolled around, he took special interest in their new dog.

"He hasn't been here long," Berkley explained. "He's still terrified, as you can see." As she said it, the dog spotted Oliver, and amazingly, he perked up.

Both Berkley and Whitley were surprised when Oliver went down on one knee and offered his hand for the dog to sniff.

An even bigger surprise was how the dog crept toward him, tail tucked, ears back...but he was moving forward, not backing up.

"My God," Berkley whispered. "He's shied away from everyone."

"No wonder," Oliver said in a low croon. "You haven't been treated well, have you, bud?"

Berkley explained the situation the dog had been in. Sometimes it wasn't easy for her to keep the anger and frustration from her tone when discussing a mistreated animal's history, but it was necessary when dealing with the public.

At night, though, she often cried for the animals who'd been through too much.

"What's his name?" Oliver asked. He lowered himself to sit cross-legged in the grass as an invitation for the dog to inch closer.

"He doesn't have one yet," Berkley said.

"I'll sponsor him," Oliver stated, his tone light and friendly.

"He obviously needs some care, and I'd be happy to pay for it." He looked up at Berkley. "I couldn't do what you do, but I can do that. I can give money. Will it help?"

Okay, then. Oliver Roth just became one of her favorite people. Deciding they were friends, whether he knew it yet or not, she lowered herself to sit beside him. "I think that's a wonderful and generous idea. The shelter runs largely on donations. Thankfully, the vet— Have you met Henry Upton?"

"He just joined my facility. Friendly guy."

She wasn't surprised. Henry liked to stay fit, saying it helped his golf swing. "He treats most of the animals for free, but in this dog's case, with the dental work he needs, there will be some costs. Nothing astronomical, but—"

"Let me know how much and I'll take care of it."

Berkley blinked at him. "Don't you want an estimate first?"

"I'm single. I'm comfortable." He lightly stroked the dog. "I'm grateful to people like you who do the tough work. Paying for his care will make me feel better, so I hope you'll accept."

"I do, thank you." She chewed her lip a moment, but watching Oliver and the dog bond fascinated her, and she wanted to do something for Oliver in return. "Why don't you name him?"

"Handsome," he said immediately, while continually petting the dog's neck, ears and back with a large, very gentle hand. "I'll name him Handsome."

"A fine name," she managed to choke out, because seriously, this particular dog was a touch on the hideous side. He had some bald spots because his fur had been trimmed out in chunks to remove mats. On top of some bad teeth that needed to be removed, he had a severe overbite. One of his eyes was forever squinted, and the other eye always held a look of panic. But she had to agree he was a sweetheart. "Handsome it is."

"What does he need? Special treats? Toys? Dog bed?"

Oh, if Lawson hadn't already caught her attention, she might have been drawn to this man. He was a picture of contrasts with his unmistakably fit body beneath the conservative clothes of a polo shirt and khaki pants. His hair and glasses made her think of a stereotypical clerk, but with warm compassion for a helpless dog.

Yup, he was the whole package... If a gal was looking. She was not.

"We can discuss everything." She glanced at the time on her phone. "Come on. I'll show you the rest of the shelter and the space where Handsome sleeps."

The dog cautiously walked with them, giving everyone worried looks, while Berkley showed Oliver the limited space of the dog's home. Concrete floor, utilitarian dog dishes, isolation... True, it was so much better than many shelters, but it still wasn't what a dog deserved. It wasn't a permanent home. A position in a family.

Oliver obviously knew it, too. He ran a hand over the back of his neck while looking things over. "Do you have limitations on what I can bring to him?"

"No, but we don't yet know how destructive Handsome might be. For instance, if you get him a fancy dog bed and he rips it up—"

"Then I'll get him another."

"If you bring him toys—"

"I'll make sure they're soft, at least until he gets the dental work he needs, but nothing that he might choke on."

Grinning, she said, "Sounds like you have a plan."

He nodded, all serious and sincere. "Thank you, Berkley. I can tell that you care, and that matters a lot. I'll come by whenever I can to visit him, to volunteer with him." He dug out a card. "In the meantime, if he needs anything, if anything happens, will you let me know?"

"If only all our visitors were as generous as you."

He looked sheepish for a moment, then dipped his head with

a laugh. He removed his glasses and used the bottom of his shirt to polish them. "I'd completely forgotten the reason I'm here."

"Visiting a dog is a good reason to forget." She led Handsome into his living space, gave him a few more of the soft treats and waited while he got comfortable on a blanket. She secured the chain-link door, then gestured for Oliver to follow her into the shelter's office.

They'd be closing soon. Lunch had been a long time ago and she was already thinking about dinner, but she didn't want to rush Oliver. His kindness to Handsome meant he deserved her patience.

Fortunately, he had things to do, too, so they did a quick tour of the space she could offer for cat yoga. It was basically the lobby, which had both an interior and exterior door to keep pets from getting out unattended when guests visited. She'd brought Oliver in through the back, where they had open spaces for the dogs to play and get used to leashes, but they also had an indoor training area.

Her shelter, if she did say so herself, was pretty darned amazing—almost as sleek as Oliver's fitness facility, but not nearly as large.

As he looked around, he asked, "Am I correct that you live in the small house on the property?"

Her warning sensors went off unexpectedly, which left her unsure how to answer.

Immediately, he said, "I'm sorry. I didn't mean to pry. I was just..." He shrugged. "Impressed? That the shelter is bigger in comparison. Not that your house isn't terrific—"

Damn it, she'd made him uncomfortable, and over ridiculous concerns. "No, I apologize. Everyone in Cemetery is aware that I live here, so I have no idea why I..." Freaked out? She hadn't, not really, but her heart had definitely lurched a little. Berkley shook her head. "Bad experience once, that's all."

"Then I hope you have good security set up, not just at your house but here at the shelter, too."

"We have the basics." Heck yeah, she did. Out here alone in the woods, with all the animals to protect? She worried about them more than herself. "Thank you." For the next few minutes, they discussed a possible schedule that would work for the cat yoga, and finally decided on a start date.

"I'll see if Lark has any suggestions on signs we should create." He smiled at the mention of her name. "So far, she's had incredible ideas."

"I agree."

"Did she talk to you about a parade?"

They spent a few more minutes discussing the requirements to be a dog walker, but so far, Berkley loved the idea. It'd be a great way to get the dogs out for attention and exercise, and maybe it could become a special event for Cemetery. They could even get Kathleen involved. Maybe create a wagon for her to ride in.

She grinned, imagining what Lawson would think of that.

By the time Oliver left, the dogs were all put away. Whitley brought Hero to her. He'd helped out with the other animals, playing peacekeeper and making sure they each felt included. He was such a great dog for welcoming other canines.

She thanked Whitley for all the extra help, waving to her as she drove off.

Erin had already left for the day, but she'd left a stack of notes for Berkley on the front counter. She picked those up, glancing through them as she headed out of the office building with Hero. On the way, she set the alarm codes and locked the doors.

They closed to the public at six o'clock, but it was always seven or later before she finished up. Not that she minded. For her, it truly was a labor of love. After all, she'd put her heart and soul into her work.

She had nothing else. No family. No significant other. No children.

She reminded herself that she was okay with that. It was a choice she'd made.

As they always did, she and Hero walked the perimeter of the play yard, ensuring that everything was properly secured. They had two layers of eight-foot-high fencing—an interior layer of fences that provided individual runs for the dogs, surrounded by a second fence that enclosed it all to ensure the safety of the animals, and anyone visiting.

The sun hung a little lower in the sky, but it wouldn't get dark for a few more hours. Lawson hadn't shown up yet, so maybe he wouldn't visit.

She refused to be bummed about that.

On the way over to her house—which, as Oliver had noted, was probably half the size of the shelter—she realized that her side door wasn't secured. It never was, because she'd never seen a reason. Friends and neighbors surrounded her, and she often went from her home to the shelter and back again.

Yet now… Now it felt like maybe that was a bad idea. She glanced down at Hero, but he just looked anxious for dinner and his bed.

With added tension squeezing her lungs, she stepped into the laundry room, and then the kitchen, pausing to listen.

Hero stared up at her curiously, unsure of this change in their pattern.

Everything was quiet. Closing and locking the door behind her, she walked through to the front door, but it was always locked because she seldom used it. Cheese, who had been sleeping on the back of the couch, stared at her with wide yellow eyes. Berkley gave her a stroke, telling herself to stop fretting.

When the house had been renovated and the shelter built, she'd specifically requested that the laundry/mudroom be at the back, closest to the shelter, to make it easy to clean up when things got messy.

A good, solid plan.

There was no reason to use the front door. She didn't entertain, so she didn't have invited guests. Visitors to the shelter drove around to the gravel parking lot near the side of her house.

Damn it, she was spooked. She unleashed Hero and gave him food, then refreshed his water. Cheese, of course, trotted into the laundry room, wanting her dinner, as well. They were at ease, so she should be, too.

With the animals taken care of, Berkley forced one foot in front of the other, going around the corner, peeking into her bathroom, then into the guest bedroom. It'd make her feel better, she reasoned, just to double-check that all was secure.

She opened the closet, but all she saw was her winter clothes hung on the rod, and her boots and extra shoes on the floor.

Forcing a deep breath, she went into her bedroom. The closet stood open because she often left it that way. The bed wasn't made, because she rarely made it. Feeling ridiculous, she knelt down and peered under the bed. Nothing but dust bunnies and a couple of boxes of keepsakes.

Calling herself a fool, she plopped down to sit on her butt, her back against the mattress and box springs. Why was she suddenly jumpy? It was almost like the static from an incoming storm, making the fine hairs on her arms stand up. She hadn't been this nervous since she was eighteen, after she'd lost her mother and had to sleep alone in her house until it could be sold.

Hero heard everything, and he could be protective. If there was any reason for nervousness, he'd have sounded a loud, barking alarm.

To distract herself, she looked at the notes Erin had left her. Another shelter wanted to know if she could take an expectant cat, due to give birth any day. Yes, she would. She put that note aside.

Another was a note from Yardley, asking if she'd please join them for tea. She did like Yardley. Heck, she liked everyone she'd met so far. Hmm… She could *try* to make that meeting. That note went to the side also.

Lastly, the director from the shelter she'd previously worked at said they'd gotten a call—from Chad Durkinson. For the longest moment, her eyes stayed glued to the name, trying to convince her brain that she'd seen it incorrectly.

Chad Durkinson.

No mistake.

Her heart shot into her throat and managed to lodge there. *No.* It couldn't be true. Chad had no reason to seek her out. None at all.

As she read the rest of the note, her hands shook.

He'd tracked her down because he wanted to see her. For what purpose? She wanted absolutely nothing to do with him. She gripped the paper, and thankfully saw that the director had told him she'd changed jobs, but he'd had the good sense not to tell Chad where she'd gone. He'd kept all her information private.

Dropping her hands to her sides, she closed her eyes in stark relief.

She tried to draw a few deep breaths, telling herself to get it together—and her phone buzzed in her rear pocket. She nearly shot off the floor.

Her heart punched back into her chest and started a furious, almost painful pounding. Fumbling, she withdrew the phone and stared at the screen with dread.

Lawson. Relieved beyond measure, she answered with a strangled, "Hello?"

After a beat of silence, he said, "Berkley? What's wrong?"

Seriously, was he psychic? It wasn't like he could see her sitting on the floor, completely rattled. "Nothing," she denied, trying to make her voice stronger. "Why?"

"You whispered."

Oh. She cleared her throat. "Yeah, the phone just startled me."

"Sorry," he said. "I'm here, but I can leave."

"Here?"

"At your door. I walked over, saw the place was quiet and realized I'd missed you. I didn't want to knock in case it got Hero and Cheese stirred up."

As soon as he said it, Hero barked. She knew and understood the sounds her dog made, and that was not a grumbling bark of warning, but rather a happy and excited greeting. Clearly he knew it was Lawson who'd come to visit.

"Hang on." She scrambled to her feet and started back through the house. Seconds later she found Hero standing at attention by the door, ears up, his entire body jiggling with the force of his wagging tail. Cheese sat atop the washer—on the clean and folded laundry she hadn't yet put away, which would now be covered in cat fur. Oh well.

The cat watched with mild interest.

If only she could adopt Cheese's aloof attitude, but unfortunately, Berkley was in the happy camp with Hero. Thankfully, she didn't have a betraying tail to give her away.

She peeked past the curtain covering the little window on the door, just as an extra precaution, and tried to school her features at the sight of him standing there, backlit by the late-day sunshine, looking sexy as sin in a black T-shirt and well-worn jeans.

Grabbing Hero's collar with one hand, she opened the door with the other.

Lawson, being awesomeness personified, quickly stepped in and immediately knelt to say hi to Hero. "Hey, buddy. How are you? You knew it was me, didn't you? Such a smart guy."

His silly voice made Hero ecstatic.

While they greeted each other, she secured the door and reset the alarm. When Lawson stood, it was to give a mock frown to Cheese, who stared back with a look of defiance. "Cheese, sweetheart, I don't suppose you know anything about a missing hat of mine?"

The cat lifted a paw and began to groom herself.

Uh-oh. Berkley offered a shrug. "I haven't seen a hat, sorry."

"She's taken to leaving my things in the woods. I've found socks there, a receipt I needed to return a faucet, and a promotional screen-cleaning cloth."

Leaping off the washer, Cheese sauntered away, tail in the air and head held high, to return to the back of the couch. Hero gave a giant yawn, showing all his strong white teeth, then he headed to the couch also. Clearly, both animals were ready to rest.

"Now," Lawson said, putting his hands to her shoulders and beginning one of those toe-curling, magical massages. "Want to tell me what's wrong?"

Out of habit, she replied, "Nothing."

He continued to knead her muscles, working out the knots, but he didn't say anything more. Once again, she'd brought tension into their conversation.

It struck her that she *could* talk to him. She *wanted* to talk to him.

Stepping away from his hands and the pleasure they gave, she turned to face him. "Actually, I'm hungry. Are you hungry? If you're sure you want to know, I could tell you all about it while we eat."

Surprising her, he cupped a hand around her neck and stroked his thumb along her jaw. "A great idea. I was going to ask you if you wanted to go out for pizza."

Immediately, she shook her head. If Chad had found out where she was, he might be in Cemetery. Not likely, but still, she didn't want to risk running into him. Not until she had a plan. "I have a frozen pizza." She winced. What a lousy offer. "Or I could make grilled cheese."

"You want to stay here?"

He asked that so simply, as if he knew that was the crux of her issue, so she nodded. "I do, yeah."

"Frozen pizza works for me. Or…" He pulled out his phone to check the time. "We could order a pizza. Usually only takes thirty minutes or less."

Berkley blew out a breath. He made this so, so easy. "Yeah, let's do that." She hadn't realized that was an option. How little did she know about her town? "Is that from Saul's restaurant?"

"No, a little place farther away from the lake. Pepperoni and sausage okay? Or are you an all-veggie pizza lover?" He frowned. "No anchovies, okay?"

How was it that a discussion about pizza could be so fun when it was with Lawson? "I'm fine with pepperoni and sausage, and if they have a salad, I'd enjoy that, too. If not, no biggie. I have colas here." She shot him a teasing look. "Unlike someone I know, I keep plenty in the fridge."

While he ordered a large pizza and two side salads, she got out glasses, added ice and poured them each a cola. It occurred to her that she'd been around him enough now to know his preferences.

They sat at her little table, and Berkley wondered how to begin.

"It's okay," he said. "If I overstepped, you don't need to—"

She shook her head. "No, you didn't." Now seemed like a good time to be truthful, so she admitted, "I'm glad you asked. I'm glad you're here with me and that you, hopefully, don't mind listening."

"I asked because I'm interested." His eyes, light brown and framed by darker lashes, were extra intent as they studied her. "I asked because I care."

Oh, way to make her heart do another flip. That particular organ was getting quite the workout today. "Thank you."

With a small laugh, she shook her head. "I mean…" Better just to get it said. "Chad is looking for me."

"Chad?" Doubt gave way to incredulity and he asked with a frown, "Chad *Durkinson?*"

See, he was as shocked as she was! "Yes, and I have no idea why. He called the shelter where I used to work and they told him I'd changed locations."

Slowly, Lawson stiffened. "Did anyone—"

"No, thank God. The director said they didn't give my new address, but Lawson, The Love Shack is on social media. We have a website. I'm listed as the director and my name hasn't changed…" Saying it out loud made it all so real again, twisting her stomach into knots and making her pulse race. "He could do a search and find me—easily."

Lawson reached out for her hand, and she gladly gave it. How amazing was it not to face this alone, to be able to share her worry with someone?

"First," he said, "I need to know. Are you afraid of him?"

"Of him personally, no. Of having it all dredged back up, most definitely yes." How to put it into words? "Being here, in Cemetery, has been amazing. I love my house. I really, really love the shelter. I've gotten close to Betty. Today I met with Oliver and we discussed the ways we can help both our businesses. Plus, he took a lot of interest in one of our new dogs. Yardley invited me to tea…" Everything had seemed so wonderful, yet now she was sick with dread.

"You're worried that if Chad comes here, he'll bring the past with him."

"You know people will whisper. Some of them will think the worst."

"Will Betty?" he asked—and the look in his eyes said he already knew the answer.

"No." Berkley didn't have any doubts on Betty's part. "She's like the grandmother I never had. She has my back."

"And she has a great BS monitor, right? She'd peg Chad in an instant."

"I'm sure you're right." Betty had incredible insight.

"Do you think Oliver will change his plans?"

Berkley shook her head. "I'm not worried about that." No one who took such an immediate interest in a needy dog could be callous enough to bother with gossip.

"Lark?"

"She doesn't strike me as the gossipy kind." The woman was far too upbeat and happy. "Lark takes an interest in everyone, and she chats freely, but only in the best possible way."

His last question came, soft but gruff. "Me?"

There was so much behind that single word, things that warmed her, that made her both tearful and happy. "No." As she said it, Berkley accepted it, deep down to her soul. "You don't think less of me for what happened."

"Just the opposite. I'm damned proud of you. The world—or at least our small part of it—came at you in the most hateful, ugly way, but look at you. More beautiful than ever, inside and out."

Her thoughts stuttered to a standstill. Beautiful? *Her?* Never in her life had she felt that way.

"Berkley," he chided. "How can you not know that? Even if you weren't so fine to look at—and you are, very fine—the amount of care you give would win over anyone. People are drawn to you."

"They're drawn to you," she countered. She, with her private, reclusive ways, they probably considered standoffish.

"Are you drawn to me, Berkley?" he asked with a small, confident smile.

She snorted. "Hero sure is. And I think Cheese secretly has a crush on you, and that's why she keeps stealing from you."

Brushing his thumb over her knuckles, he said, "She doesn't steal from anyone else?"

"She used to, but you're the only one she's targeted lately."

"I'm glad your pets like me, since I'm hoping to hang around a lot more."

Anticipation caught her breath. She wanted to reciprocate, to say something witty in return, but she'd never been good at this type of banter. So why not be truthful?

Wrinkling her nose, she confessed, "I'm bad at this."

The corner of his mouth curled. "At flirting?"

Having it confirmed made her even warmer. "Yup, that." He looked so pleased that she grinned. "I like it, though."

"So you don't mind having me around?"

Since they still held hands, she gave his a squeeze and admitted, "I'm glad you're here, and you're welcome anytime."

"From now on, I'll let you know if I'm coming by." As he said it, a knock sounded on her front door and Hero went into warning mode, shooting off the couch with a bark, followed by low growling. "Case in point," he said. "The dog isn't thrilled to have someone just show up, and you went white." He lifted her hand to his mouth, kissed her knuckles and reminded her, "Pizza delivery."

Her bones wanted to melt. "Right. Pizza." Grumbling, she released him and stood. "I'll get my wallet."

He stood, too. "This is my treat, so let me."

"Then I owe you a meal… Or maybe two."

"Count me in."

He started for the door, but Hero blocked his way. When Lawson started around him, Hero moved, too.

Quirking a smile, Lawson said, "Bud, it's okay. No rescue needed." He stroked Hero, speaking softly.

That he took the time to reassure her dog meant a lot.

"Trust me," he said to Hero.

Ears twitching, Hero read his mood, then moved to his side and accompanied him to the door. Money in hand, Lawson glanced at her. "Anytime you want me to visit, tell me, and I hope you know you're welcome to drop by my place, too."

Would she? She wasn't sure. Catching Hero's collar just in case, she waited while Lawson paid for their food and, she noticed, gave the delivery guy a great tip. Everything he did only made her like him even more.

It occurred to her that there was no welcome mat for the front of her house, but then, she didn't welcome people.

Except Lawson, and in a dozen different ways, that felt incredibly right.

9

They finished off nearly the entire pizza and as the evening wore on, Lawson took pleasure in watching all the tension ease out of Berkley. They'd both have an early day tomorrow, but he didn't yet want it to end. She worked too hard, felt too deeply, for Durkinson to disrupt her now.

Seeing her like this, relaxed and joking, especially with the way she'd been when he first arrived, made him want to protect her. A sentiment she probably wouldn't appreciate.

She stretched, then stood from the table, and he thought he was about to be sent home, but she said, "I want dessert. How about you?"

Glad that she, too, wanted to extend the evening, he asked, "Whatcha got?"

"Ice cream, or packaged cookies."

He raised his hand. "Ice cream."

She grinned, leaned toward him and said like a taunt, "Ice cream *and* a cookie."

"Now you're talking."

When she opened the cabinet to get down bowls, he saw a plastic storage container. Reaching over her to get it, he asked, "Okay to put the last two slices of pizza in this?"

"Sure, thanks."

He stored the leftovers in the fridge, crushed the pizza box and rinsed their glasses in the sink.

While putting two cookies in each bowl, she said, "You can stick those in the dishwasher if you want. I need to run it tomorrow anyway."

He'd always been responsible for his own messes, so of course he didn't mind pitching in, but it seemed extra nice that she was comfortable enough with him to give him directions.

With that done, he came to stand at the counter beside her. The house was quiet and dim, the pets sleeping, the sun all but set. It was a hell of a pleasant way to spend an evening.

Near her ear, he whispered, "Another scoop of ice cream for me. I'm bigger than you."

She snickered. "And that means you get privileges?"

He'd like a few privileges—with her, not her dessert—but he was wary of pushing for too much, too soon. "I had a rough day."

"Oh?" Now looking worried, she glanced at him and apologized. "I'm sorry. I was so caught up in my own drama, I didn't even think—"

Why not? Lawson leaned down and pressed a barely there kiss to her mouth. "Don't do that. Don't apologize for letting me in, okay? I'm glad you shared with me." Lightly, he fingered the hot-pink tips of her silky hair. It was pretty, and unique, just like Berkley. "Really glad."

Blue eyes stared up into his before she suddenly turned back to her task.

Well, hell. He'd rushed her after all. "Berkley…"

She closed the ice cream carton, dropped a spoon into each bowl and then faced him once more. "You could do that again if you want."

Dare he hope? His body certainly did, but to be sure, he asked, "Do…?"

"This." She came up on tiptoe to press her mouth to his.

Just that, nothing else. A press. Two heartbeats, three.

It was…eye-opening. Fighting a smile, Lawson caught her shoulders and eased her away, his gaze searching hers. "Berkley, when was the last time you kissed someone?"

Heat rushed into her face. "Was it that bad?"

"No." God, no. "Let me make it clear—you touching me is never bad. You kissing me, any way at all, has my never-ending approval."

Amusement replaced the worry in her gaze. "So then why the question?"

He rubbed her shoulders. "That felt like your first kiss."

Issuing a half groan, half laugh, she dropped her forehead to his chest. This time he didn't hesitate to fold his arms around her.

"Hey, I wasn't complaining, believe me. I just want to make sure I do this the right way."

She went still, and said against his shirt, "This?"

He tucked a knuckle under her chin, tipped up her face and kissed her. *His* way. Gently searching. This kiss carefully explored the texture of her mouth, from the corner to the peak of her upper lip and the sweet center of her bottom lip. Her breath quickened, her lips parted, and he tilted his head for a better fit, increasing the pressure while coaxing her to relax. The slow, easy kiss grew warmer and deeper until she settled against him, chest to thighs. Breathing faster, her fingers gripped his shoulders.

He spread his hands over her narrow back, keeping her close, acutely aware of her past experiences and current reservations. When she made a small, eager sound, he coasted one hand to the bare skin of her arm, up to her shoulder and then her neck beneath her hair. Her dyed strands felt silky and cool, teasing him with the need to hold her head, crush her close and let them both get carried away.

Because this was Berkley, fragile in her own unique ways, and he was just beginning to understand how much she mattered to him, he resisted the urge. Instead, he chose to gradually ease up.

Breathing fast, she murmured, "Now."

"Now?"

She still clutched at him, and her eyes appeared dazed. "You asked the last time I was kissed. I think that might've been my first because nothing before it can possibly count." She licked her lips and smiled up at him. "So I'm going with 'now' as the answer." Turning away, she asked, "How about that ice cream?"

That quick about-face nearly gave him whiplash. "Sure. Ice cream." He could hear the rasp in his voice, but damn, his brain and his body definitely had other priorities.

She grinned at him, then picked up both bowls and moved to the table. "I think I need time to consider a few things."

Of course she did, especially given the news she'd gotten about Chad. "Things like me and you?"

"Is that okay?"

"Of course it is." Never mind that his thoughts were halfway to the bedroom already; he would never pressure Berkley. She'd had enough of that in her life already. "Always feel free to tell me what you want."

"Lawson?"

"Hmm?"

"Thank you. For everything."

He quirked a brow in question.

"Being here, perfect timing." She lifted her bowl in a modified toast. "Sharing food and conversation." Her lips, pinker now, lifted in a smile. "That killer kiss. It was…devastating, but in a good way." Getting serious, she watched him, and added quietly, "And for understanding."

Her words helped to ease the constriction in his muscles. At the moment, he wanted to be anything and everything she needed. How that had happened to him so quickly, he wasn't quite sure. He only knew that when Berkley needed someone, if she *wanted* someone, he hoped it would be him. "If I tell you it was my pleasure, will you believe me?"

"I'd like to, but it's hard to imagine."

"I don't know why. You're great company. Funny, easy to talk to, smart and sincere." He looked past her to the couch visible in the family room, where Hero and Cheese slept. "Compassionate, too, and loving." He looked at her. "Lovable."

A sweep of red climbed her throat and settled into her cheeks.

Watching, enjoying her reaction to his compliments, Lawson ate a scoop of ice cream.

"I, um, thank you."

"You know that's all true, right?" Her ice cream remained untouched in front of her. "Betty clearly adores you. I'm sure Oliver was impressed by you. Lark has had nothing but wonderful things to say about you."

She picked up her spoon, toying with it. "I thought about some of that, about how friendly and caring everyone is around here. I know I need to be a little more open, especially if so many people are going to volunteer and be involved at The Love Shack. We need that. The animals need it. So I was thinking of putting myself out there a little, maybe hitting up one of the town council meetings, and joining Yardley and the other women for their tea."

He understood without her having to say it. "But now you know Chad is looking for you and that worries you?"

Nodding, she put a big bite of ice cream into her mouth.

"What do you think will happen if he shows up?"

The spoon landed in her bowl with a loud clink. Head in her hands, she stared down at the tabletop.

"Berkley?" *Was* she afraid of Chad? If so, Lawson would love the chance to intercede on her behalf.

"When I read the note, I panicked. Even if Chad was nice and only wanted to catch up, I think I'd freak out." Finally she lifted her face, letting him see her beautiful blue eyes, dark with worry. "I don't want everyone to know about the scandal. I want it behind me. I want all that ugliness kept private."

"I understand that." If their chairs were closer, he'd be tempted to pull her into his lap and hold her. Much as he'd enjoy it, he knew it wasn't the right move to make. She was opening up to him, and every time she did, it felt special. It felt right—between them. "It's not really a scandal, you know. Not now. It shouldn't have been back then, either, and wouldn't have been if Chad's wife hadn't been a local celebrity."

She squeezed her eyes shut, a picture of misery. "I slept with her husband."

"You didn't know he was married."

"But I should have known. I should have found out."

"Know how I see it? Durkinson is a bastard for using you. If his wife had any backbone, she would have kicked his sorry ass to the curb, not taken out her anger on you, a teenager."

"I appreciate the sentiment, but I'm not blameless."

"Actually, you are. That's how anyone with a brain will see it. No, don't tell me what Durkinson's wife thought. My guess is she reacted on pure emotion." If he put his anger aside, he could almost understand her reaction. But understanding didn't make it right. The woman should have seen that Berkley was a shy, backward girl, and that she'd been a victim, too. Instead, she'd salvaged her own pride at Berkley's expense. "You were convenient—too young and innocent to fight back."

She whispered, "I haven't felt young or innocent for a very long time."

Of course she hadn't. Their neighborhood hadn't exactly fostered those softer illusions. People either hardened their hearts or they became prey. "Well, you were." In many ways, she still was. Strong, yes. Independent, absolutely. But she hadn't yet learned how upside down the world could be. If she had, she'd know that her innocence, her fresh outlook on life and her big heart were as unique as each animal she adored.

With sudden determination, Lawson sat forward. "Do me a favor if you can."

"Sure," she said without hesitation.

Hoping to give her a perspective on her past, by showing her the awesome present, he said, "Give this town a chance. Let them all know you as well as Betty does." *As I do.* "I promise you once that happens, there's not a damn thing Durkinson can say or do that will turn them against you."

Her lips, those incredibly soft lips he'd kissed moments before, lifted into a slight smile. "You sound awfully cocky about that."

"I'm cocky about your appeal." He saw another blush coming and had to smile over it. "Tell you what. Let's make a date night at Saul's barbecue. We can fit it in around the monthly town council meeting and the tea gathering you'll attend."

"That I'm thinking of attending," she amended.

"Go," he encouraged her. "Give it a try." *Give the town a try.* "If you don't like it, then you don't have to return, right?"

"Says the guy who won't be drinking tea with dozens of women." The second she said it, she groaned. "That sounded horrible. And unappreciative. I didn't mean it like that."

"You're busy," he said, understanding her in ways others might not. "You keep a full schedule and when you have free time, there are certain ways you want to spend it."

Appearing amazed at his insight, she nodded. "I will go,

at least once, just to see what it's about. Same with the town council meeting." She hesitated, then asked, "I don't suppose you'd want to go to that with me?" As enticement, she hurriedly added, "We could do dinner at Saul's after."

So she wanted his company, did she? He wanted her. Sounded fair. "I like that plan. Will there be more kissing?"

"I hope so."

Looking into her eyes to gauge her reaction, he asked, "How about if I guarantee it?"

"Better and better. So it's a date?"

A date. With Berkley. Yeah, he liked that a lot. "One condition."

She frowned at him.

"The town council won't meet again until the second Thursday of next month."

"Oh." Concentration deepened her frown. "The tea club meets every first and third Monday."

He was going to need a calendar to keep up. "How about we do dinner this Friday?" That was only a few days away. Before she could speak, he said, "I'll happily claim every Friday if you're free. Weekends optional for whenever you have time."

Her eyes widened, but she said, "Done."

Well, that was quick and easier than he'd expected. "It's getting late." He stood from the table, thinking he should go before he took things too far.

Like to the bedroom. Or the tabletop. "It'll be another long day tomorrow."

Berkley smacked her palm to her forehead. "I did it again! You said you had a rough day, and I went right back to talking about me."

Gently, he tugged her from her seat. "Actually, I steered that conversation, because my issue was embarrassing."

Her brows lifted high. "You don't want to talk about it?"

Trailing a finger over the multiple earrings in her ear, he

said, "That wouldn't be fair, would it?" He wanted her to share with him, about anything and everything. "And with you, I don't mind."

Relieved he felt that way, Berkley stepped closer. He was right, it was late and she should be winding down. The time with him had flown by, because he made her so comfortable. More than that, he entertained her, and around him she felt more alive than she had in... She couldn't remember ever feeling like this.

Free. Happy.

Everything with Lawson was unique; it was a relationship unlike any she'd known. "You didn't pressure me, so I don't want to pressure you. But if you feel like talking, I'd love to know." And then, maybe, she could help him, too.

With an awkward laugh, he explained, "Kathleen was back." His mouth twisted. "Actually, she's always there. She seems to live in front of my shop now."

Berkley fought a smile and lost. "It still bugs you?"

"What bugs me most is that someone keeps putting signs in her hand."

"Signs?"

Fanning out his arms in a grand gesture, he intoned, *"Why don't you like me?"*

"Oh, um..." She tried not to grin, but it was pretty funny.

"There was another, too." He frowned. *"Why won't you be my friend?"*

Berkley didn't mean to, but she barked a surprised laugh. Slapping a hand over her mouth didn't help, especially when Lawson grinned, too. Someone was really egging him on.

Catching her wrists, he gently pulled her hands away and then tugged her into close, full-body contact. "I love hearing you laugh, Berkley." He kissed her, a long, steal-her-thoughts kind of kiss, and as he straightened, he said, "Mmm. Love the taste of your laugh, too."

That sobered her real quick. Tonight had been shattering in many ways. Contact from Chad, her first kiss with Lawson.

Her *second* kiss.

And now all those special words…

He pressed a kiss to her forehead. "I'm right through the woods, okay? If you need me, for anything, will you let me know?"

Anything, huh? She nodded, her thoughts already scrambling, but no. She did need time—time to assimilate this new version of herself, to think about how to handle things with Chad if he dared approach her. And to decide how far and how fast she wanted to take things with Lawson.

"Thank you."

He leaned in for one last, firm peck. "As always, my pleasure."

She could really get used to the kissing. How had she gone so many years without realizing how incredibly wonderful, and hot, and stirring a kiss could be?

Chad certainly hadn't affected her like this—not that there was any comparison between Lawson and Chad. Lawson engaged her mind, her heart, her body… Whereas she'd seen Chad as a port in the storm. Safety. *What a laugh.* Comfort. *So ironic.*

"Friday," he reminded her.

She knew she shouldn't, but this was new and exciting and she couldn't resist. Going on tiptoes again, her hands against his chest, she put her mouth to his once more—and didn't want to stop. Honestly, she could have stood there by the door and kissed him for hours.

It wasn't fair to him, though. She wasn't yet sure how much she wanted, or how far to go, so she reined it in, dropped back to her heels and smiled up at him. "Friday."

With a small, bemused shake of his head, he went out the door, and then waited while she locked back up. Berkley watched through the kitchen door window until he rounded the corner between the house and the shelter, and disappeared from sight.

Floodlights automatically came on at dark as part of the security, but they didn't reach far into the woods. Lawson would have to walk through the dark to get home and she was suddenly worried. She had a second of reservations and, deciding it would be okay because it was Lawson, she called him.

He answered with "Miss me already?"

Even now, he kept her smiling. "Yes," she answered honestly. Her small house—a house she loved—felt suddenly empty now that he'd gone.

Of course, he'd probably think she wanted him to come back for...well, sex, so she rushed to say, "It's dark. Can you see okay?"

"Using the flashlight app on my phone, actually."

"Right." Yeah, she should have thought of that. "Not to be a pain, but would you mind—"

"Not at all."

She couldn't help but laugh. "I haven't told you yet what I want."

Voice an octave deeper, he said, "Whatever it is, Berkley, I don't mind."

Happiness filled her in a way she hadn't known was possible, like a warm glow, giddiness and contentment all mixed together. "Then you'll call me when you get home? Just so I know nothing got you?"

"Ah. No problem at all, but those small favors have to be reciprocated. That's how it works, you know."

"Really?" She could hear the rustle of the woods around him and hoped he'd left some lights on at his own place. "So what favor would you want?"

Without hesitation, he said, "If Durkinson bothers you, will you let me know?"

"Um..." Any problems with Chad she'd prefer to keep private.

"If he calls, texts and definitely if he shows up."

Curious, she asked, "What would you do?"

He cleared his throat, and this time he did pause, but not for long. "I'd be there with you."

So I won't be alone. "Nothing else?"

"Well... Not unless you gave me permission."

For some reason, that struck her as funny and she laughed again. She could just imagine what he'd like to do, and to be truthful, she appreciated it. "Okay, sounds like a deal."

"I'm home now." She heard the opening and closing of a door. "Good night, Berkley."

"Good night." She disconnected, then stood alone in the darkness for a minute, smiling, thinking that saying good night to Lawson was an especially nice way to end her day.

Even nicer would be if he stayed over.

Friday. Now she could hardly wait.

Their first day of cat yoga happened sooner than anyone expected. Once Betty got on board with the idea—boom!—it was happening. Lark had known it would be popular, but the number of people who signed up right away made it possible to get the ball rolling. It helped that Berkley was also accommodating, but then she had a feeling Berkley would do almost anything for her animals, and for Betty. The two of them were close, and seeing that made Lark miss her own family. When she'd moved away, she'd tried to do so on good terms, but it wouldn't hurt if she called her mother and father, just to say hello.

With the class going, Lark noticed that Berkley looked both pleased and frazzled. She didn't take part in the yoga, choosing instead to constantly monitor the cats and how the guests were interacting with them. To Lark, it seemed like a big hit. Everyone, including the animals, appeared to be having a great time.

The cats were social and excited, as well as impertinent. No matter how the women tried to guide them, the cats did as they pleased, climbing over, under, atop and behind anyone attempting to follow Oliver's instructions. It made for a lot of laughs.

As she attempted to follow along, Lark wondered if it was actually Oliver who drew the crowd of fifteen women instead of the cats. He looked far too fine standing there in loose linen pants and a tank that exposed stellar shoulders, honed biceps and strong, hair-dusted forearms. When he'd first begun, a few cats had tried crawling up his legs. Without missing a beat, Oliver had scooped up first one cat—giving it several affectionate strokes while talking to the class—before setting it down and then taking up the other cat.

He was so comfortable in his technique that even a few women flirting with him didn't throw him off. His smile never changed. He laughed easily at the adorable antics of the kitties. And he was very clear on what to do and how to do it without losing his train of thought.

Lark felt a little self-conscious. Everyone, except she, Berkley and Betty, wore trendy outfits of tight yoga pants and supportive crop tops. They looked amazing. Even Betty and Berkley blended in, since they wore their usual clothes and were mostly just involved in watching over the cats.

And here she was, wearing loose-fit drawstring pants and an oversize T-shirt that she'd bought from Lawson's shop. At least it promoted Oliver's facility, but still, she made a sloppy advertisement in comparison to the others.

For the first half of the class, Oliver led everyone doing mostly standing and balancing poses. Then at the thirty-minute mark, he had an assistant take over and he went to the back of the room to watch, every so often kneeling by someone to offer more detailed guidance.

For Lark, it became harder to concentrate. For one thing, she wasn't used to being quiet this long. For another, she literally felt Oliver behind her. Not that he was focused on her. Surely he wasn't. He was serious about the class, playful with the cats, and he had plenty of women to draw his attention.

So why did it feel like his dark gaze was on her more often than not?

She glanced back—bam. They looked at each other, or at least they did until Oliver said, "Eyes forward."

Right. She was supposed to be concentrating on her pose. As she quickly glanced around, she realized she'd lost her place. Her stance was nothing like everyone else's.

When Oliver spoke directly behind her, she nearly jumped. He had approached without making a sound!

"Square your hips to the front of the mat. That's it. Face your back toes in. Good. You want them aimed at the corner of your mat."

She tried to do it, she really did, but then he put his hands on her, much as he had while instructing others, and she seriously wanted to melt.

Clearly she'd been far too long without the touch of a man. No way should she be obsessing about a guy while surrounded by a class of women and with cats crawling everywhere. Cats! Right, she could use that as an excuse. Quickly she dipped to pick up one kitty that brushed against her ankles.

"Good diversion tactic," Oliver murmured, and moved on to another person.

Giving up, Lark carried the cat and went over to Berkley. "Hey."

Berkley smiled at her. "Thanks for being here."

"My pleasure." She propped her shoulders against the wall next to Berkley. "It's a hit, don't you think?"

Betty took up a position on Berkley's other side. "I've gotten some terrific photos."

Eyes widening, Lark asked, "Photos?"

"The paper you signed when you came in? It included per-

mission for me to take some photos to post on our social media
so everyone can see what they're missing."

"Er... I'm a mess. I hope I'm not in your pics."

Betty just smiled, but Berkley protested, telling her how
cute she looked, that she could never be a mess, on and on,
until Lark laughed.

When Oliver glanced at them, she quickly quieted herself
and lowered her voice to a mere whisper. "I'm often a wreck
these days. Before coming to Cemetery, I almost never was."
Of course, there were those few weeks when she'd shut herself off from the world. No one had seen her then. No one had
known how she'd cried, how she'd so badly wanted...

Berkley put a hand to her forearm. "We got a new cat today."

Effectively drawn from the memory, Lark asked, "Oh?
Which one?"

"She's not out here yet." Berkley turned to Betty. "Would
you mind keeping an eye on things? We won't be long."

With her phone raised again—this time aimed at Oliver—
Betty shooed them away. "Take your time. I've got this."

Berkley indicated the door to leave the training room, so
Lark followed along, wondering about this mysterious cat. They
entered the cat room, currently empty since all the cats were
at yoga, but at the other end there was a larger, separate room
enclosed with a secure gate, and Lark immediately heard the
tiny mews of kittens.

Her breath caught. She'd just been thinking of babies, and
tears immediately clouded her vision as she followed Berkley
into the room, then sank to her knees before a deep cardboard
box. Inside, a yellow tabby lovingly licked on a gray kitten's
head while three other kittens nursed. They were all different colors.

Softly, Berkley said, "We took her in from another shelter,
and two days later she gave birth. I hate that she was moved,
but she's better off here."

Lark wasn't sure she could speak, not with emotion clutching her throat, her heart. She nodded, reaching over to pat Berkley's arm to let her know that any animal was better off with her.

Apparently, Berkley understood. "You can pet her if you like. Or the kittens. She's amazingly gentle, and she's a wonderful mama."

Oh God, Lark wasn't sure she could. She knew tears were rolling down her cheeks, but she couldn't stop them.

"It's okay." Using the back of one finger, Berkley stroked the cat's head. "She's here now, and we'll take very good care of her and her babies."

Lark wanted to explain, but she couldn't. She did manage to say "Thank you."

For the next few minutes, she and Berkley sat in silence.

Then Berkley said, "I've been meaning to ask you something."

Not so subtly, Lark wiped the tears from her cheeks and drummed up a smile. "Oh?"

"Are you good with color?" To explain that, she lifted a lock of her hair. "I need a refresh, and I usually do it myself, but it's a whole process, and now I'm so busy—"

"I would *love* to do your hair." Thrilled with the distraction, Lark drew a breath and half turned to face her. "Your hair is beautiful, fun and it totally suits you. You have great style, Berkley."

Her smile looked more like a self-deprecating smirk. "Style wasn't really my goal when I changed everything. Mostly I just wanted to be different."

"From other people?"

Berkley shook her head. "From myself, from who I'd been." Wrinkling her nose, she said, "I was a very mousy girl, somewhere between plain and homely."

"No way. I will never believe that."

"It's true."

Skeptical, Lark said, "Your bone structure says otherwise.

Maybe as a girl you just didn't know how to feature your assets, like your eyes. You have gorgeous blue eyes."

With a startled laugh, Berkley said, "Thanks. I think your gray eyes are really pretty, too."

Lark grinned at her.

"And you always look great."

She certainly tried. "My style is quieter, sort of soft, but yours is edgy and bold and I'm envious because you totally pull it off."

Musing, Berkley looked her over. "I'd call your look romantic. I love the way your dark hair rests on your shoulders, and your eyes look dreamy with your pale peach skin and all those dark eyelashes. You don't even need mascara."

What wonderful compliments. "You've certainly made me feel better." It was only a partial fib. She didn't like being down; she much preferred to be upbeat, to be happy and to make others happy, too. Berkley had her well on her way. "Now, let's talk about your hair. The pink is incredible. I really, truly mean that, but have you ever thought of going with something darker? Maybe red? That'd complement your skin tone, too."

"Sold," Berkley said. "When can I set an appointment?"

Surprised by her enthusiasm, Lark laughed. "You can come to the shop if you want, but I'd be happy to do your hair at your place if that's more convenient for you." This time she brushed the tears away for real, not caring if she'd just smeared her mascara once more. "We're going to be friends, right?" She grinned hugely. "What am I saying? We're already friends. But we could be better friends. I'd like that."

"I'd really like that, too." Berkley's gaze searched over hers. "You've got a little... Wait right here, okay?" Popping to her feet, she left the room, went through another door and returned seconds later with paper towels, one of them damp. Kneeling in front of Lark, she asked, "Do you mind?" And then Berkley dabbed at her cheeks. "You got emotional seeing the kittens, something I do sometimes, too, and I didn't want you to leave here with streaks."

"It's the curse of makeup," Lark said, looking up at the ceiling to make it easier for Berkley to get beneath her eyes. "Babies of any kind get to me." And damn it, that almost set her off again.

Berkley saved her by fanning another paper towel in front of her face. "Breathe," she whispered. "I hear everyone filing out, so the class must have ended. My guess is that Oliver will come looking for you any minute."

"Do you think so?"

"Are you kidding? He couldn't take his eyes off you during the class."

Oh, she hoped that was true. "Am I wrecked?"

"No." Berkley stood, then offered her a hand. "If he asks you about it, laugh it off and blame it on the kittens."

Er… "It was the kittens."

Expression gentle, Berkley said, "Okay."

"You don't believe me."

"I do." Berkley looked down at the mama cat. "You were already looking a little sad, though, and that's why I brought you back here to see them. It's okay. Believe me, I have my own stuff I'm dealing with, so I won't pry into your business. Maybe… Maybe just know that if you ever want to talk, I'd be happy to listen."

Oliver came into the cat room, looked around, and once he spotted them, he headed in their direction.

"See," Lark whispered. "We're going to be very good friends, I can tell."

As soon as he reached them, Oliver said, "There you are," and his concerned gaze went from one to the other. "Everything okay?"

"Babies," Berkley said, pointing down at the box. "You can pet, but don't pick them up yet."

"Kittens," Lark specified, hoping she didn't get weepy again.

"Want to see?" She could show them to Oliver, talk a few minutes, then head home, where a warm shower, a brownie and a book would help her to regroup.

He said to Berkley, "Betty is waiting to talk to you."

"Thanks. Make sure the door is closed securely when you leave this room."

"We will," Lark said, and moments later, she and Oliver were alone.

10

Oliver glanced at the mother cat, smiled at seeing how she slicked the fur on top of one tiny kitten's head and then he turned back to Lark. He could see she'd been crying. Ridiculous as it seemed, her tears took him back to his father's funeral with his mother quietly weeping, his brother withdrawn, his sister-in-law red-eyed and stone-faced.

He'd failed them. He'd failed his brother most of all. Uncomfortable with the memory, he asked Lark, "What's wrong?"

Confusion tweaked her brows, but she smiled anyway. "Nothing now. A sad memory had hit me, that's all. It happens now and then."

Good God. Her explanation was exactly what had happened to him. Shaking his head, he said, "I'm sorry. I…" He rubbed a hand over his mouth and deliberately lightened his tone. "You're okay now?"

"Yes."

He should ask her if she needed to talk, but he couldn't quite make himself say it. "I'm going to walk Handsome. If you're not busy, do you want to join me?"

Tipping her head, she asked, "Handsome?"

"A sweet dog that was brought here. He needs extra love and a gentle hand. I can't adopt a dog right now, but I figured I could do other things for him, so I—"

The way Lark suddenly embraced him took him off guard. Slim arms fit around his waist and she squeezed him tight, her cheek against his chest, her soft hair teasing his chin, her scent enveloping him.

Hands on her shoulders, Oliver tried—and failed—to decide what to do.

"That's wonderful. *You're* wonderful." Smiling up at him, she said, "I'd be thrilled to join you on your walk. Thank you for inviting me."

He wasn't sure, but Oliver thought he might have just set himself on a course of no return. Sure felt like it. He cupped a hand to Lark's cheek, relishing the softness of her skin and how right her small body felt against his. His gaze was drawn to her mouth, and he saw her lips part.

He leaned down, she stretched up, and—Berkley and Betty came into the room, each of them carrying a cat.

Pretending she hadn't noticed them quickly stepping away, Berkley said, "The cats had fun. Thank you for this."

"And two people asked about adoption."

Whispering, Lark asked, "Should we offer to help put the cats away?"

"We should," he whispered back, and then on impulse, he touched his mouth to hers in a quick, light kiss.

Betty remarked, "Darn it, I wasn't ready or I'd have gotten a photo of that."

Thank God she hadn't, Oliver thought as he stepped out of the separate kitten room to join them.

Right behind him, Lark laughed. "Whatever release I signed didn't include anything other than the class."

Her humor was preferable to seeing her upset any day.

As he secured the door behind them, Lark, Berkley and Betty went after more cats. He took a moment to look in at the mother cat again. She appeared very peaceful with the little fur balls tucked up to her side. He watched her yawn, rest her head on the bedding and close her big green eyes.

This shelter, and Berkley especially, was responsible for so much love. This was what he needed in his life. The signs of positive action. The ability to make a difference, to see it happening and to take part.

"Hey," Lark said. "Get the gate for me, will you?"

He turned to see her with two cats in her arms, both of them purring. Soft, loose pants fell around nicely rounded hips. And her shirt advertised his business.

Damn, but she hit him on several levels. He hadn't stood a chance, he realized that now.

Stepping over to assist her, he saw how easily Lark fit in here. With the town, the people, the close community and the overall sentiment. He had a feeling she'd fit in anywhere. *Why had she been crying?*

He might have messed up before, but he wouldn't make the same mistake. Not here. Not now.

Everything in his life came down to priorities, and this time, he'd make the right choices.

His new business *was* a priority, but it wouldn't be number one.

That would be the people. Starting right now.

Possibly...starting with Lark.

★ ★ ★

It was an unusual occurrence for a guy to pick her up, so no wonder she kept looking out the window. Hero insisted on looking with her each time, though the dog didn't know Lawson was coming by. Berkley had wanted to meet him at the restaurant, but he'd insisted this was an official date, and as such, he wanted the whole shebang.

Berkley wondered what the full boat entailed. Hopefully everything she imagined and more.

Over the last few days, he'd stopped in several times for visits, and now Hero and Cheese considered him part of the family. Sometimes Lawson deliberately brought along things that Cheese could steal. A soft key-chain fob. A foam can Koozie. Lanyards. Once he brought a visor, and they later found Cheese curled up inside it, her fluffy body contorted to fit.

Each time they saw Lawson, they welcomed him with enthusiasm, but Hero no longer went bonkers with glee, and Cheese, after a brief greeting and a little thievery, left to do her own thing. They were used to him, and his visits.

While she impatiently waited, she wondered how Oliver and Lark were getting along. After the yoga class, they'd shown up together a few times to walk Handsome. Thanks to all the love and attention the dog received, he was making great progress. His dental work was tentatively set for two weeks from now with Dr. Upton. Once that was done and the dog had recovered, he'd be available for adoption.

One of the good things about running the shelter was that Berkley could make the final decisions, and she had a feeling Handsome had already found his forever person. Oliver just didn't realize it yet.

Sunday the salon was closed, so Lark would be coming over to do her hair. Berkley was both excited and nervous about the idea of changing it. She'd donned the pink tips years ago as a way to camouflage herself, a type of statement that the old Berkley—the doormat, the pariah, the dog-faced girl who'd stolen a married man from a princess—was gone for good. All hail the new Berkley.

Except…she hadn't been new. She'd been the same old downtrodden, fearful person—with different hair. Big whoop. So much for her bold change.

This time she'd do things right. An outward change would be a good start, even fun, but it was the inside she had to work out. A less fatalistic attitude, an openness to friendship, a willingness to take part.

Animals had been her lifeline; now she needed to include people. A makeover with Lark was top of the list.

When she heard a car pulling up, nervousness and excitement gripped her. She smoothed her hair, tugged up the neckline of her sleeveless sundress, stared down in dismay at her unpainted toenails in her casual flip-flops, and had the wild urge to run to her bedroom and change. Everything.

Hero, who'd jumped at the closing of a car door, barked happily. He wanted the door open *now*.

Too late to change her mind about her outfit. With a bracing breath, she caught Hero's collar, pasted a smile on her face and opened the door.

Betty stood there.

Before Berkley could say a word, the older woman announced, "I've come to get Gladys. I'm ready. Completely ready and totally committed and I want her. You can't refuse me, Berkley. You just can't." She ended with her wobbling chin held high and defiance in her eyes.

It all struck Berkley as hilarious as she started to laugh.

"Humph," Betty said indignantly.

"Oh, Betty." Berkley awkwardly embraced her with one arm while still controlling Hero. "I'm sorry I laughed. You just took me by surprise. And of course I wouldn't refuse you! You're perfect."

Betty now tucked in her chin. "I'm not."

"You are. In every single way."

"There are quite a few people in this town who would strongly disagree with you."

"So?" Berkley said, drawing her inside and closing the door. "Who cares? I think you're perfect." When Hero snuffled against Betty and received a friendly pat, Berkley added, "Hero agrees that you're perfect. Best of all, Gladys, who has the most important opinion in this scenario, loves you so much. If you want her, and if you're sure you can handle it, I'd be happy to process the adoption."

Until Betty's face lit up, Berkley hadn't realized there'd been any doubt on the matter, and now she felt terrible. She and Hero both lavished the woman with affection. Even Cheese sauntered in, brushing Betty's legs once to let her know she approved, as well.

Hands clasped tightly together, Betty asked, "Could I take her now?"

Oh, boy. Erin and Whitley had already left for the day, and Lawson was due any second now—but Berkley couldn't disappoint Betty. "Of course you can. We just need to fill out the paperwork."

"Already done," Betty said, opening her small white purse and digging inside to produce a folded sheet of paper. "I got this from Erin a few days ago, and yesterday I went shopping. I have a big cushy dog bed for my Gladys, piddle papers randomly placed around, dog brush, two dishes, the food Erin said she prefers and—"

Another knock sounded at the door, and Hero abandoned Betty so he could bark and turn a few circles in glee.

"That'll be Lawson," Berkley whispered. "We have a *date*." She bobbed her eyebrows.

Betty blinked at her. "You do?" In a rush, she said, "Well, for heaven's sake. Of course you do. Look at you! You look incredible, all fixed up and..." She leaned in with a sniff. "Young lady, is that perfume?"

"Cherry blossom body mist. Do you like it?"

"Yes, I do. Lawson will love it." Turning away in a flurry, Betty said, "Let's not keep him waiting."

Berkley caught Hero's collar again as Betty opened the door.

To his credit, Lawson barely missed a beat at finding Betty instead of Berkley, even when she said, "And look at you, all handsome and—" again she leaned in to sniff "—also smelling good."

Lawson grinned at her. "I'm not wearing cologne."

"Mmm. Apparently, you don't need to."

Seeing Betty with her nose near Lawson's chest sent Berkley into snickers of hilarity. There were times when Betty could be so outrageous, and it seemed to be happening more as time went by.

As Lawson stepped in, he dipped his appreciative gaze over Berkley and whistled. "Nice."

She felt like doing a curtsy or something, and instead she shifted her feet. "I felt like wearing a dress."

"Good choice."

Betty's gaze bounced back and forth between them. "I have rotten timing, clearly."

"Oh." With Lawson looking at her like that, she'd almost forgotten herself. "No, your timing is never off. We can get Gladys right now." Quickly, she explained the situation to Lawson.

Pleased with Betty's decision, he jumped right in, offering his help. "I can go with you, Berkley, while you get Gladys, or I can visit with Hero and Cheese a few minutes so they don't feel left out. Your pick."

For once, Betty appeared humbled. "Seriously, you don't mind?"

"It's only six-thirty and Berkley isn't a teenager. She can stay out late, so a half-hour delay isn't a big deal, especially when it means Gladys gets a forever home."

"I'll be eighty-eight soon," Betty pointed out. "Not sure how long forever will be, but—"

"No, don't say that," Berkley protested, her chest going tight. "You have years and years yet." Both Betty and Lawson watched her, and she realized she'd almost shouted. Forcing her lips into a smile, she added, "You were just sniffing Lawson. Obviously you have a lot of life in you yet."

That got the response she wanted, with Lawson grinning and Betty laughing.

"Both of you wait here. The less confusion, the better, because the dogs are already settled in. I'll only be a minute." Grabbing up her keys, she slipped out the door. At the shelter, she entered as quietly as possible. She wrote out an adoption slip with a note and left it on the desk for Erin in case she forgot to tell her right away.

Gladys was sound asleep when Berkley silently opened her individual kennel, but the dog jerked awake with a start when Berkley whispered her name. Poor thing. It was rare for them to be disturbed once they'd been put to bed, and Gladys gave a cautious woof, her ears flat and her belly to the floor. The second she recognized Berkley, she jiggled with relief but still seemed really confused.

The dog had been using the same bed since she arrived, so Berkley scooped it up, along with a couple of Gladys's toys, as she led the dog out on a leash. In her mind, she was already listing all the suggestions she routinely gave to new dog owners. She trusted Betty completely, and she knew Gladys would be far better off in a real home than at the shelter, but that didn't seem to matter. In Berkley's heart, Gladys had become her own, and Berkley felt wholly responsible for her well-being.

A few of the dogs barked as she and Gladys went by, and it broke her heart anew. They all deserved forever homes, damn it. If she had to see one more designer dog, or another TV show on breeders, she'd scream. There were enough dogs in the world. They only needed to be seen.

Thank God *this* dog had found her person. And what a person she was.

Berkley whispered sweet words to the animals as she passed them, and she vowed never to do this again. It wasn't fair to them. To her heart, it felt like every dog was watching, and wishing they were the special one.

Gladys still seemed confused as Berkley reset the security system, left the shelter and locked the doors. Then the dog spotted Betty's car, and her ears shot up. Betty and Lawson were at the back door waiting, but Betty stepped out and suddenly Gladys was jumping around in joy. She and Betty met halfway to the house, and they were both ecstatic.

Despite the makeup Berkley had so carefully applied, she felt tears gathering. Happy tears, of course. She laughed as she brushed them away. "Gee, I think you two were meant to be."

"Yes, we were," Betty said in a teasing voice to the dog. Gladys licked her face in agreement. "I'm taking you home, Gladys. We belong to each other now."

Berkley pressed a hand to her mouth.

Lawson, bless his heart, took over for her. With a kiss to her forehead, he said, "Let me help while you say your goodbyes." She nodded agreement, so he relieved her of Gladys's things and put them into Betty's car. Then he ensured Cheese was in the house, took Hero out one more time to use the bathroom and grabbed her purse for her. After he secured the house, he returned to help Betty and Gladys into the car.

To Berkley, he asked, "Would you like to follow Betty home to ensure she gets everything inside?"

God love the man, could he be any better? "Great idea." *He* was a great idea. "You're sure you don't mind?"

After pressing a kiss to her forehead once more, he whispered, "I think you need that, right?"

Drawing in a shaky breath, she nodded. Having someone know her so well was unsettling, but in a good way. As if, after all these years, she was finally being seen.

Their date had definitely gone awry. By the time they'd finished getting Gladys settled, it was much later than they'd anticipated.

Lawson held her hand as he drove to Saul's restaurant, his thumb constantly coasting over her knuckles.

Watching his profile, she said, "I'm okay, you know."

The corner of his mouth lifted. "You're far better than okay, lady."

Even though she wasn't sure what that meant, she found herself smiling, too. "I'm thrilled that Gladys has a forever home. Betty will be so good to her."

"And Gladys will be good for Betty—but you'll still miss her."

"Yes." She missed every animal that found a home.

"And worry about her."

"Yes, only because, as Betty said, she's getting older. Gladys has gotten used to our routine." To people coming and going throughout the day, to other dogs and cats, with regulated feeding times and—

"I bet she'll adapt quickly."

"She will." Berkley knew that. "I'm being silly."

"No, you're not. You give your whole heart to these animals. Letting go isn't easy. I get it. So does Betty. That's why she told you to feel free to check up on Gladys whenever you want, but she also promised to bring her with her whenever she visits."

Turning her hand over, Berkley gripped his fingers. "Saul's will be closing soon."

"I know." He pulled into the parking lot, which had already emptied out significantly.

"I wouldn't mind ordering takeout. We could eat it on the beach."

Lawson turned his head to look at her. "That sounds great."

Berkley felt the reverberation of her heart beating, as it drummed harder than usual. It wasn't nervousness. More like… sizzling anticipation. "Or," she said, "we could eat at your house."

His gaze locked on hers.

She couldn't tell what he was thinking, so she launched into explanations. "I haven't seen it lately and you've been doing a lot of work, so—"

"Let's do that." He opened his truck door and jogged around to her side. The second he had her door open, he said, "Let's grab food and head to my place."

Now that he seemed in a hurry to get things underway, she grinned. "Looks like we're as adaptable as Gladys."

With a firm kiss, he stole her humor. "Don't compare me to a geriatric dog, Berkley."

And…that brought the humor right back.

Lawson grinned with her. "Tease. Come on."

As packed as it had been last time she was here, tonight there were available tables. Still busy as customers lingered over their dessert or just chatted, but not wall-to-wall and chaotic.

Across the room, Lark waved to them. She sat at a table with Oliver, and like many of the guests, their food dishes had already been taken away.

Lawson asked, "Want me to order while you visit?"

It almost felt like a verbal nudge—but she accepted. "Sure. I'll take whatever you get, but I wouldn't mind something simple, like a sandwich?"

"They have a terrific turkey club. Want to share fries?"

"I do," she teased, then caught what she'd said. "I mean—"

"Milkshake or cola?"

"Mmm. Vanilla shake."

"You've got it. I'll only be a minute."

Right there in front of God and everyone in the restaurant, he put one hand behind her neck, bent down and kissed her.

She was still blinking when he strode away to the bar to put in their order.

Feeling pretty awesome about her life, she glanced at Lark again and got double thumbs-up. Oliver was smiling, too. Moseying toward them, Berkley smiled at this person, and that person, and discovered she knew more people than she'd realized.

When she reached Lark, she said, "Hey, you two."

Oliver stood. "Do you and Lawson want to join us?"

"Actually, we're just getting food to go." She quickly explained about Betty adopting Gladys. "I'm thrilled, but it put us a little behind on our official first date."

Lark said to Oliver, "Berkley starts work early, well before six, every single day."

"No days off?" Oliver asked.

She shook her head. "I don't mind. It works for me."

"Impressive. I used to be that way, but I have a feeling we were driven by different things. Me, I just wanted to get ahead, to make my practice the best."

Unsure what he meant by that, Berkley asked, "The fitness studio?"

He shook his head. "I was a physical therapist. Most of my clients were well-known athletes."

"Wow." Berkley noticed that Lark looked equally surprised. "You gave that up?"

"To come here." His gaze skimmed the restaurant as if he saw things other than everyday people, before it returned to Berkley and then shifted to Lark. "To start over."

Nodding, Lark said quietly, "I'm also starting over."

Berkley felt like an interloper. These two obviously had things to discuss. She was about to excuse herself when Lawson stepped up to the table. "Food will be ready in a few minutes."

"Wait with us," Lark insisted, pushing out the chair beside her.

Oliver seemed in agreement, and Berkley figured a few minutes more wouldn't hurt. Before she could offer up any topics for conversation, Mila, one of the servers who also helped manage the restaurant, came over to them.

Berkley had only met her once, but Mila had been all smiles then. Now she wore a concerned frown.

"Hey, Berkley, right?"

"Yes. We met once before when I stopped in."

Mila nodded. "So…earlier today, someone called asking about you."

Everything inside her went still—her lungs, her pulse, even her heartbeat. It was Lawson's hand on her back, rubbing between her shoulders, that got her breathing again. She choked out "Oh?" even while thinking that it made no sense for Chad to hunt her down now.

Oliver asked, "Someone looking to adopt an animal?"

"I don't think so." Mila dug in an apron pocket, sifted through a few pieces of paper and finally handed one to Berkley. "Wheeler took the call. It was a guy, asking if you lived around here. Wheeler's a sharp guy, so of course he didn't say that everyone in Cemetery knows you, or of you." Her shoulders lifted. "The Love Shack is a huge hit, you know?"

Lark asked, "So what did Wheeler tell him?"

"He got his name and number and said he'd ask around. Not that he will," she assured Berkley. "But Wheeler figured he could at least find out who was looking for you. He got a bad vibe off the guy." She nodded at the paper now crumpled in Berkley's hand. "That's your caller's info."

Twisting her lips into a smile, Berkley looked at the paper. Sure enough, it had Chad's name and a number. "Thanks, Mila." She shoved the note into her purse. "Will you thank Wheeler for me, too?"

"Sure." She hesitated. "No one here would give out personal info, but Cemetery has a lot of businesses, and if that dude starts calling around…"

"It's fine." It would be. Somehow Berkley would see to it. "I'm listed with the shelter, so he's bound to locate me sooner or later."

"Trouble?" Oliver asked, his expression so dark that Berkley did a double take.

"Nothing I can't handle." That became truer by the day. "He's a creep I knew years ago. I haven't heard from him in nearly a decade."

Still Mila hesitated. "If you need anything, let us know."

"Us?"

Her smile went crooked. "The town? Anyone here?" Giving a pat to Berkley's shoulder, she said, "We've got you, okay? Cemetery takes care of its own."

With those profound words, Mila got back to work.

Undone by the generous statement, Berkley sat there in awe. *I am part of this town now.* Guess that came with some perks.

Unconvinced, Oliver sat forward. "Would you like me to have a word with him?"

The offer took Berkley off guard.

"You don't think I've offered?" Lawson asked.

"I didn't think about it. Just gut reaction, I guess."

That made Lark snicker. "Rushing in to save the damsel in distress. You're both so sweet."

"Not *save*," Lawson corrected. "Offer backup."

"And options," Oliver added.

Lawson faced Berkley. "Stand with you."

Oliver nodded. "Or in front of you, if it was necessary."

Laughing even more, Lark leaned into Oliver, hugging his upper arm and batting her eyelashes. "Will you be my hero, too?"

He blinked at that. "Of course."

That even got Berkley laughing.

Lawson was not amused. "Go play caveman with Lark. If Berkley needs anything, I'll be her caveman."

All eyes turned to her, making Berkley grin.

"You're not insulted?" Oliver asked. "Because I didn't mean it that way."

"He's just an old-fashioned guy," Lark said, sighing as if she liked it.

Shaking her head, Berkley followed Lark's lead and leaned into Lawson. "Honestly, it feels amazing to have friends." She glanced around the table at each of them. "Thank you."

Dinner on the beach turned out to be a better idea. Lawson was feeling so damned territorial, which was unheard-of from him, that if he got her alone right now, he'd probably end up rushing things. Plus, Berkley was shaken. He saw it whether she admitted it or not. The fresh air, he hoped, would help her to relax.

"The sunset is amazing."

He'd been so lost in thought, her small hand in his as they walked along, that he hadn't noticed. "Pretty."

"I like how the orange sunlight reflects on the water, except closest to shore where it looks deep blue. It's like a painting."

He couldn't talk about the sky when he had other things on his mind. "I don't want you worrying about Chad."

"I'm not, or at least, not as much as I had been."

"What Oliver said..."

"I'm curious about his backstory now. What do you want to bet he's an older brother or something like that? He seems really protective."

Unable to bear it, Lawson stopped. He set down the bag of food he carried and turned Berkley to face him. "I'm protective, at least when it comes to you." Kissing felt like the right move, but even if it hadn't, he needed to taste her again.

With them out on the beach, even though they weren't near others on the shoreline, he was careful not to take it too far. Cupping her face in his hands, he fit his mouth gently to hers, slow and easy, and still his heart kicked against his ribs. He wanted her, but what she wanted mattered the most. "If you need anything—"

"What I need, you're already giving me." Here, with the setting sun behind her, her blue eyes looked dark, but not in any way distressed. "Not to put you on the spot, but around you I feel like a different person. A better person."

He kissed her again, because damn it, she'd always been a good person. That business with Durkinson hadn't changed anything. "Listen to me, Berkley. I remember that girl from years ago." Sunlight in her colored hair drew his fingers, so he stroked his hand over her head, then cupped the back of her neck. "She was shy and quiet, but good-hearted. Loyal to her ailing mother and a little aging dog. Kind despite the violence all around us. You're still you, just a little older and more mature, and even more beautiful."

Her self-conscious smile made him want to hold her close, but instead he picked up the food, careful not to spill their drinks, and took her hand again. As they walked on, he said, "I'm glad you had your mom as long as you did. I think she must have been a really terrific person, for you to be who you are now."

"We were really close." After a minute, Berkley asked, "What about your mom? What kind of person was she?"

The kind he didn't want to talk about.

But that wasn't fair to Berkley. Multiple times now, she'd opened up to share about her past. Each time he'd known it was difficult for her, yet she'd done it. She'd taken those strides, so how could he do any less? Sure, he'd hinted a few times—all in an effort to get her to talk. He could easily discuss the past in the abstract, as a thing that had happened but was no more. But discussing the day-to-day grind of it... That was what it had been for him. A grind. A struggle to survive. He'd managed in the only way he knew how: by separating himself from it, physically when possible, emotionally all the time.

Overall, it had worked, and at the same time, it had left him feeling completely alone in the world.

While he weighed how much to share, they chose a quiet spot on the beach, away from the waves but with the sunset still in view. He spread out the jacket he'd brought from his truck. "That should protect your dress from the sand." His jeans would be fine either way.

"Thanks. It's been so long since I wore a dress, I hadn't considered that."

"I'm glad you did." She looked amazing. His only problem was that he couldn't stop thinking about getting his hands under the dress. Shoving his fingers through his hair, he looked out at the lake and said gruffly, "You have gorgeous legs."

Making light of the compliment, she replied, "They're strong, and they get me where I'm going."

The second she'd finished arranging herself, kicking her sandals off her small feet and crossing her legs at the ankles, he dropped down beside her. He dug out their drinks and handed one to her with a straw. "These will melt soon."

"I don't mind." Relaxed and smiling, she said, "I'm enjoying this enough that even a melted shake will be good."

Yeah, he felt the same—because he was here with her. He started to get out the sandwiches, but hesitated. He set the bag aside, glanced at her, then turned toward her and leaned back on one elbow. "My mother was a train wreck."

Berkley shifted to face him, saying nothing.

"A drunk. An addict. Sometimes worse." Scooping sand into his hand, he considered his words. As he let it pour through his fingers, he added, "Both of my parents worked with a gang and different dealers. Nothing huge—mostly because they weren't trustworthy. They'd do little jobs. Hide the product. Deliver it. It became this huge fight between us because I wouldn't do the same."

Berkley's lips parted, then firmed. "They actually wanted you to—"

"First time they asked, I was fifteen."

"I can't imagine," she whispered.

No, most people couldn't, thank God. "When I refused, they accused me of not helping out." They hadn't given him money for lunch, and had refused to let him pack anything. Pressure tactics. "There were times…" Christ, he hated talking about this, only because it made him feel like that person he was back then. Still a boy on the threshold of being a man. Determined to be better than the examples he had. Desperately wishing he had a mom and a dad, instead of adversaries.

"I always felt like I was up against the world."

Berkley stretched out next to him in much the same position. On her, *in a dress*, it was a sight to see.

She kept her voice soft when she said, "I'd had no idea. From the outside looking in, you seemed to have it together, like you were above it all."

He touched her warm cheek, breathed in the fresh, sweet scent of her. "I worked wherever I could, but I couldn't save my money at home. Mom or Dad would have found it. They trashed my room regularly looking for money. I couldn't get a bank account without one of them signing on, not until I was eighteen, so I used to put the money in cans I got out of the garbage, and I'd bury it down by the river."

"Resourceful."

He half smiled. "A cop busted me once. He was a big guy, probably in his midfifties, out of shape and wheezing with every step. He thought I was doing something shady and was barking so many questions at me, I started feeling guilty, like I was burying a body or something."

Humor teased her lips. "Is that what he thought?"

"Not sure. When I showed him my pay stub, proving the cash was mine, he sat down on this fallen tree and started asking me questions. Where I worked, why I didn't get paid with a check, stuff like that." Lawson rubbed his ear. He'd never shared any of this before. Not with anyone. "I wasn't trying to rat out my parents, but I also didn't want to get arrested."

"I hope that didn't happen."

"No. He was a cool guy. Gave me a card and told me if things got too rough, to give him a call. He swore there were places that could help, but you know how that goes."

"I'm sorry, I don't."

Lawson gave a gruff laugh. Thank God she didn't know. Somehow, even while wasting away, her mother had managed to shield her. "Half the kids in our neighborhood were homeless, fostered or mistreated. The system is great when it works, but a lot of the time it doesn't."

Berkley surprised him with a hug. She simply put her arms around him, paying no attention to her dress, and squeezed him hard.

He started to tell her he was fine, but instead, he lowered to his back and returned the embrace.

On the beach, he reminded himself. *Definitely not alone.* Even now, he could hear distant voices. Still, it felt special, because he knew it wasn't a show of pity, but understanding, the same that he'd given to her.

Trailing his fingers through her hair, he finished the story. "The cop suggested I find a better place to hide my money, because the river could swell with a hard rain, and my cans could float away. I hadn't considered that. I had six months more before I turned eighteen and could get my own bank account, so I thanked him for the advice. After he left, I collected my cans—I had twelve of them—and put all the money in one."

Berkley pressed back to see his face. "What if you'd gotten mugged?"

The setting sun created a shadowy halo around her, half hiding her expression. "Probably would have if I'd headed home. Instead, I went into the woods, found an old rotted tree stump and hid the money in there. The next day I bought a lockbox. Every so often, I found a new hiding place." He was always careful that no one had followed him. "The day I turned eighteen, I had it out with my folks."

Cautiously sitting up, her gaze studying his face, Berkley asked, "What does that mean?"

Damn. He'd enjoyed holding her, but he supposed being horizontal on a public beach in the town they lived in probably wasn't a great idea. "I told them no more pressure to drag me into their messes." He, too, sat up. "I wanted to finish school, so I said I'd pay them rent, but if they kept trying to involve me in their schemes, I'd leave." He shook his head. "I knew they were both too far gone to get clean and hold down honest jobs. My mom looked twenty years older than she was. Sickly, like she'd just come off a bender. Honestly, I'd given up on them years before that. I'd tell myself that it didn't matter, but it was a lie. It always mattered, too much." He took a breath and stated, "I just didn't let it stop me."

This time her smile was small and tinged with sadness. "You amaze me."

He huffed a laugh. "I have no idea why."

"Lawson, you did all that as a *kid*. You saw how messed up things were and made a conscious decision to forge a different path. Grown adults struggle to do that."

"I guess." He'd had bad examples, and knew that to survive, he had to be different. For him, the choices had been simple. Hard, yes. Painful, sure. But he'd wanted more out of life.

Her brows tweaked together. "When did you move out?"

"As soon as I graduated high school. Like—that very day. No ceremony, no celebration. All I needed was my diploma.

I didn't go far, though." He hadn't been able to, not with his limited means. "I still worked and lived in our neighborhood."

"Right. Because you were there for my big headlines."

She'd been seventeen, but he was older. A man when she'd still been a teenager. "I'm glad I was still around, because as a firsthand observer, I have a perspective you don't have."

She acknowledged that with a nod. "Eventually, you left, though. When did you make it out?"

"It wasn't long after that, when I'd just turned twenty." He heard a splash and they both glanced at the lake. The night was still warm, with a humid breeze stirring the air. "I'd been working construction when another guy offered me a job."

"That job where you traveled?"

"Yeah. It was like a lifeline. Got me out of our neighborhood, paid me well, let me see things in the world I'd never imagined." It was the first time he'd felt any real hope. "Gave me the opportunity to learn a lot, too." Closing his eyes, Lawson recalled how liberating it was to leave everything, and everyone, behind. "Standing up to my parents was the first step for me."

"Toward being free?"

He lifted one shoulder. "After that, I knew I could handle everything else. Moving out, earning enough to make it on my own." Touching his fingers beneath her chin, he tipped up her face. "You've done the second, hardest part already. It impresses the hell out of me." He kissed her, and didn't want to stop. At every second, he was aware of her dress, of the flirty skirt and how easy it'd be…

Unable to help himself, he rested one hand on her thigh and felt her shift that leg toward him. He stroked his palm a little higher, drawn by the silkiness of her skin, then forced himself to stop.

It was getting darker by the minute. If he wasn't careful, they'd be eating their food under moonlight.

Easing away from her, he whispered, "I'd be happy to put

myself between you and Durkinson. If you want that, say the word and I'm there." He'd take great pleasure in making sure Durkinson never bothered her again.

"I know," she said softly. "But—"

"But." This was the point he wanted to make, what he really hoped she would believe. "I know you can handle it, Berkley, just like you've handled everything else." If it was a confrontation only.

Anything more, if the bastard dared to touch her, Lawson would destroy him and deal with the consequences later.

11

Berkley thought that was the finest compliment anyone had ever given her. "Your faith in me means a lot."

"I'm a good judge of character," he assured her. "You'll be fine."

Hearing him say it with such belief made her believe it, too.

With a quirky smile, he added, "I have a feeling Durkinson is in for a big surprise. But if you decide to see him face-to-face, I'd like to be with you."

A wonderful offer, except she'd prefer to dodge Chad if at all possible. "I have zero interest in being anywhere near him, so I was thinking I should call, just to make that perfectly clear." Hopefully, that would keep him from showing up in Cemetery.

It was a silly request, but with Lawson, she didn't mind being silly. "If I call him, would you want to be there with me—"

He swooped in to give her a firm, enthusiastic kiss. It happened so quickly that she laughed. "Is that a yes?"

"I'm glad you asked." With one more kiss, he said, "I want to be there with you, and I agree. Telling him to get lost before he shows up is a good plan. Just remember that you're past the hard part already. After everything you've accomplished, facing the past will be easy."

"Maybe." She wasn't Lawson, and so far nothing had seemed easy to her—except loving animals.

And talking to him.

Wanting him. That came pretty easily, too.

She stroked his jaw, liking the slight rasp of his beard shadow. His fair hair, a little messy and a little long, drew her fingers next. Who knew a man's hair could be so sexy? She never had before, but everything with Lawson felt new. Seemed appealing. And turned her on.

Lawson held perfectly still, watching her intently, before he caught her wrist, turned his head and kissed her palm. "What are you thinking, Berkley?"

Many things, decisions that involved the immediate future. She hoped he would continue to be agreeable. "That talking with you is easy, maybe because you share, too. Thank you for trusting me." That's what it was, she knew. Trust. He'd told her things no one else knew, awful things that a boy should never have gone through. She'd had her mother, she'd known love and concern and caring. He hadn't. Compared to what he'd gone through, her own worries felt smaller.

And Chad... Well, Chad felt like nothing at all.

"Thank you for listening." He opened the bag and dug out their food, handing one thick sandwich to her. They ate in comfortable silence, hearing only the distant, barely perceptible drone of voices from the main stretch of the beach. Occasionally a bird sang. Repeatedly, the lake washed against the shoreline in a lulling hush.

"Did you see that fish jump?"

He nodded. "Looked like a big carp, maybe. Or a bass."

She finished off half of her sandwich and gave him the other half.

"You don't want it?"

"I'm full." She finished off her shake, then nodded out at the sunset. "It looks like it'll sink right into the water."

"Pretty."

Berkley watched him polish off the sandwich, then use a napkin to wipe his mouth. "It's not that late yet."

Pausing, Lawson gave her his full attention for several arresting, heart-stopping moments. "Not late at all." With his light brown eyes extra alert, he asked, "Something else you want to do?"

Oh, boy. Yeah, there were several other things she wanted to do, but not here in public. To give her something else to look at, she gathered up the wrapper from her sandwich and her empty milkshake cup, and put them back in the larger bag. "We could maybe go to your house."

His voice went deeper when he said, "We could."

She studied him, trying to gauge that simple reply, and realized at once that he wanted her, too. It was there in his heated expression, and that gave her the confidence to say, "I want sex."

His eyes flared, then narrowed. "Hell, yes," and suddenly he was on the move, grabbing up his own empty wrapper and cup, urging her to her feet, shaking out his jacket.

His rush was flattering enough that she laughed as she hurriedly brushed off her feet and stuck them into her sandals. She caught Lawson's hand and, while dragging him along at a fast clip, said, "We could jog to your truck," and she was only half-joking.

Holding her to a walk, his own smile warm with anticipation, he said, "No way, lady. We'll continue like two sedate adults just finishing our casual stroll. Don't forget how quickly news spreads in Cemetery."

She nodded, but after a minute or two, asked, "You want to keep our relationship private?"

"No, but I don't want it advertised, either, not until you and I figure it out."

That made sense, and yet as they moved along, a few reservations set in. "So… Do we have a relationship?"

His brows pinched together, his look serious and firm. "Damn right we do."

She nodded again. "And that relationship is…what?"

As if he'd just run into a wall, Lawson stopped. It was so abrupt, she went a step past him before she realized it.

Tugging her around, he said, "If I haven't made it clear, I care about you."

The words were a balm, softening her heart. "I care about you, too."

His frown eased away, replaced by satisfaction. "I haven't done any serious, one-on-one relationships that I wanted to last. If I miss a beat, just tell me."

Biting her bottom lip, she wondered how to reply to that. They'd only been reacquainted for a month, but the history they shared made it feel longer. Definitely deeper and more meaningful.

"This, with you," he stressed, "is serious. It needs to be one-on-one. Just me and you."

Well, that certainly explained it, and made her want to rejoice. Nodding, she said in a whisper, "Me, too."

Apparently forgetting that he didn't want their relationship advertised, he bent to kiss her, crushing her close and practically lifting her off her feet. Someone, somewhere, gave a loud whistle and he abruptly stepped back.

Feeling dazed, happily so, Berkley glanced around and saw that they'd gotten closer to the parking lot than she'd realized.

It was Wheeler who'd whistled, standing there with a trio of blondes who were maybe sisters, all of them beautiful. He waved as he laughed.

"So much for that plan," Lawson said as he waved back.

Berkley hugged up to his side and got him walking again. "We have an exclusive relationship, it's serious, and we both want it to last. That covers the bases, right?"

"Does for me."

"Me, too. So who cares what others think?" Given that much of her life had been colored by negative judgment and condemnation, not caring was a new attitude for her.

Just as they reached his truck, he completely stole her heart by asking, "Will Hero and Cheese be okay for a few more hours?"

Affection filled her heart when she whispered, "Yes. Hero is chill and Cheese will sleep. No worries."

Smiling, he jogged to a trash can to dispose of their bag, then hurried back so they could leave.

A few more hours…

It had been a perfect first date, and it seemed her evening was about to get even better.

When they stepped into his house, Lawson glanced around, glad that he'd put away tools and cleared construction messes. His house was almost done, minus some decorating.

"Ooooh," Berkley said, walking through his now tidy living room, eyes wide as she took in the cathedral bookcases, track lighting and built-in seating. "This is amazing!"

Shifting, Lawson tried to see it as she would, freshly completed, but his mind was more on getting her upstairs to the bedroom. To that end, he stepped up behind her and looped his arm around her waist. "You know I read a lot."

"I do, but this…" Tilting her head back, she stared up at the top shelves.

He had a rolling ladder to reach the uppermost books. "Those are all collections. I like to revisit some of them once a year."

She said "And the seating" with a touch of awe.

"It's a small space." Damn it, he was starting to feel embarrassed and he had no idea why. "It made sense to build them to fit the lines of the house."

She glanced over her shoulder at him. "They look comfortable."

A hint? Hey, he could be spontaneous. He wanted Berkley, and a bed definitely wasn't necessary. Urging her to the nearest couch, he drew her down and said, "Why don't we test it out?"

She giggled—a sound he'd never thought to hear from Berkley—then slapped a hand over her mouth.

Grinning at her, he tugged her onto his lap and into his arms. "I like seeing you happy."

"I like being happy. I thought I always was, but now, with you, it's so different."

"Easier, I hope."

"Surprisingly so." Looking at the material on the couch, instead of him, she asked, "Will we mess it up?"

At the moment, he didn't even care. "No." Leaning in, he nuzzled her throat.

Her breath caught. "It's soft."

Gently, he let her feel his teeth on her shoulder. "And not so soft."

Turning her head, she murmured, "I meant the material you used."

He gave a soft growl and said, "I don't want to talk about the furniture or my house anymore." Taking her mouth in a deep, hungry kiss, he showed her his priorities of the moment.

And actually, when it came to Berkley, the priorities of his future. In so many ways, they were intrinsically tied—by a past location, a difficult history, understanding and drive. Yes, he had his hands full with a new business and the work on his house and property.

Didn't matter. He would always make time for her.

Lowering her to her back on the cushions, he settled his weight half over her. Thankfully, the custom-built couch ran the length of the wall, offering room for guests—or one reclining woman with sex on her mind. "This dress…" Sliding his hand over the material, he explored along her waist, down her hip, her thigh and to her knee. The fabric was no barrier at all, and in fact served as more of a tease, giving hints of her warmth, her softness, as he explored her curves.

"My dress?" She opened her mouth on his neck, tasting his skin with an innocent greed that threatened to incinerate him.

"I like it." More than liked it, he thought, as he brought his hand back up, this time under the material. He felt her wiggling and lifted his head.

Flushing, she said, "Just kicking off my sandals. Proceed."

How had he never realized her sense of humor? Earlier, stating flat out that she wanted sex? And now telling him, more or less, to get on with it?

He'd worried about rushing her, but clearly Berkley didn't mind making herself clear. "Yes, ma'am." Taking her mouth in another deep kiss, he did some exploring of his own.

Her hands went around his neck, into his hair, then down to his chest, where she plucked at his shirt. Freeing her mouth, and taking a few deep breaths, she said, "Not to be shallow, but could you remove this? It's the truth you look better than most men and I enjoy seeing you. A lot."

At this point, everything she said reeled him in even more. After levering up to a sitting position, he reached back for a handful of the shirt, stripped it off and tossed it to the side of the couch.

Her gaze devoured him, followed by her hands, fingers spread, feeling all over his chest. Keeping her attention on his body, she said, "Until I saw you without a shirt, I had no idea that chest hair was so sexy."

Since she was in a teasing mood, he replied, "Mostly on men."

"Ha! Yeah, no chest hair on me."

Grinning at that, he lifted the hem of her dress. "Why don't you show me? Pretty as the dress is, I'd like to get it out of the way."

As if in confession, she whispered, "I'm not wearing a bra."

A fact he'd already noted. Not sure a bra would have worked under that wispy material anyway. "Not a problem for me."

That got him another huffed laugh. "Because you're not the one getting naked in front of someone for the first time."

The admission brought out his tenderness. Bold as she might be, he had to remember that this was new for Berkley. She'd been badly burned once, and needed this experience to be different for her. With that thought in mind, he stretched out alongside her, then trailed a fingertip over her collarbone. "I'm not just anyone, right?"

Her tension ebbed away. "No, you're not."

Slowly, he pulled one strap off her shoulder, down her arm and lower...until he exposed a breast.

"Say something."

Leaning down, he whispered into her ear, "I want you so much, I'm holding on by a thread."

"Me, too." In a new rush, she slid off the couch to her feet, struggled to get the dress up and over her head, and she tossed it toward his shirt.

Okay, that was a shocker. Slowly he sat up, but he couldn't take his gaze off her pale breasts, her narrow rib cage and slim waist that flared out to rounded hips. "I wasn't expecting that."

"Surprise."

Joking was no longer possible for him. Not with Berkley standing there, naked except for tiny panties. "I hope you know you're perfect."

"I'm not, but I don't even care." With that said, she pushed down her panties and stepped free, then gestured at him. "Jeans off."

The sudden rush threw him. When he got his attention off her body and onto her face, he saw the heat there. "Berkley..."

"Do you have a condom?"

"I do." No lie, she was gorgeous, and she really had to stop expecting him to carry on a conversation. He fished out his wallet, took out the protection and handed it to her.

"Er..."

Shoving down his jeans and boxers at the same time, he kicked them away. Once he straightened, he took the condom from her, then pulled her into his arms.

Thankfully, all dialogue ended there, because he didn't think he could have strung two words together. Berkley stopped being shy, and probably would have taken over if he hadn't been in such a rush himself.

The thing was, everything clicked.

Her quirkiness, his lust. Her demands, his delivery.

Her gasps and his growls.

It was all in sync. He'd had sex plenty of times, but he'd never experienced anything like *this*. Like her.

Realizing how much he cared for her, that the inevitable had somehow happened lightning fast, gave him a sense of peace he hadn't felt before. Like his past and his future had collided, and in the process every decision he'd ever doubted now made perfect sense.

When she clenched around him, when she arched and cried out, he felt it everywhere, especially in his heart.

For the first time in a long time, maybe the first time ever, it felt like he was home.

Held loosely in Lawson's embrace, her heart still racing and her breath yet uneven, Berkley smiled. She'd done some foolish things in her lifetime, and she had more than her share of regrets. But this, with him, she would never regret, no matter what twists and turns the future took.

Talk about an eye-opener.

She rested half atop him, her cheek on his chest, and she heard the heavy cadence of his heartbeat as it gradually slowed. She was naked and didn't care. Her hair and makeup were wild, and she didn't care.

She'd been demanding—and noisy. And she didn't care.

She cared about Lawson. About them together.

A few minutes passed. Lawson's fingertips teased over the bare skin of her bottom. She liked it that even now, after they'd just expended all that energy, he still touched her.

Once she thought she could speak coherently, she tried to find a way to put her thoughts into words. She lifted her head and saw that his eyes were closed, his hair even messier. His mouth, so talented, wore the slightest of appeased smiles.

"Lawson?"

"Hmm?" His light brown eyes opened, sated, lazy, happy.

It filled her with contentment. "Even at the worst of times, I was glad to be alive, so please don't misunderstand."

Concerned, he brought his hand up to lightly touch her cheek, his fingers drifting over her skin before stroking through her hair. "And now?"

"Now I feel like I'm really alive." That didn't quite cover it, and she knew her words wouldn't be adequate, but she gave it a try anyway. "I had no idea what I was missing."

"You were missing me." He brought her forward for a warm smooch. "So many times, I've thought that I never should have left you."

"What?"

"Back when we were both still young. When the world wasn't treating you kindly."

A short, soft laugh of surprise escaped her. "You didn't leave me." How silly. "You got on with your life and I'm proud of you for it."

"I left everyone. For a while there, after seeing you again, I felt bad about that."

"You shouldn't. I wasn't your responsibility."

"I know." He sat up, drawing her up with him.

Okay, now she felt naked. It was one thing to be sprawled over him in the aftermath. This was altogether different.

As if he saw her dilemma, he reached over the side of the couch and grabbed his shirt. To give her an out, he even said "The air-conditioning is chilly" as he pulled it over her head.

She gladly pushed her arms through the short sleeves and tugged it down to cover herself. It was large enough that it slipped off one shoulder and hung nearly to her knees.

"Be right back," Lawson said, and took his sexy self to the bathroom.

His jeans and boxers were still on the floor. Interesting. She waited, her gaze glued to the short hall, and sure enough, he returned only half a minute later, still without a stitch. Not only that, he detoured into the kitchen.

Berkley wasn't sure if she should follow, maybe take his boxers to him—nah. She had no issue with his nudity. In fact, she'd consider it a gift to herself. After the opening and closing of the fridge, he came back with two bottles of water.

Stepping right over his jeans, he handed her a water, then pulled on his boxers and took the seat next to her.

Naked was better, but he looked pretty darned fine in his shorts, too. "Thanks." Apparently, the bathroom trip was to dispose of the condom. Naturally, that was a priority, although she hadn't thought things through to that logical point. Her limited experience with sex had been fast, less than satisfying and in the dark, followed by shame.

This was a whole new ball game.

"Now..." He brushed a knuckle over her cheek. "I think

I've run the gamut of emotions since finding you here in Cemetery. Like you, I hadn't wanted any reminders of the past, but there you were."

She nodded. "I had planned to avoid you."

"Same." He smoothed her hair. "But I couldn't. When I didn't see you, I thought about you. And your thieving cat kept taking my things."

"She'll probably continue doing that."

"I don't mind anymore. Cheese and I are coming to an understanding."

So the quickest way to a woman's heart was, apparently, to love her pets, and provide some truly stellar sex. Lawson was winning on all counts.

"After getting to know you again, I kept thinking about that mess you'd been left with. I could have done more."

She pressed a finger to his lips. "Again, not your responsibility."

Taking her wrist, he drew her hand down to his chest. "I'm not sure the male brain works that way. At least, mine doesn't. The second I started to care about you, I wished I'd done things differently. The thing is, I'm not sure I could have. If I'd stayed, we might not even be here now. Maybe I'd have fallen into the same pattern as so many others who grew up where we did."

"Hurting others, or being hurt," she agreed.

"And you." He cupped his palm to her face, pressed his mouth to her lips, then her cheek, the bridge of her nose, her forehead. "Maybe you wouldn't have discovered your path in life, and all those animals who depend on you would still be lost and alone."

Such a wonderful way for him to see things. "I'd gladly go through it again to make sure I could be where I am right now."

The corner of his mouth hitched. "Naked on a couch with me?"

Humor had her own lips twitching. That, too, was new.

She'd never expected to have so much fun following sex. "I wouldn't mind ending up right here...often."

"Plan on it."

Oh, she definitely would. "I suppose you've had women from numerous countries?"

"Had?" His grin challenged her.

"You know what I mean. Sex."

"I haven't been marking conquests off on a world map or anything."

That wasn't a denial. "But?"

Rolling a shoulder, he said, "I'm damn near thirty, so yeah, I've been with a few women. Doesn't matter, because none of them were you."

"I wasn't complaining." Exactly. Just curious about how she'd measured up. "I guess if you wanted something, from me, I mean. During sex. You'd say so?"

He rubbed a hand over his face, then shoved his fingers into his hair. "You don't have a lot of experience—"

Immediately, she felt defensive. "That's what I'm saying."

Pressing a finger to her lips, then replacing it with his mouth, he gave her a kiss at first meant to quiet her, but he lingered, she pressed closer, he adjusted, drawing her against his chest and turning his head to take her mouth more deeply. It went on and on, until they were both nearly panting again.

"Without experience," he said, "you can't know how special this is between us." His gaze was so close to her own, filled with heat. His hand held her bared shoulder, his fingers long, warm against her skin. "I don't even know how to describe it, except to say that if you were any more perfect, I'd probably incinerate, and I wouldn't even mind."

Dazed by that confession, Berkley set her bottle of water on the table and happily snuggled back into his chest. "Thank you."

"Don't second-guess yourself. We're good together. If you want something, feel free to tell me and I'll do the same, but you can trust your instincts, too." He nuzzled against her ear and whispered, "You're smoking-hot, and don't forget it."

Hiding her grin against his throat, she said, "That sounds like an invitation, but I can't stay much longer. Hero and Cheese are used to me being there in the evening. They're like little alarm clocks. They know when it's bedtime."

His hand returned to her bottom, stroking her skin. "And you have to be up early tomorrow. You work too hard to go without sleep."

He was more than worth a little tiredness. "You do, too."

"I start later than you. Most of the Cemetery shoppers don't seem to get going until nine, and my shop doesn't get busy until ten or so. Before that, I think they're visiting the coffee shops." He gave her a hug. "Not true of animals. I've seen them all demanding attention at the same time."

Accurate. "Dogs wake earlier than cats. So many of the cats are practically nocturnal, but they all have to be fed, water dishes cleaned, messes removed."

"When did you know you wanted to take care of animals?"

She thought about it for a moment, then shook her head. "My mom knew before I did. I'm sure you remember that I was awkward."

"Not awkward," he corrected. "You guarded yourself, a smart move, all things considered."

"Maybe. I was a little friendlier in school, but outside of school, everyone reverted to their street cred—and I had none. I think, like you said, that's because my mother and I were so close. I needed to be home to take care of her, but we talked a lot, too. About everything. Even at her sickest, she watched over me, reminding me to be kind but safe, to stay alert but have an open heart. She always encouraged me to share my worries. I'd sit beside her to do my homework and she'd take care of bills, doing what she could online and using a lap desk to write checks when she needed to. She taught me everything that had to be paid and when so I'd be prepared. I'd moved a twin bed into the living room for her, because she was rarely well enough to sit in a chair, and we'd sometimes watch a movie while eating dinner."

"What did you talk about?"

"School, groceries, everyday stuff, but also plans for the future. I know she was afraid for me." It had always been hard to talk about her mother's health, but now, tucked against Lawson, the words flowed. "She was afraid she'd die before I was eighteen, and that I'd have to rely on strangers. We only had each other. There was no other family to turn to."

"Rough," Lawson said.

She pressed back to see his face. "We owned that house, inherited from my grandfather before he died, along with a decent savings account. Mom probably could have moved us, but without enough money coming in, she was afraid we wouldn't be able to keep up, and when she was gone, she wanted me to sell it so I'd have the funds to start over."

"The house couldn't have been worth that much."

"No." Not where they'd lived. "If we could have moved it somewhere else, a nice suburb or something, I'd have gotten three times what it sold for. Maybe four times more. But Mom's plan was solid and I never questioned it. In the end, it worked out."

"So how does that factor into you taking care of animals?"

She winced at the memory. "Every day, Mom would ask me what I might like to do, where I'd like to live. She was hoping to get everything worked out in advance, but I never had any answers, especially after everything that happened with Chad. Then Sabrina Durkinson dropped in on us."

His arms tightened around her. "I remember."

She understood his supportive embrace. It was the first time she'd mentioned Chad's wife by name. Even more so than Chad's, Sabrina's name dredged up regrets. "She pounded on our door like she wanted to break it down. At first I wasn't going to open it. Any loud banging was a bad sign in a place where people got robbed so often. It scared my mother, and Baby, her dog, started loudly yapping. I peeked out a window, and when I saw it was Sabrina, I figured I might as well get it over with."

Displeasure brought his brows together and flexed his jaw. "It still pisses me off that she came after you instead of Chad."

"I figured I deserved it," Berkley said. "So I let her in and then took the shouts and insults, even though they made me feel about an inch tall. Mom tried to speak up, but Sabrina yelled at her to butt out." That had already put Berkley on the defensive. "Mom's energy was fading, and the whole scandal had left her weak and upset. I hated that, too, hated that I'd brought so many problems to our home."

"I didn't realize the princess's visit was that bad."

"Oh, it got worse," she admitted. "In the middle of screaming that I was trash and should just die and do the world a favor, Baby got too close to her." Heart aching, Berkley whispered, "She kicked him."

Outrage widened his eyes. "That sweet *little* dog?"

"My mother cried out as if she'd been kicked. Baby squealed over and over again, cowering in the corner..."

"Was he okay?"

She nodded. "Mostly scared, upset, but no lasting injury. It didn't matter, though." Still bemused over her own reaction, she confessed, "I lost it. One minute I'd been shrinking with shame, and then bam, I saw red. I was in her face, backing her up to the door with terrible threats. Apparently, I was convincing, because she ran out."

Lawson made a strangled sound, and when she met his gaze, she realized he was trying not to laugh. Humor pulled at the corners of her lips, and she shoved his shoulder. "It isn't funny."

"Funny, no, except that I'm cheering you. Damn, Berkley,

I wish I could have seen it." He grinned. "And right after you chewed her a new one, she met up with me on the sidewalk. At least she had the good sense never to return."

"I still feel bad for not knowing Chad was married."

"That's on Chad, not you. And it had nothing to do with that poor little dog. Anyone who mistreats an animal won't get sympathy from me."

"That's what my mom said. Baby had already limped over to her and she was cuddling the dog, reassuring him while also praising me."

"Poor dog."

"Baby had never heard anyone shouting like that, and no one had ever struck him." Even now, it enraged her to remember it. Sabrina had deserved to be blasted, but the dog had been entirely innocent; his only fault had been trying to defend Berkley. "Mom claimed I'd just met my calling." Smile going crooked, Berkley said, "At first I thought she meant shouting—because I got really loud and mean. Then she explained that I was meant to protect animals. Turns out, she was right."

"Yes, she was. So maybe when you remember that twisted tale, you can find something positive in it."

"True. Because of that conflict, I found my way. After I lost Mom, I sold everything as quickly as I could. It was enough money for me to get a used car and get set up on my own, with money in the bank. Baby and I relocated to a small, pet-friendly apartment, and I got a job with a shelter." She had poured herself into that job. During the day, the different dogs and cats had kept her preoccupied and given her purpose. They'd also entertained her and made her feel loved. At home, she'd had Baby for company to help get her through the first, most painful year. "I was at that shelter a long time, and I was content, but it didn't pay much. I was starting to worry about the future, thinking of things I couldn't afford."

"Like a house?"

She nodded. "After Baby passed away and I got Hero, I knew he needed a yard. I worried endlessly about Cheese sneaking out and maybe getting into the road. Then I met Betty, and she told me she wanted to build a shelter here in Cemetery." Holding out her arms, Berkley said, "Now I'm here, and I feel so lucky getting to run my own place, still with minimal pay but an adorable little house that I love." *And you*, she wanted to say, because he was definitely a big perk. But she didn't want Lawson to think she was pinning him down, so she kept that part to herself.

Being here with him, tonight, making plans for a relationship, it was enough.

"Unlike me," he said, "you didn't have to go halfway around the world to figure it out."

"But how exciting to get to visit so many different places."

"It gave me a healthy perspective on life, that's for sure. After seeing so many disasters, I decided to settle down in one place."

"What made you decide on Cemetery, Indiana?"

He looked off as if recalling something amusing. "I knew I wanted the Midwest. Familiar territory, you know? But I didn't want to deal with a lot of crime, and I wanted that old-time vibe, where people pulled together and cared about each other. I saw that a lot in the more depressed areas of other countries. Community was big and people relied on each other."

"Friends instead of adversaries."

"I saw the ads for the lake, came to spend a few days to check it out and didn't want to leave." His gaze traced over her face. "I thought it would be entirely different from where I grew up, with more opportunity than the ravaged areas I helped rebuild."

"You didn't expect a blast from the past."

"Or involvement. With you, both are nice surprises."

It really was late, and Hero would start to worry, but she couldn't resist. "Do you have another condom?"

"I have a whole box."

"Think you could manage a quickie?"

Interest, and confidence, gave him a sexy smile. "Yeah, I can handle that. But then I'm walking you home, and I want your promise that we'll get together again soon."

Since she was having a hard time leaving, she knew that wasn't a problem. "Guaranteed." Next time, she'd get him to her house, and hopefully Hero wouldn't mind. She figured if she could adjust, the dog could, too.

And she was adjusting just fine.

12

It was bright and sunny on Sunday when Lark knocked on the back door of Berkley's home. She immediately wondered if she should have gone to the front, like an actual visitor, but she'd never seen Berkley use that entry and—

The door swung open and Berkley welcomed her with a huge smile, Hero and Cheese at her side. One of the things she liked most about Berkley was her love of animals. The other was her warm way of greeting people. She wasn't a chatterbox like Lark, but her reserved manner felt cozy.

The cat shot out before Lark could step in. "Oh, no!" Juggling her supplies, she reached out, but she wasn't even sure how to catch a cat, and it was already too late anyway. Cheese raced off as if being chased.

"It's fine," Berkley told her. "Cheese is a free spirit. I long ago gave up trying to keep her contained."

"Where do you think she's going?"

"Probably to steal something else from Lawson." As they went inside, Berkley explained about her cat's history of swiping things. It was an amusing story.

While Berkley poured them each iced tea, Lark took a few minutes to greet Hero. Unlike Cheese, the dog tended to stick right with Berkley most of the time.

"Where do you want to do this?" Lark asked. "I can set up anywhere."

"I guess just the kitchen, if you're sure that's okay." Wrinkling her nose, Berkley said, "My bathroom is really tiny."

"No problem at all." After digging around in her enormous tote bag, Lark located a small towel that she opened on the counter, set out two bowls, mixing brushes, tubes of hair color, scissors, combs, clips and foils. Lastly, she withdrew a large clear plastic shower curtain and spread it over the floor. When she realized Berkley was watching with interest, she said, "To avoid any drips and to catch any hair."

"This is all new to me," Berkley admitted. "I've always done my hair myself, and it shows."

"Are you kidding me? Girl, you have hidden talents. Your hair looks amazing. I totally thought you had a high-end stylist."

Dubious, Berkley slanted her a look. "I have gotten it trimmed a few times, but just at those supercheap walk-in places. I'm kind of excited for this new experience."

"Me, too. I actually love doing hair, so yay me. Not everyone can say they enjoy their job."

"I feel the same about my job, so I know what you mean." Berkley tugged at a hank of hair over her ear. "I was thinking…"

"Hair idea? Lay it on me. I'm flexible."

She eyed the products Lark had set out. "If you already had a plan, I don't want to throw a kink in the works."

"Ohhh, a kink," Lark teased. "Seriously. Let's talk about it." She took a seat and tried to look solemnly interested, when really, she couldn't wait to get started. She hadn't lied about Berkley's hair. It was gorgeous and thick, and Lark wanted to play with it, style it, be adventurous with color and give her a great cut.

"Well." Berkley took the seat opposite her. "What would you think of me going back to my natural color, which is sort of a plain medium brown, but still with some color to jazz it up?" Rushing on, she said, "I dyed it so long ago just to be different, to look like someone other than myself. But now..." A slow smile appeared. "Now I'm kind of reconnecting with the old me, but meshing it with the new me, and I think it'd be easier to maintain if I just—"

Shooting out of her seat, Lark exclaimed, "Love it!" She threaded her fingers into Berkley's hair and examined her roots. "I can see the color under the bleach. It's beautiful! Not plain brown at all, but more auburn." Turning to the counter, she located her phone and began scrolling. "Oh, *this*. What do you think?" She turned the screen for Berkley to see an image of a woman with brown hair, but with a few lighter, more golden streaks around her face. "It's still bold, but it would be beautiful with your coloring."

With new excitement, Berkley sat forward to view the image. "Oh, wow. Yeah, that's stunning." She twisted her mouth. "It won't look like that on me, though. That woman has really healthy hair."

"Your hair isn't unhealthy. I think you're just tired of it. Admittedly, this style will look a little different, though," Lark agreed. "Your hair is wavier, which I actually think will be better. Trust me?"

A grin that turned into a laugh preceded Berkley's enthusiastic nod. "Tell you what." She threw out her arms. "Do as you like. Surprise me. I trust you completely."

Such simple words, but they meant a lot to Lark. Pressing a hand to her heart, she said, "Thank you." At the most critical moment of her life, her own family hadn't trusted her, but Berkley, a new friend, did.

Sure, the differences were there, yet it still felt substantial. "It's going to take a few hours," Lark warned.

"Okay by me. Erin and Whitley offered to hang around to see about the animals, so I have time if you do."

"Are you kidding? I've been looking forward to this all week." Moving a chair to the center of the shower curtain on the floor, she gestured where she wanted Berkley. She clipped up her hair, wrapped a towel around her neck, followed by a long cape to protect her clothes front and back.

For the longest time, they chatted about everything while Lark worked on her hair, first applying the base color. As the color processed, they each had a cup of coffee and a few cookies.

At one point, Erin came to the door with a question, then seemed totally intrigued by the work in progress. Soon after she left, Whitley showed up "just so she could get a look."

Lark felt downright popular.

Apparently, Berkley did, too, but she smiled and said, "This is so different for me. I was always pleasant to customers, but I didn't really do friends."

"Do?" Lark asked.

"I was antisocial."

"No way."

"It's true." After the briefest hesitation, Berkley shared her heartbreaking background, telling her all about Chad Durkinson and his wife, Sabrina.

And Lawson. Wow. Lark had known there was more than a spark there. Apparently, it was a full-blown wildfire.

"So," Lark asked, while checking the color, "you and Lawson are now together?" When Berkley didn't reply, she leaned around to see her face. The happiness, the glow, was answer enough. "I see you enjoyed yourself."

"It was..." Berkley softly exhaled. "Unlike anything I thought possible."

"That good, huh?" Lark had missed this, chatting with a girlfriend, sharing secrets. "I'm not surprised. Lawson looks like a guy who'd know how to do things right."

"What about you?" Berkley asked, as Lark urged her up so she could wash her hair. "Any stupendous sex in your life right now?"

"Maybe if I can win over Oliver."

With a startled laugh, Berkley stuck her head into the sink, and for the next couple of minutes, they were silent as Lark washed and conditioned her hair. After wrapping a towel around Berkley's hair, Lark urged her back to her chair.

Immediately, Berkley asked, "So you like Oliver?"

"I took one look and I've been thinking of him nonstop ever since." She sighed. "There's a superhot man under that buttoned-up facade. I can feel it."

Finding that hilarious, Berkley laughed some more. "Does he know how you feel?"

"If he's paying attention, he does. I've practically thrown myself at him." Lark combed out her hair and began to snip. "Can I tell you something, Berkley? Something really private?"

"I'd be honored if you did."

Seconds ticked by while Lark struggled with the truth. "The reason I came here is because I had a miscarriage."

Berkley twisted around, gazing up at her with eyes full of sympathy. After a moment, she said, "I'm so sorry."

"Me, too." Nudging Berkley back around, Lark continued shaping her hair. "I hadn't known I wanted a baby. I was in a semi-serious relationship, but we'd never discussed marriage, definitely not kids." She heaved a sigh, still confused by her own emotions.

After doing hair for so long, she could practically work by instinct alone, so baring her soul didn't hinder her progress. "At first, when I found out I was pregnant, I was devastated. Scared, worried, unsure what to do. I love my parents, but they're pretty old-fashioned and I knew they wouldn't be happy with the news. It was even worse than that, though."

"Worse how?"

"They made assumptions on how I'd handle things, and when I didn't immediately agree, they were furious. My mother claimed I'd ruin my life, my dad said I was too young. I understood their sentiments, and I know they were only thinking about me and my happiness." Emotion lowered her voice. "My mother said I was *her* baby, that she loved me and wanted more for me. I was twenty-three then, not fifteen. I felt like it had to be my decision, not anyone else's."

Berkley was quiet a moment before asking, "And the baby's father?"

"He was okay at first, understanding and supportive, because he assumed we'd do certain things, and that'd be that. He offered to pay half the bill and thought that was generous." Her stomach knotted as she remembered that awful confrontation. "I wanted time to think about it."

"You deserved that," Berkley assured her.

"He told me I was being selfish, thinking only of myself when it involved him, too. I agreed, but... It didn't change my indecision."

"Having a baby is a big deal. Of course you wanted to think about it. That only makes sense."

Well, Lark thought, at least one person understood her. No one else in her life had. Somehow she'd been painted as the villain, selfish, immature, dramatic—she'd heard a lot of odd insults during that difficult time, all from people she had thought cared about her. "He said if I wanted to make the decision on my own, I could deal with the consequences on my own, too."

"He *ditched* you?"

Lark appreciated her outrage, but honesty compelled her to admit, "It was by mutual agreement. At that point, I realized we had some very big differences that I'd never considered."

"Still..." Berkley persisted.

"My parents were hassling me, too. My friends thought I was being ridiculous and wanted me to carry on as usual." She'd felt completely cut off from her usual support system. "I just wanted some space, a little peace and quiet to come to terms with my new reality." Pausing, Lark rested her hand on Berkley's shoulder and swallowed heavily. "I was home alone when the cramps started."

Berkley reached up, their hands connecting. A *human* connection. Something she'd wanted so badly on that trip to the hospital. But she'd been at odds with her parents, so pride had kept her from calling them. By the time she'd let them know, the damage to the relationship had been done.

"I wasn't very far along when they told me I'd lost the baby, but then I realized how much I'd wanted it." Tears clouded her eyes. "I'm sorry," she said with a sniffle and a huff. "I didn't mean to unload on you. We're supposed to be having fun."

Berkley was out of her seat in the next second, flowing cape and all, and she drew Lark in for a firm, secure hug. "Don't apologize. Just... Don't. I'm glad you're here and that we're friends and we can share this stuff, the good and the bad."

Lark gave a sniffling laugh. "The good being some really hot guys."

"Yes, them. But also this. You doing my hair. Girl talk. All the stuff I missed out on when I was growing up. My mom was sick for so long, and once she passed away, I didn't have anyone I was close to. Not even any casual friends. Then I met Betty, and she's like a grandmother to me, and Lawson is just special in so many ways. Now you." She held Lark's shoulders and stepped back to see her face. "Thank you for telling me. For trusting me."

Lark nodded. "I haven't really trusted anyone in a long time."

"Then I'm doubly flattered. I swear, I won't make you regret it."

"I know. I mean, I sort of sensed that from the start. You know how some people just click?"

Pleased, Berkley asked, "We've clicked?"

"Absolutely." She gestured at the chair. "Let's get back to it so I can finish your hair." Now that she'd told Berkley everything, she surged with new energy. Sharing was a wild, invigorating activity. "I'll blow-dry and style it before you see it, okay?"

"I can't wait." Berkley dutifully sat.

They continued to talk, the conversation now lighter, mostly about the guys. She made a few risqué jokes, and Berkley laughed each time. They talked about the shelter and the mama cat who'd had kittens, the town council meetings and the monthly tea group.

Many plans were made, and by the time Berkley's hair was finished, Lark knew they'd chosen correctly. Berkley's natural hair color complemented her skin tone and made the blue of her eyes even brighter. The subtle red streaks added a lot of depth to her hair and made it shimmer. With some trimming and shaping, her hair now fell in perfect waves to frame her face, still long enough for a ponytail when convenience was key, but easily tousled into sexy disarray.

"Well?" Berkley said.

Proud of the finished product, Lark took her hand and said, "Come on. Let's go look in the bathroom mirror."

Hero jumped up from where he'd been napping in a ray of sunshine on the floor and trotted after them.

At the bathroom door, Berkley braced herself with a deep

breath and then stepped into the room in front of the vanity. Awe widened her eyes, and her lips parted.

Bouncing on the balls of her feet, Lark asked, "Do you like it?"

Turning her head this way and that, Berkley whispered, "Wow."

"Gorgeous, right?"

Color rose in Berkley's cheeks. "I can't say I look gorgeous because that'll sound conceited, but I feel gorgeous. My hair is beyond beautiful and I *love* the change."

"Way to stress me out!" They both laughed. Lark couldn't resist fussing with Berkley's hair, pulling a little forward, tucking a little back. "No matter what you do, those subtle red hues, and a few that are more golden, show. You look amazing, if I do say so myself."

They were both staring at her reflection when the knock sounded on the door. A mere moment of silence ensued, then shattered as Hero broke into frenzied barking, jolting around to race to the door, which forced Berkley to hustle after him, with Lark hot on her heels.

At the kitchen doorway, Lark could see straight through to the laundry room—and the man standing at the door.

Oliver. What was he doing here?

Somehow, their gazes locked and she couldn't force herself to look away. "He's here," Lark whispered. He seemed as surprised to see her as she was to see him. Giving Oliver the "just a second" sign of one finger, she turned to Berkley.

"I think I'm going to blush." Looking back and forth between them, Berkley laughed. "Yeah, you two definitely have a thing."

"But *what*?" Lark would like to find out.

"Definitely physical." Berkley kept her voice low so he wouldn't hear. "But there's a lot of other stuff going on."

Lark sighed. "I hope so." Every time she saw Oliver, she wanted him more.

Touching her arm, Berkley whispered, "With all these sparks going off, maybe you should tell him why you moved here?"

"What?" Lark snapped her gaze to Berkley. "I couldn't."

"Why not? You don't think he'd understand?"

She had no idea, and she wasn't sure if she was willing to chance it.

Oliver lifted his brows, watching them both whispering together and probably wondering why one of them didn't let him in.

Lark bit her lip. "You really think I should?"

"I'm hopeless when it comes to figuring out relationships, but I know that talking to Lawson about the stuff that worries me made me feel better, like I had a fresh perspective."

Oliver, however, was nothing like Lawson. For one thing, they didn't share a past. For another, he was seriousness personified, while she enjoyed laughing and teasing, which was the main reason everyone had been so surprised over her reaction to being pregnant. "What if I tell him and it scares him off before we've even gotten started?"

"Then maybe it's better to know that now, before you're more invested." Berkley turned so that she blocked Oliver's view of Lark. "I'm the last person on earth who can give advice about life. So this is just a thought, maybe a gut feeling. You won't be happy casually dating Oliver. You want to know he's open to a relationship, too, right? Doesn't mean it will work out, that you two will elope, have kids and retire as old people together. But it should be a possibility, right? If he's invested in the success of his fitness studio and wants to avoid involvement, better to find that out up front, don't you think?"

The thought of losing him already made her stomach clench, but Lark nodded. "You're probably right." Oliver knocked again, a little harder this time. Peeking around Berkley, Lark took in his exasperation, his dark brows pinched behind his glasses. "We should let him in."

"Before Hero has a conniption."

The dog really was confused, running from Berkley to the door and back again as if to say *Come on!*

Mustering up a smile, Lark led the way. She unlocked the door, pulled it open and was about to greet Oliver when he spoke.

"What's going on?" His gaze went over Lark's face, hesitated on her mouth, then stared into her eyes. "What's wrong?"

"Nothing." Guilt sent a flustered wave of heat to her cheeks. "I was doing Berkley's hair."

Berkley, bless her, struck a pose. "What do you think?"

His attention briefly transferred to Berkley, but came right back to Lark. "Looks nice."

Beaming at him, Berkley said, "Thanks. I'm glad she added more pink."

"Yeah."

Snickering, Berkley said, "She's a wizard—who *removed* the pink."

Dragging his gaze from Lark once more, he glanced at Berkley's hair. "Ah, yeah. I see. It looked great either way."

"So much enthusiasm," Lark teased.

Aggrieved and not bothering to hide it, he dutifully turned to face Berkley again. "Gorgeous hair. Lark did an amazing job."

"Better," Berkley said, giving a pat to his shoulder.

Attention shifting right back to Lark again, he doubled his frown. "Why were you two just staring at me and whispering?" While rubbing Hero's neck, he looked beyond them, through the laundry room to the kitchen. "You two are alone?"

"Yes, definitely alone." Confusion had Berkley frowning now, too. "Were you expecting to find someone?"

He shook his head. "I just have a bad feeling about this joker who was looking for you. He hasn't contacted you again?"

"No." More forthcoming than she'd been before, Berkley said, "Lawson and I talked about it, though, and I'm going to call Chad—when Lawson is with me—just to tell him to get lost."

"Cut him off at the knees before he comes sniffing around?"

"Something like that."

Crossing her arms, Lark showed her doubt. "So you came here, on a Sunday, just to check on Berkley?"

"What? No." Oliver's gaze never left her face when he said to Berkley, "I was going to see about visiting with Handsome. I know it's an off day, so I'll understand if you'd rather I not, but I have the rest of the day free, so—"

"Great idea. Lark, do you want to go with him? I can put away the rest of the mess."

She'd already cleaned up her supplies while the color processed, so there really wasn't that much except to ball up the shower curtain, pack it away and put the chairs back in place. "I can do it. You can get the dog for him."

Nonplussed, Berkley stood there. Clearly, she'd hoped to put them together.

"Sorry." Lark explained, "It's a habit of mine to put everything away after I've done a client's hair in her home. I'll need to store my stuff in my car, too."

"I'll help you," Oliver said. "Then we can walk Handsome together." Almost like a lure, he added, "The dog likes you, and he can use all the attention he can get." His dark eyes shifted to Berkley. "No offense. You're doing a great job."

"None taken, because I agree." She looked down at Hero. "Stay, bud. I'll be right back." And then to Oliver, she said, "Get yourself a drink in the kitchen, if you'd like. I'll have Handsome out in five minutes." Using more haste than necessary, Berkley slipped away, leaving her alone with Oliver. For some reason, Lark couldn't seem to move.

Hero's astute gaze bounced from Lark, to Oliver, and then he sat down with a bored yawn.

Oliver grinned. "He's so well-behaved. I wonder how protective he might be."

It wasn't jealousy she felt—no, absolutely not—but something
spurred Lark's irritation. "You seem more than a little interested in Berkley's safety."

"You aren't?" He had no problem moving. With a pat to his
thigh, Oliver called Hero to him and they went into the kitchen
together.

Leaving her standing there in the laundry room alone.

Closing her eyes for two seconds, Lark struggled to suppress
the disturbing emotions clamoring inside her. When she opened
them again, it was to see that Oliver had turned back and was
now watching her.

In mild query, he asked, "Ready?"

It was almost laughable. Oh, she was ready all right. For many
things. The bigger question was, how far and how fast could
she get him to go?

After some bookkeeping and inventory, Lawson headed out
of his shop, pulling the back door shut behind him and securing
the locks. He turned and nearly tripped at the sight of Kathleen. The mannequin had been moved from the front of the
shop when he wasn't looking, and now stood near his truck.

A note had been taped to her hand. Trying to spot any guilty
faces, he glanced around, but Sunday in Cemetery was fairly
quiet, especially on this small strip. Nearer to the restaurant
and the lake, people still enjoyed the day, but here, at the back
end of the shops, he didn't see a single soul.

Annoyed, he strode up to the mannequin, trying not to look
at her face and unseeing eyes, and pulled the note away to read it.

It's no fun if you won't take part. If you don't want me
here, put me somewhere else—where people will appreciate me.

Snorting, he crumpled the note and tossed it into the trash bin. Not a bad suggestion, though. He should have moved the mannequin a week ago.

Hands on his hips, he tried to decide what to do with her. Another furtive glance, and he came up with a plan. Quickly, because he didn't want to be late seeing Berkley, he went back into his shop. After creating a sign with a bold black marker and a sheet of white cardboard, he located the shirt he wanted, along with a pair of shorts. Others might dress the mannequin in loose clothes, but what the hell—if he was going to do this, he might as well do it right.

He grabbed extra small shorts since Kathleen had almost no hips at all, but a small shirt—Kathleen had been made with a rack. For good measure, he grabbed a sweatband, too.

Cautiously, he looked outside, but he was still alone. Didn't matter. He felt like a perv changing Kathleen's clothes outside, so he moved with haste. The shorts were easy. He just put her in the truck bed and slid them up her long, narrow legs, then tightened the drawstring so they'd stay in place. The shirt, with her unbending arms, proved a little trickier. At one point, he almost took off her head, but finally he got it done.

Sliding the sweatband over her forehead, and grinning, because yeah, this was a little fun, he finished off her look. He hefted Kathleen completely into his truck, secured a tarp over her, closed the gate and drove away from his shop.

Nearer to Oliver's fitness center, people milled about, but with a little effort, he managed to get Kathleen and the sign set up. She looked very trendy in her sportswear with Oliver's logo on the front.

Come on in and get fit like me. You know you want to.

Fighting a grin, Lawson took a pic with his phone, then headed home. Kathleen was no longer at his shop, and it hadn't been that much trouble to change her clothes and move her.

He'd just enjoyed taking part in Cemetery's nonsense—and it was fun.

Now to grab a shower at home, then join Berkley for some one-on-one time.

He couldn't think of a better way to spend his day.

13

Lark was in an odd mood, and Oliver didn't like it. He was used to her friendly chatter and smiles, but now she seemed... Shy? No, that wasn't a word that would ever apply to Lark. But something was wrong. He could damn well sense it.

She was as sweet as ever with Handsome, telling the dog how cute he was, that he was such a good boy, praising him when he sprinkled the grass, when he darted after a butterfly and even when he led them under the shade of a cluster of trees.

For Oliver, she'd been slightly distant.

"You did a great job on Berkley's hair."

She flashed him a smile that wrapped around his heart. "Not that she didn't look awesome already. She wanted a change, and I really like how it turned out."

Since Handsome plopped down on the grass near a tree,

Oliver meandered closer and leaned back against the trunk. He studied Lark. "You've got a little smudge of mascara under your right eye."

"Again? Ugh." She reached up to rub, but he stopped her.

"Let me." He lifted his pinky finger to her lips. "Little lick."

"Excuse me?"

He'd probably excuse her anything, but the idea of her tongue touching him had his thoughts in a riot. "To dampen the end of my finger. Then I can remove the smudge."

"Oh." She took hold of his wrist, her hand so small that her fingers barely managed to encircle him. He could have sworn a wicked gleam entered those gray eyes before she lowered her lashes and, bringing his hand closer, swirled the tip of her tongue over his finger.

He felt it everywhere, and almost forgot what he was doing until she gave him such an innocent look. "Chin up," he gruffly ordered.

Dutifully, she tipped her face, staring up at the tree to make it easier for him. One small swipe, and the mascara was removed.

She still held his wrist.

If Handsome wasn't right there, held on a leash between them, Oliver would have kissed her. Didn't matter that they were in the shelter yard on a Sunday, or that Berkley had glanced out at them several times.

Lark might not be aware of her friend's attention, but he was. "Did Berkley have plans? Are we holding her up?"

"No. She's having dinner with Lawson tonight, but we have another hour before she'll want to put Handsome in his area and lock up the shelter."

"Want to sit, then? Handsome is done walking, I think. The ground is dry, and you're in jeans." Cute jeans, snug enough to hug her behind and showcase her waist. Her sleeveless top was some kind of sheer pink material that draped over her breasts and fell loosely from there.

Lark Penny had showstopper looks, but that wasn't what drew him.

"Sure." When she started to lower herself, he took her hand under the guise of assisting her. She smiled her thanks, and sat cross-legged.

Once Oliver sat at the other side of Handsome, the dog scooted closer, then rested his shaggy head over Oliver's thigh. The pooch definitely knew how to steal his heart.

He was a lot like Lark that way.

"Aww," Lark breathed softly. "He loves you."

"I'm fond of him, too." Much of Handsome's fur had returned but it was still uneven. The dog gave him a gruesome smile, thanks to his perpetually squinting eye and dental issues, but it was adorable all the same. "He no longer looks panicked when I visit."

"Are you kidding? He's thrilled to see you." She leaned closer as if to share a secret. "He's your dog now, you know?"

"Yes, he's mine."

Brows shooting up and eyes widening, she showed her surprise.

"You thought I'd deny it?" He gently rubbed one of Handsome's bristly ears. "I think Berkley already knows, but either way, she said she'd talk to me first if anyone was interested in adopting him. I'd like to take him soon, but until he's gotten through his dental work, I don't want to disrupt him. I thought I'd be putting in sixty hours or more at the fitness center, but it's all coming together more easily than I'd imagined and my schedule isn't near as strict as I'd anticipated."

"Somehow, you and a strict schedule seem to fit."

Very true. Before moving here, he'd been rigid in his work ethic, determined to get ahead, to build a name for himself, fatten his bank account and set up his future.

Here, in Cemetery, he was trying to learn to live more, plan less. There was a reasonable balance, and he was finding it here.

"Things aren't as regimented as I'd expected." That was in part due to Lark's incredible marketing talents. "You can take some credit for that."

"Me?"

"I thought I'd spend at least a month just drumming up business, but we've been nearly maxed out since opening. With so much clientele, I've been able to adapt the business hours to accommodate the busiest times. Lawson and I are doing some shared promotions, and thanks to you, I'm meeting new people through the shelter. The cat yoga was a massive hit and we're already booked up for the rest of the summer. Now other businesses here are reaching out."

"Glad you could use some of my ideas." She gave him a cheeky grin. "Any time you want to discuss business, let me know."

He wanted to discuss business, all right. Among other things. Like how she'd taken all his plans and so easily turned them upside down. He wanted his new career to be a hit, but he also wanted Lark, the sooner the better. "When I came here, the very last thing I counted on was a—"

She inhaled and held it.

"Dog."

"Oh," she said on a long, relieved exhale.

"Or a woman," he added, knowing that was what she'd expected.

Scrunching her nose, she said, "I did sort of push myself on you that first time at Saul's restaurant."

He couldn't help that his voice lowered. "You can push yourself on me anytime you want."

"Ha!" Her laugh startled Handsome, who could still be skittish, so she spent a minute apologizing to the dog, bending down to talk to him and hugging him—which put her very close to Oliver's lap.

"Lark?" Settling his hand over her dark hair, he let his fingers sink into the heavy locks. She had amazing hair, not that long, but so silky it was almost liquid. He'd never paid that much attention to a woman's hair before. It either suited her or it didn't. He noticed redheads, but then noticed blondes, too. Lark, with her rich hair and pale gray eyes, gave off a uniquely innocent but mischievous vibe—and somehow was scorching hot at the same time. Especially with her smiles and "we *will* be friends" manner.

With Handsome now reassured, she peered up at him. "I'll be on my best behavior now. I hate that I frightened him."

"He'll get used to you." Oliver tugged her a little closer. "I want to kiss you."

Nodding, she said, "I was hoping you would."

He almost grinned, but getting his mouth on hers took precedence. They met over the dog, each leaning in, and he knew he was a goner.

Her lips, slightly parted, touched his tentatively. Their breaths mingled, each savoring the moment. When she started to pull back, he closed the distance and kissed her again, warmer, firmer. Deeper.

It went from a getting-to-know-you kiss to a prelude-to-sex kind of kiss. Everything he'd expected from Lark—a heated punch to his senses, a mere taste that made him want more— was in that kiss.

Need tensed his shoulders, but he gently brushed his thumb over the smoothness of her warm cheek. Slowly, he straightened. "I need more of that."

"Yup, me too."

Her eagerness made him feel guilty. "I should tell you something."

All that warm excitement faded from her expression, and a mask of polite interest fell into place. "Okay."

The last thing he wanted to do was overwhelm her, but it wouldn't be fair to her to start something she might not want. So, he settled more comfortably against the tree, stared out at the yard and said, "I'm not into casual sex." For her, though, he might make an exception—if it was the only way he could have her.

"Me, either. Go on."

The ready agreement was promising. "I always wanted a dog."

He sensed more than saw her confusion. "Pets are awesome."

"I wanted a family, too. You're right that I'm a serious-minded person, always have been. Even in college, I had an end goal in mind. Good job, house, wife, kids, all in that order."

Behind Handsome, she settled against the tree, her shoulder touching his, her attention rapt in a way he hadn't expected. "You want kids?"

He couldn't tell if she was appalled or intrigued.

"Eventually."

"So not now?"

"Pretty sure I can't just snap my fingers and produce a baby." By the expression on her face, his joke fell flat. "I'm thirty-four." Couldn't help the way his gaze dipped over her, seeing all the signs of her youth. "Ten years older than you."

"Practically ancient," she quipped. "Go on."

Smart-ass. He fought a smile, because this was serious and yet, she'd just made it clear the ten-year difference didn't factor in for her. "I thought I'd be married long before now. My brother and I grew up in this nice, upper-middle-class home. Two professional parents with important jobs, but they always made time for us. My mom was a school superintendent, my dad a lawyer. They were strict, but I think also fair." When Handsome turned to his side and dozed off, Oliver continued to lightly stroke him. The dog responded to him, to his touch.

He wanted Lark to do the same, but in a very different way.

He definitely didn't want her dozing off.

"Everything was going according to plan. I was a physical therapist with a six-figure income at a well-respected practice, working with college athletes and some professional players. Dating a woman in the same practice. Then my dad died." They'd been close, and he missed his father still. "He was playing golf when a massive heart attack took him."

"That had to have been an awful shock."

"He was gone before the ambulance arrived. It's been a little more than a year now. My mom was lost. They'd been a team for so long that she couldn't seem to get her footing back. She retired from her position, and I think it gave her too much time to focus on her loss." He huffed a quiet laugh. "That sounds heartless, doesn't it? I don't mean it that way. She'd always been a doer, but after losing Dad..." His mother became a sedentary stranger, almost a recluse. "She ignored invitations from her friends, and when I visited her, she barely seemed to know I was there."

Resting her hand on his arm, Lark sympathized. "Almost like you lost both parents."

That was how it had felt. "My brother's been hurt more by it. He's a few years younger than me. Always the baby, you know?" Imagining how Gordon would react to being called the baby, he half smiled. "Not that he wasn't a great guy. He just relied on Mom more. Losing Dad was hard enough on him, but Mom withdrawing like that... I'm not blaming her. Please don't think that."

She waved that off. Interested and concerned, she leaned closer. "You said your brother *was* a great guy?"

So she hadn't missed that emphasis? He hated thinking about it. That was a problem, too. He'd shut them all out, all their struggles, so he could focus on his own life and moving forward, sticking to his plan. He'd own up to it now, because he was done turning away from problems, especially his own.

"Gordon is married, has a sweet baby girl, everything to live for...but he started self-medicating." What a shitty way to describe drug addiction. "That's what my mother called it at first.

She thought it'd be a simple problem to fix and she wanted me to do something. So did my sister-in-law. Gordon spiraled out of control so fast that it took us all by surprise. I talked to him so many times, trying to get him to see a specialist. Nothing I said mattered, but then, I was a physical therapist, not a professional who deals with emotions."

"You do pretty well with emotions, too," Lark said, nodding at Handsome.

"Animals are easier than people." No one expected them to understand. But a grown man? Yes, he'd had expectations for his brother. "Instead of seeking help, Gordon turned into a hothead, blowing up on everyone."

"Including you?"

"Me, his wife, our mother." Frustration gathered, making his temples pound. "He got fired, started mixing drugs and alcohol. The last time my sister-in-law called me, I didn't want to go."

"But you did anyway."

It had felt pointless. And in the end, things would have been better if he hadn't. "Gordon was out of control. He had the car keys, planning to go out. When I tried to stop him, he took a swing at me, and I…" He tightened his jaw.

Lark filled in for him. "You swung back? So? Was he a little guy?"

"My size, but stockier."

"Oliver." Gray eyes conveyed acceptance and understanding. "For a fit guy like you, I imagine it was almost instinct."

"That's no excuse. Especially because it made everything worse. He went wild, throwing things, cursing my sister-in-law when she tried to calm him down. The baby woke up screaming, but he didn't seem to care about that, either." His hand on Handsome stilled, and his free hand curled into a fist. God, he'd wanted to pound his brother. By sheer force of will, he hadn't. "It was one of the most disgusting displays I've ever seen from a man. Honest to God, it shamed me that he was a Roth."

Lark leaned against his shoulder, her expression both under-standing and sympathetic. "I can see why." After a thought-ful moment, she added, "You're his brother and you love him. You, too, had lost your father and you were worried about your mother. You wanted the best for Gordon, and the all-consuming destruction of drug dependency wasn't it. Plus I'm sure you love your sister-in-law and niece."

"Very much." He missed them, especially his niece. She'd be three soon. Would he get to see her for her birthday? Didn't seem likely. "Over the next month, his addiction got worse, until he completely bottomed out. Mom claimed he was only grieving, like her."

"Sounds like he needed some tough love."

That's what Oliver thought, but no one else had agreed. "Mom didn't understand how I was functioning fine with ev-erything. She accused me of just carrying on as if we hadn't lost Dad."

"Oh, Oliver," she said softly. "I imagine she was hurting, so she verbally struck out at you, but she should have known that falling apart isn't your way."

The words, stated with such confidence, drew him like a lifeline. "You're sure about that?"

"Of course. You loved your father as much as the others. You love all of them, I can tell." She rubbed his arm. "Every-one's grief is different. I bet you stayed busy and tried to be productive."

How could she already know him so well? "It was the only thing I knew to do." He'd pushed through, refusing to let him-self dwell. "I didn't want to add to Mom's upset." He'd thought he was doing the right thing, only to find out he was wrong.

"It's obvious that's how you coped. You couldn't understand your mother and brother, just as they couldn't understand you."

Grateful that Lark so easily understood him when his own family hadn't, he nodded. "We haven't even spoken in so long."

"I'm sorry." She drew a breath. "You'll be in touch with them soon, or they'll contact you. I'm sure of it."

"Tonight," he said. "I'll call Mom tonight. It's been two months since I left." And for a month before that, they'd been at odds, barely speaking.

Too damn long. For all of them.

"Does she live far?"

"A few hours south." He dropped his head back. "After things fell apart with my brother, I wanted out of there. I gave up my job, emptied my accounts, sold everything and came here." To start over. "I wanted a complete change from the city. I know drugs are everywhere, but this town feels…"

"Wholesome." Lark smiled up at the oak leaves overhead, at how the sunshine left dappled shadows everywhere. "Safe and welcoming. The air is fresh, everyone knows everyone else, and the sunsets on the lake are inspiring."

"That's about it."

"Fewer reminders here, too."

Another bull's-eye. "You're pretty perceptive, Lark Penny."

Her slim hand curved around his jaw. "How is your brother doing now? Do you know?"

"He OD'd, damn near died, but thankfully pulled through." That was what had sent Oliver packing. He couldn't stick around and watch his little brother kill himself. "He'd been drinking all night, hooked up with a woman in a bar, took a pill someone gave him…"

"Oh, no."

"So damned irresponsible." Oliver had thought it then, and he thought it now. How could a man—his own brother—dishonor his wife like that? Risk his life when he had a child to care for?

No, he didn't understand, and sadly, he never would. He'd be there, he'd help if he could, but he knew he didn't have the knowledge to help Gordon get through addiction.

"Your poor sister-in-law."

Yeah. "Once he got out of the hospital, Gordon had court-ordered rehab, and he hated it, and he hated life." The entire thing had been ugly, but Oliver knew he couldn't help his brother. Whenever he'd tried, it'd just made it worse. "For a while, she blamed me. So did my mom." *You should have done more for him. You could have tried harder.* So many things he should or could have done.

Skipping right past that, Lark asked, "Are they still together?"

"Last I heard." But he knew it was dicey, understandably so.

"Who'd you hear it from?"

"My sister-in-law, but she was still dazed and hurting. Her parents are terrific. She was going to stay with them for a while." It was a relief to him to know his niece would have others looking out for her. "Once he finally got out of rehab, Gordon was going to stay with Mom." Closing his eyes, Oliver said, "At least Mom started seeing and feeling again."

"She'd had to, to take care of Gordon."

It had given her a new purpose. "She insisted he'd be fine, that they'd work through things together."

Gently, Lark said, "I hope that's true."

"At that point, I knew I needed a change. I wasn't going to be a help to anyone." A sad truth. "So I walked away."

She rubbed his shoulder. "What else could you do?"

"I don't know. That was the problem. I had no idea what to do. Still don't."

"So you decided to live." She said it decisively, and with admiration. "This is *your* way, Oliver. Here, you can help people without the family strife. You're offering physical fitness for an outlet, for others, and for yourself."

Exactly what he'd told himself. "Or maybe that's just a cop-out so I don't have to go back and do the hard work for my family."

Lark heaved a sigh, then rested her head on his shoulder. "It's not a cop-out. It's reality. I think Gordon needs professional help."

"Me, too." He'd suggested it, but the idea wasn't well received.

"You're here, a wonderful, smart, talented man with so much to give to the community and a lot of life ahead of you. Making yourself miserable won't help anyone." She went quiet, then straightened again to ask, "What did you say to them all when you left?"

"That I wouldn't be far, I loved them, and if I could help, if they needed anything at all, to let me know."

Soft understanding filled her eyes. "That's wonderful, Oliver. A generous offer and the perfect way to leave things." She brushed a quick kiss to his mouth. "Now that a little time has passed, if you're feeling like you need to connect with them again, I vote for a plan of action. If you wouldn't mind my input—"

"I would love your input." He drew her hand from his jaw to his mouth, pressing his lips to her palm. "Got a marketing plan for me? A way to salvage my family ties?"

"I'm positive your family ties are as strong as ever. You don't need any help with that." Lower, she muttered, "And I wouldn't be the one to give that advice anyway."

What was that? Was Lark also at odds with her family? He wanted to ask, but then she continued.

"How about some objective thoughts from an outsider instead?"

"Objective is good."

"Sometimes family is the best of us, and the worst of us."

Coming from experience, no doubt. Cradling her hand in his own, Oliver teased the pad of his thumb over her delicate knuckles. She was small in stature, but he had a feeling Lark was strong where it mattered, in her loyalty, her convictions, her honesty and her pride.

"Invite your mother here to visit. Cemetery—the name alone, right?—is a topic starter. Make it a casual, open-ended invite and tell her you've missed her."

"I have." A lot. "She might be intrigued by the town."

Cautioning him, Lark added, "She'll either agree to come or not, but you're connecting either way. Then get hold of your brother, tell him you've been thinking of him and you hope he's doing well."

"Also true, but the last time I tried that, he blew up on me."

"Last time, he hadn't yet hit rock bottom." A wealth of sincerity darkened her eyes, showing her vulnerability. "He hadn't yet lost you."

Oliver frowned. Who had Lark lost? Hopefully there wasn't a guy he didn't know about. "Have you—"

She cut him off. "If he loves his wife, and I assume he does, hopefully he took rehab seriously and is trying to get his life in order. It won't be easy, but it's on him, not anyone else. You said he was a great guy before sorrow and drugs got the better of him, so I'm giving him the benefit of the doubt. By now, I'm sure he has a lot of regrets."

Regrets. Everyone had them, right? Surely, he wasn't alone in that. There'd been a time where he and Gordon were buds as well as brothers. "Family was always important to all of us."

"And your family took some hard blows." Her gaze tracked over his face, his eyes, his jaw, his mouth—where she lingered a moment—before returning to meet his gaze. "Don't apologize to him. That's the wrong road to go down. Even if he isn't receptive, just tell him you're wishing him well. Nothing deflates anger faster than someone who doesn't reciprocate."

Was that why Lark stayed so happy? To deflect any negativity? "Thanks for the great suggestions. I appreciate it."

"He's your brother," she said. "So if he's anything like you, he has to be pretty awesome. He'll come around."

Talk about reciprocal... "Does that mean you like me?"

Wearing a "get real" expression, she said, "I more than like you, and you know it."

A lazy smile curled his mouth. "Good to know, because I more than like you, too." He tugged at a lock of her hair. "Now that we've cleared up our interest, will you tell me about your family?"

The heartfelt groan conveyed her feelings on that.

He was disappointed, but said, "If you'd rather not—"

"How about the shortened version?"

"Whatever you're comfortable sharing."

Suddenly talking at hyperspeed, she said, "My parents and I love each other, that's not in doubt, but I went through a miscarriage and we were at odds over the pregnancy, and like you, I came here for some space, for time to work out my feelings."

The rushed explanation hit him like a sucker punch. Of all the family issues she might have shared, that never factored into his thoughts. "You were pregnant?"

Still avoiding his gaze, she nodded. "My parents were concerned, but we differed on what to do. It...caused a lot of conflicts."

Emotions bombarded him, concern first, and then a touch of possessiveness. Using two fingers, he stroked along her jaw, then nudged up her chin until she met his gaze.

Worry-filled gray eyes stole a chunk of his heart.

"The guy?"

One shoulder lifted in dismissal. "He was history before I lost the baby."

"He knew you were pregnant?"

A smirk came and went. "That's why we split up."

Meaning it, he said, "I'm sorry."

"That he took off?"

"No." Good riddance to him, as far as Oliver was concerned. "I'm sorry that he let you down. That you went through that." And it sounded like she'd handled it alone. Instinct made him want to gather her close, but they had a small, needy pooch between them.

Memories softened her tone. "It was an unpleasant eye-opener for sure. Until then, I'd been without direction. Just enjoying life day by day, with no thought of the future or what I really wanted."

"You're young. No one expects you to have it all figured out."

Her sunny smile didn't quite meet her eyes. "Old enough now to know that I want to be with people who matter." A nudge, shoulder to shoulder, made it clear that she included him in that. "I love my job, I love the people here, and someday I'd love a family."

If she thought that would scare him off, the opposite was true—it encouraged him. "That day you were upset, after cat yoga, it's because you saw the kittens?"

Self-conscious about it, she rolled her shoulder again. "The babies dredged up the memory. Someday, with the right guy—"

"With commitment and love."

They stared at each other, until she continued lightly, "As you said, I'm only twenty-four, so I have time."

Which meant he had time to win her over. "How would you feel about dinner?"

Gaze warm and direct, she asked, "How would you feel about a sleepover?"

"My place or yours?"

The quick reply parted her lips. "Really?"

That deserved a laugh. "Did you honestly think I wasn't interested?"

"I don't know. You were talking about your grand plan and everything." Her eyes widened. "Not that I expect you to rush me into marriage or kids or anything like that."

A little rushing sounded fine to him. "How about we see how it goes?"

"Right." Pragmatic, she said, "I'd like a chance to fall in love with you, instead of merely in lust."

Just seeing her lips form the word *lust* ratcheted up his temperature. He touched her mouth. "One step at a time."

She was nodding when Oliver closed in, his mouth taking hers, soft and easy for, oh, two seconds. Then he angled for a better fit and she did the same, the kiss turning ravenous.

Hearing heavy footsteps, Oliver glanced up sharply.

"Damn." Lawson stalled midstep. "Sorry to interrupt. I can just—" He started to pivot toward Berkley's house.

"It's fine." Scrambling, Lark got to her feet and brushed off her backside with more energy than necessary.

Heaving a put-out sigh, Oliver gathered the dog into his arms and got to his feet, as well. "We were walking Handsome."

Deadpan, Lawson said, "Exactly what it looked like." He reached out to scratch the dog's chin. "How's he doing?"

Handsome tucked up against Oliver's chest, cowering but also wagging his tail.

"Mixed signals, bud," Oliver said, gently sheltering him. It was the first time he'd held Handsome, but the dog appeared to like it.

Lark said, "I didn't hear you pull up."

"I walked over through the woods. My house isn't that far from here."

"That's convenient," Oliver said. "And actually, I'm glad you're close by."

Eyebrows lifting and suspicion clear, Lawson waited for an explanation.

Seriously, he'd just been devouring Lark, so Lawson had to know where his interests lay. "Look around. This place is isolated enough that I didn't hear you until you were already close. As you just pointed out, she has woods around her instead of neighbors. Some guy from Berkley's past is looking for her and he could walk right up on her without her knowing until it was too late."

"Too late?" Lark repeated. "You really think he's that dangerous."

Lawson's dark, level brows came together. "Berkley doesn't, but neither of us have seen him for damn near a decade. He was worse than a cowardly creep back then, and I have serious doubts that time has improved him any." He did his own survey of the area. "You're right. She needs more lights out here, and probably a better security system."

Snorting, Lark turned away. "I'll let Berkley know that the menfolk are taking care of her problems for her."

"Hey." Lawson fell into step with her. "Don't make it sound like that."

She tossed an impish smile over her shoulder. "I'm sure she'll understand the concern."

Shaking his head, Oliver followed along. "I'm only offering advice. Wouldn't you do the same for someone if they had a hair question?"

"A hair question?" With both men now following her, Lark snickered and hastened her pace. "I wouldn't presume to tell someone how to wear their hair." She shot Lawson another look. "If they asked, I'd be happy to share suggestions."

Lawson had to lengthen his stride to keep up with her. "Racing, Lark?"

She grinned and jogged the last few steps to the door. "You have a surprise in store and I want to be there to see it."

"A surprise?" He looked back at Oliver.

"Hair," Oliver said, earning a scowl from Lark. "Well, you're worrying him for no reason."

"Not worried," Lawson denied, but his frown darkened.

After a quick knock, Lark ducked inside the house and shut the door. Oliver had to admit that he liked how she teased. Liked how she ran, too. And how she defended Berkley.

He stood there, holding Handsome, smiling, until his thoughts circled back around...

She'd lost a baby.

Knowing Lark now as he did, he could imagine how difficult that had been for her. She had an open way about her, a contagious enthusiasm and optimism, and she freely offered help wherever she could.

Who had been there to help her?

Going forward, he would.

Lark Penny, a tenderhearted woman with a positive way of looking at life, hadn't factored into his plans. When he'd set out for Cemetery, a new relationship was the last thing on his mind, especially with his already established relationships in tatters.

But now he knew her, and he wanted her.

Plans changed. With Lark, they changed for the better.

14

Lawson loved her hair. He'd told her so numerous times, even when she invited Oliver and Lark in to visit for a few minutes. Lark beamed at the praise, and Berkley couldn't stop smiling.

According to Lawson, she always looked gorgeous.

Maybe that was because when she was with him, she felt prettier. Not that she'd ever been that displeased with her looks. But who she was? Yes, that had displeased her a lot. Now, as she'd told Lark, she was learning to forgive her mistakes, and to accept a happier future.

She was glad Oliver and Lark decided to stay for just a bit. It allowed Handsome to spend some one-on-one time with Hero. The skittish dog was always more at ease with animals, but Hero was special in many ways, as they witnessed with how he carefully led Handsome into playing. Hero wrangled, teased, yapped at and taunted Handsome until finally the smaller dog got the hang of it. Now they had the zoomies around the couch, under the coffee table, through the kitchen and to the laundry, where they both did a little skidding before wheeling around and racing out again.

The commotion had Oliver standing protectively, as if he thought he might need to rescue Handsome. Berkley assured him it was fine, that Hero would never hurt the smaller, shier dog. As they shot past again, each with a tongue hanging out, Oliver relaxed and said, "So when I adopt him, maybe I need to think about a buddy for him, too."

That wonderful sentiment had her sharing a look first with Lawson, who winked at her, and then with Lark, who appeared to be falling in love.

Funny that when she'd accepted the position of director at The Love Shack, she'd had no idea of the massive changes in store.

Then boom, instead of being a recluse who associated only with animals, she was assisting cat yoga, entertaining friends in her home—and enjoying stupendous sex with a smoking-hot guy who knew the worst moments of her life, and liked her anyway.

That last perk, the incredible sex, was her favorite.

It was getting late when Oliver and Lark left, but they'd all had such a great time. Berkley hoped to have them over again soon.

Handsome was happier than she'd ever seen him, and he was also worn out from all the vigorous playtime. The second she got him into his area in the shelter, he curled up on his bedding, ready to nod off. Berkley gave him a few extra pets, made sure he had his blanket and on impulse kissed the top of his little furry head. This one would have a very happy life, thanks to Oliver.

"Hero is good for him," Lawson said quietly as they left the shelter.

"Hero is good for everyone." That was why he had his name. He rescued people, animals and, in her case, her heart.

The moon was high, the air humid, when they stepped outside. Berkley locked up the shelter, saying, "It's getting late." They'd both be up early tomorrow—and still she didn't want the day to end.

Lawson kept a hand on the small of her back as they walked the short distance to her house. "Are you tired?"

"No." If anything, she was invigorated. "You?"

His mouth curved in a small smile. "Not even a little."

"Good. Then can I convince you to skip dinner so we can go straight to bed?"

"A genius idea," he teased, nuzzling her neck while they both hurried into her house. He secured the door behind them. "Will Hero or Cheese mind?"

She took his hand and led him into the living room. Hero was asleep on the couch, with Cheese curled up by his rump. "No," she whispered, "they won't mind."

Each time with Lawson was somehow better, but nearly two hours later, hunger drove them to the kitchen. They kept it easy with grilled-cheese sandwiches and chips—and conversation. Lots and lots of quiet talking, about important things, and mundane things. As they finished up the dishes, Berkley couldn't stop smiling. Not a big smile, but she was so content, her lips just naturally curved.

She was drying her hands when Lawson stepped up behind her, his arms wrapped around her to keep her close. "Not to ruin an incredible day…"

"It was incredible." All of it, every moment—including this one. She leaned into him, and he kissed her ear.

"How about we get to that phone call?"

A heartfelt groan disrupted her contentment.

"I know," he commiserated, turning her to face him. "I'd rather not mention Durkinson's name, but he needs to be dealt with."

"I know." She smoothed her hands over his chest. "He's been lingering there in the back of my mind, too." Oliver's concern had affected them both. "You don't think it's too late, though?"

"It's only late to those of us who get up so early. Besides, do you care if you inconvenience him? Because I don't."

No, she didn't really mind, either. "I may as well get it over with." Keeping the dread from her tone, she pointed to the top of the fridge. "The card is up there." Out of sight, but never really out of mind. Like an impending storm, the issue with Chad wasn't going away. How bad it'd be, that was what she didn't know.

Lawson reached it easily and tossed it onto her table. "You sure you don't want me to call him?"

"I appreciate the offer, but I feel like this is something I need to do."

Giving a gentle squeeze to her shoulder, he accepted her decision. "You've got this."

If only she had his confidence. She got her cell phone from the counter and sat down at the kitchen table. Feeling a bit like a coward, she asked, "How about if I put it on Speaker?" That way, she wouldn't feel alone. Anything Chad said, Lawson would hear, too.

"I was going to suggest it."

Grateful that he made this so easy, she put in Chad's number, then hit the speaker button and set the phone on the table. After the third ring, she said, "Maybe he won't answer—"

"Berkley!" Absurd joviality resonated in his greeting. "You got my message."

Just that, the sound of his voice, and a deluge of memories flooded over her. Visions of the past, of how he used to act with her, compressed her lungs and nearly stole her breath. He'd taken part in almost ruining her life, yet he acted as if they'd parted good friends. As if he hadn't lied to her, used her.

As if she hadn't been the "other woman."

When Lawson's hand came to rest on her thigh, it jolted her back to the present. She wasn't a kid anymore.

And she wasn't alone. "Yes, I got your message."

"What's wrong?"

That had to be a joke. She let out an unsteady breath, drew in fresh air and covered Lawson's hand with her own. "You shouldn't have contacted me."

"I had to." Concern lowered his voice. "I've been thinking of you, of how you've been."

Right. Nearly ten years had passed without a word, but now he thought of her? She wondered what had happened. How his life might have changed.

"I saw your photo listed for that shelter, but when I called them, they said you'd moved."

She didn't want him thinking of her, and she wouldn't discuss any part of her life with him. "We have no reason to talk, Chad."

"Of course we do. I've missed you."

Of all the... Beside her, Lawson narrowed his eyes on the phone. Tension and obvious anger tightened his shoulders.

Now it was her squeezing his hand. His gaze shot to her face, and his expression eased.

Giving her attention back to the phone, she said, "Lose my number, Chad."

Sliding right past that, he suggested, "Let's have lunch. Talking in person will be better."

"Absolutely not." She went for total honesty. "I have no interest in seeing you, not now, not ever."

Three seconds of shocked silence preceded his crooning tone. "You don't mean that. I've just surprised you."

"Oh, I mean it." Though her hands were shaking, she picked up steam. "Don't ever contact me again."

"You sound hurt, Berkley, and defensive."

Because I am. Not that she'd ever let him know it. "Lack of interest, nothing more."

Lawson's approving gaze helped calm her rioting heart.

"You can't expect me to believe that." A nasty laugh warned of Chad's shifting mood. "You were always so hot for it."

An appalled breath nearly choked her. Heat scalded her cheeks.

Not wanting to, Berkley looked at Lawson. He'd gone rigid, his jaw ticking and his shoulders flexing.

Wow. Diverted from her embarrassment, she marveled at the change. No doubt if Chad was here, he'd be sorry for those asinine, deliberately insulting words.

Oddly, Lawson's fury helped her regain her own composure. "Goodbye, Chad."

The cajoling tone was back. "Berkley, wait—"

She disconnected, ending whatever he would have said. Heart thumping and palms damp, she stared at the phone, but he didn't call back. "I'm a coward," she admitted. "The second I heard him, I was so stressed I couldn't think."

"You should have told him to fuck off."

Her eyes flared.

His closed, and after a breath, he said, "I'm sorry. You did everything right. Cursing him wouldn't have helped anything." He peeked open one eye. "I wanted to, though."

The smile crept up on her. "I know."

"If I could have, I'd have reached through the phone and throttled him."

"Good thing you couldn't, then. That might have gotten you arrested, and I'm fond of having you around." How funny that sharing that awful moment with Lawson made it far less unbearable. "Thank you for being here with me."

Lawson pulled her from her chair and into his lap, then

wrapped his arms around her and pressed his face to her neck. "You didn't sound stressed." Lips skimming her throat, he said, "You sounded like you meant business. If he's not the dumbass I've always assumed him to be, he'll leave you alone."

They both knew better. "But he *is* a dumbass."

Straightening so he could look into her eyes, he said with apology, "Yeah, he is. And now I'm going to piss you off and agree with Oliver. You need a better security system out here."

She was thinking the same thing. Berkley lifted her chin. "I will if you will."

"What?"

"You're alone, too." Putting her palm to his jaw, she enjoyed the rasp of his late-day stubble. Before him, she'd never noticed all the wonderful ways men could be masculine. Teasing, she added, "And don't cuss in front of my dog."

Glancing through the kitchen doorway, they both saw that Hero was still asleep on the couch. On his back, head hanging off the side of the couch, tongue lolling out, Hero snored. Apparently his playtime with Handsome had really worn him out, too.

"That dog is sound asleep." His gaze cut back to hers. "I'm sorry I cursed to you, though."

"I understand." To punctuate that, she kissed him. "I don't mind that you worry about me. I worry about you, too. And I actually agree with Oliver. I'm responsible for a lot of animals. Ensuring their safety is important." This time she nipped his bottom lip and said, "Guess I've been too busy with this new guy to look into it."

"How about if the new guy—who, for the record, is actually the old guy—looks into it for you?"

"Will that keep you busy? Because if so, I might have to object."

"I'll take care of it between customers this week." He treated her to a longer, deeper, very thorough kiss, then stood, putting her on her feet before him. "In the meantime, how about you use extra caution? And call me if you hear anything at all, even if you're sure it's nothing."

No one had cared for her like this except her mother. It left her heart full. "I promise." Berkley gave him a hug. "I hate for the day to end."

Tipping up her chin, he treated her to his heated gaze. "One of these days, you need to ask me to stay over."

Grinning, she replied, "One of these days, I just might." With a dramatic sigh, she explained, "But Betty will be over early tomorrow, and I don't want to shock her."

"Shock Betty? I'm not sure that's possible."

True. Betty had been around a long time. Maybe she'd drop some subtle hints just to see how it'd go.

Lawson combed his fingers through her hair. "I know you like being right here, next to the shelter, but the setup does have its drawbacks." He headed for the door, and suddenly Hero was there, ready to visit nature one more time before they turned in.

Cheese also showed up, a credit card in her teeth, ready to sneak behind the dryer. Lawson's brows shot up. "Oh, no you don't, you little pickpocket." He whispered it gently, almost like praise, while quickly pulling a business card from his wallet. "How about a trade?"

The flashy card, in rainbow hues, caught the cat's attention. When he knelt to stroke her—while offering the new card—Cheese didn't run from him.

Successfully making the exchange, he grinned up at Berkley, then stood.

"Clever." In so many ways.

He tucked the credit card back into his wallet, did inventory to make sure nothing else was missing and then returned it to his pocket. "That cat keeps me on my toes."

"You seem to be the only target of her thievery these days."

Sending the cat a fond smile, he said, "That's because she loves me."

Love. Yes, well, apparently she and her cat were both susceptible to Lawson's charms. Which, of course, made ending the day more difficult.

Doing her best to ensure Cheese didn't slip by them, Berkley leashed Hero and stepped out with Lawson.

The sun had set over an hour ago. A tall security lamp and a bright moon lit the area around the shelter on all sides, but in her own little section of yard, her yellow porch light barely illuminated ten feet.

Shadows lurked everywhere, something she'd never noticed before. Other than the chirping of crickets and the occasional hoot of an owl, it was eerily silent.

Hero sniffed here and there before choosing a spot to do his business.

Speaking in a whisper, Berkley said, "I play soft music in the shelter so the animals don't hear every little sound when I bring Hero out. The other night, he barked and I thought for sure they'd all get started, but fortunately, they didn't."

Frowning, Lawson surveyed the area. "What made him bark?"

"What doesn't? When it's just the two of us, a wayward leaf might offend him. One night, a toad had him enraged." She smiled. "You and Oliver have nothing on Hero when it comes to being cautious."

"Glad to hear it." As Hero hurried back to them, Lawson patted his neck. "Good boy."

The evenings usually felt peaceful, but now that she'd talked to Chad, uncertainty kept her on edge. Time to wrap it up. After giving Lawson a big hug and one last kiss, she and Hero went back inside. Lawson waited until she'd locked her door, then he got out his phone, turned on the flashlight and headed back through the woods.

He was a big man, imposing enough to handle most situations with ease, and still she worried. Which meant Hero worried. Together, they stood near her phone, waiting.

As he now did after each late visit, Lawson called her once he was inside his own home. He did that for her, she knew, and she appreciated it, tonight more than ever.

After they disconnected, her phone dinged again, and she opened the photo he sent.

The laugh burst out of her, startling Hero, who appeared ready to go into rescue mode, should she require his assistance.

"I'm okay, bud." *Just falling hard for Lawson.* Kathleen, posed in front of Oliver's gym in workout gear, inviting people in. What really tickled her was the sweatband.

Her heart soared.

So did her fingers as she texted back: You did that? Wearing a huge grin, she waited for his reply.

Yes ☺

Laughing again, she started out of the kitchen, turning off lights as she went. Hero trotted behind her. I'm proud of you. ♥

Back atcha

Knowing he meant because she'd called Chad, her grin settled into a soft smile. Thx.

A second later, he added: If that's your heart I'm keeping it.

She really needed to think about keeping *him*—overnight. Maybe every night.

Would he be on board with that?

Was he, too, thinking long-term?

Either way—forever, or just for right now—they were both adults. Although she worked for the town, she didn't answer to them about her personal life.

Still, Cemetery was such a close community.

As Chad's call had reminded her, she'd been gossiped about enough to last her a lifetime.

She debated with herself for a full minute… And then, smiling, she texted along another heart—times three.

On the last Thursday of the month, Berkley met Lawson at the town council meeting, and found that Oliver and Lark had also opted to join. She'd had no idea it would be so crowded, with all the seats taken and many others standing.

The four of them took positions against the wall in the back, even when a few of the men offered seats to Berkley and Lark. They were older gentlemen and certainly needed the chairs more than they did.

Oliver muttered low, "Returned your doll to you, Lawson."

Snorting, Lawson said, "Gifts can't be returned."

"Already done."

Berkley took in his smug smile and smothered a laugh, especially when Lawson said, "Paybacks are hell."

Now both men were grinning.

These people, all of them, they were so…fun.

Lark leaned in to whisper, "Yardley, who runs the wedding business, told me it used to be torturous to come to these meetings, but now everyone loves them. It's almost like a big celebration, and afterward, everyone flocks to Saul's to eat. His wife, Emily, is already there with him."

Berkley nudged her new friend. "Do you know everyone now?"

"I'm trying, and just so you know, Betty recruited me to make sure you'll be at the next tea club meeting on Monday. Mimi has deemed it 'funny hat' day, so we'll all be wearing some weird floral hats or something. Yardley is bringing a new flavor of tea, and Sally—she owns the sweet shop—is bringing cookies."

In the last few weeks, Berkley knew she had changed a lot, because the tea party sounded like fun. "I'll be there."

Lark sent Betty a thumbs-up, and that seemed to be the official start of the meeting. With a smack of a gavel, Betty got things underway.

Impressed, Berkley watched as Betty stood at the podium like a queen, chin up, her makeup and outfit perfect to address the crowd. She spoke with authority, pride for the town and ownership of the community.

As it often did, it struck Berkley what an amazing life this one woman had carved out for herself. Memories galore, both good and bad. Friends old and many new. Betty Cemetery was high-handed but dependable, dictatorial but fun. She didn't mind telling you things others wouldn't if she thought it was for your own good.

"At my age," Betty said, "I can't pussyfoot around."

A general snickering rose from the crowd, but Berkley's heart gave an odd little skip. *At her age.* Why was Betty even bringing that up? Concern flooded her, and just like that, Lawson's arm came around her shoulders.

He was always so attuned to her moods. Gratefully, her gaze glued to Betty, she leaned against him.

Betty's gaze softened—then flashed over the crowd, and she gave a stern, "Ahem."

Everyone quieted. "I'm not fully retiring anytime soon, so you can all settle down."

Retiring. So she wasn't talking about… Spine going limp in relief, Berkley huffed a quiet laugh.

"I am now," Betty continued, "going to share the time with Yardley."

Yardley, the town's amazing wedding planner, popped up from her seat beside the podium and put her arms in the air. Edging in next to Betty, she said, "This one is still in charge."

The loud cheers turned Betty's cheeks pink.

"But we all agree she's earned a rest, right?"

More cheers, with the added burst of applause.

"Thank you," Betty said, standing close to Yardley. She bent down to pat Gladys, who snoozed beside her on the floor, and when she straightened again, she said, "More time to spend with my companion, and I owe that to a special townsperson."

All eyes shifted to Berkley, putting her on alert. Oh, hey. Warily, she glanced around at all the beaming faces. She knew many of them now, those who helped out at the shelter, some who took cat yoga or had signed up to walk a dog. Others had filled out applications to adopt a pet.

Her heart felt too big for her chest.

Near her ear, Lawson suggested, "Take a bow."

She swatted at him, then with a laugh, improvised a quick curtsy.

Lark hugged her arm, and Oliver grinned at her.

Calling order again, Betty said, "Going forward, I'll be working partial hours. We'll have a formal election in November, but until then, Yardley has agreed to step in."

Yardley leaned in to the mic again. "Not permanently, though, so anyone who is interested, let me know."

That got everyone quiet real fast.

"Now," Betty said. "Back to business." There was talk of a few town issues, updates to the elementary school flooring in the gymnasium and, lastly, she announced that funding had been approved to add additional security to the shelter.

Berkley's jaw loosened. She whispered to Lawson, "But you just added some security." Over the past couple of days, he and Oliver had put up motion-activated lighting and installed alarms to the front and back doors of her house.

"This will be better," Oliver said.

Lawson agreed.

Smiling out at her, Betty announced, "The Love Shack has

turned into a community hub, more so than we'd ever anticipated."

A murmur of agreement moved through the crowd.

"Our lovely wishing well, built and maintained by Lawson
Salder, and situated in front of his print shop, has garnered far
more profit than we'd expected." As everyone waited, Betty
let the suspense build and then announced the current amount.
Around the whistles and cheers, she said, "That's more than
three times what we were hoping for. Thank you, Mr. Salder."

Small smile in place, Lawson lifted a hand, waving to everyone and accepting their appreciation.

Unlike her, Lawson had spent much of his life helping others,
traveling the world, dealing with a variety of people. Nothing
in a small town would disturb his confidence. Watching him
interact so comfortably filled her with pride.

With her gaze back on Berkley, Betty said, "The volunteer
turnout for The Love Shack makes us all so proud, and we're
thrilled with how Ms. Carr has worked with other businesses
to not only bring in funds to help the animals, but to showcase those businesses."

Oliver started the applause, and everyone joined in. Face hot,
Berkley covered her cheeks and laughed. She was not Lawson,
so she was plenty disturbed by the attention, but also flattered.

And honored by the kind praise.

"Many of you have already signed up for the dog-walking
classes. Ms. Carr has that well in hand, I'm sure."

Betty knew she did. They'd discussed it just yesterday morning.

"Once every animal has a walking partner, we'll start planning a wonderful fall parade."

Enthusiastic whoops filled the room. Cemetery did enjoy
its parades.

"The only problem I still see is that our esteemed Kathleen
doesn't have a date."

It wasn't until everyone shifted that Berkley realized the mannequin was seated up front, a box of tissues in her hand, her head bent forward.

All eyes swiveled to Lawson.

Oliver smirked. "Told you so."

Fortunately, Lawson chuckled, then hugged Berkley to his side. "Sorry, but I'm taken."

Wow, had he just announced that to one and all? Apparently so, given how quickly Betty grabbed her phone for a photo. No doubt it'd be front and center on the local social media accounts very soon.

Did she mind? Nope. In fact, Berkley decided to lend a hand. "Lawson can only be Kathleen's *friend*, but not her date." As everyone laughed yet again, she patted his chest.

Given his smug smile, he enjoyed her possessive display.

Just imagine, she—once a scandal and then a loner—was now in a crowded council meeting, clowning around with the most wonderful man in the state, standing with friends and being heralded by the town matriarch.

A month ago, if someone had suggested such a thing was possible, she'd have given them a firm denial.

As Betty got back to business, Lark leaned around again and said with an enormous grin, "Oh man, Lawson, you're going to owe me big-time."

One eyebrow lifted in question. "For what, exactly?"

"I happen to have a brilliant idea—and you're all going to love it."

When the meeting ended, Berkley and Lark invited Betty to join them for dinner, but she declined, saying she and Gladys planned to work in the garden.

Lark couldn't help but laugh at how Betty insinuated the dog would actually assist, but it was also sweet.

Betty looked at Berkley, indecision on her face, then she

grinned widely, adding new creases to her cheeks, and hauled Berkley in for what looked like a strangling hug. When she finally let up, she surprised Lark by grabbing her, too.

The tight squeeze brought a huff of laughter out of Lark, but it was also sweet. Betty was soft, and even with her low-heeled business shoes, she was still very short. She smelled of powder and hair spray but felt warm and loving.

Stepping back, Betty gave them each critical scrutiny. "So I'll see you both at the tea, correct?"

When Berkley said "I'm looking forward to it," she appeared to mean it, and that thrilled Lark almost as much as Betty.

Oliver and Lawson got caught up talking to a few other men…as well as a couple of women.

"Business owners," Berkley murmured low.

Didn't bother Lark. "Oliver has already proven his interest most thoroughly."

Grinning, Berkley said, "Let's step outside, where we can talk."

They signaled to the guys to let them know where they'd be, then walked out together. The sun blazed overhead, and all around them vacationers moved from one shop to the next, many of them in swimsuits and flip-flops.

"I love the relaxed atmosphere here." Stretching her arms overhead, Lark smiled. "Before Cemetery, I had never styled hair on a woman in a bikini."

Berkley laughed. "Have you gotten used to that now?"

"Yes, and I think it's awesome. Imagine visiting a place that made you so comfortable—and we live here."

"It's definitely special."

"Oliver stayed the night." She hadn't exactly meant to blurt that out, but it had been bursting inside her. "Three nights now."

"I'm guessing from your grin that you're having the time of your life."

"I am. Pretty sure I'm already in love with him." She sighed. "I think it's the same for him."

"He looks at you," Berkley said, "and I see it there in his eyes."

To ensure they were still alone, Lark glanced around, then spoke in a whisper. "The sex has been amazing. I'd had no idea."

"Ha! That's exactly what I thought with Lawson."

Together, they laughed, but the buzzing of Berkley's cell phone interrupted. Because Whitley was watching over the shelter, she answered it in a rush, said "Hello" and then drew back with a gasp.

"Berkley?" Concerned, Lark stepped closer, but Berkley ended the call and jammed the phone back into her pocket with enough force to bruise her backside. "Hey. Everything okay?"

Trembling, her brows pinched and her breath coming fast, Berkley whispered, "That was Chad."

Of all the nerve! "You told him to get lost."

"I did, but do you know what he said just now? He asked me if I'd calmed down yet. *Calmed down.*"

She sounded anything but calm. "Delusional jerk. Can you block his number?"

That wiped the anger from Berkley's face. In a frenzy, she got her phone out again, pulled up the number, then blocked and removed it. "Done. I don't know why I didn't think of that before."

"Because you were already plain and that should have been the end of it." She rubbed Berkley's shoulder, feeling the tension vibrating off her. "Do you want a few minutes alone with Lawson?"

"No." Drawing a deep breath, she got herself together. "I'll tell him about the call, but not yet. Tonight we're having fun. I don't want Chad spoiling the mood."

Good plan. "Well, he's blocked now, so even if he tries again, he can't bother you." Hoping that was true, Lark pinned on a wide smile. "I'm going to end the day with Oliver again." Teasing, she added, "How about you?"

"I'm thinking of keeping Lawson over, too." Sheepish, Berkley admitted, "We haven't had an overnight yet."

Lark's jaw loosened. "Seriously?"

"I know. I kept thinking it'd be awkward because people show up so early at the shelter—"

"And your home is not the shelter."

Good mood returning, Berkley grinned. "Took me a little time to convince myself of that, but I've finally come to the same conclusion."

Of course, she understood her friend's hesitation. When Lark thought of sensitive, bighearted Berkley being treated so badly, it broke her heart. "I say go for it."

Bobbing her eyebrows, she said, "That's the plan."

The guys joined them a minute later, and no more was said about Chad.

Together they walked the short distance to the restaurant. Along the way, Lark opened her phone, did a quick search, then said to Lawson, "Ta-da."

One quick look and he snorted. "What the hell is that supposed to be?"

"Kathleen's new boyfriend."

They all stopped to crowd closer, gazes on the screen, where a cheesy-looking plastic guy—smooth as any Ken doll and with plastic molded hair—posed in a way to show off his not-so-impressive muscles.

Of course, he had the same dead stare as Kathleen.

Oliver snickered.

Berkley grinned.

Lawson gave a dramatic shudder. "He's even creepier than Kathleen."

Elbowing him, Lark said, "I'm naming him Kingston, and he's going to *love* Kathleen, and *you* are going to add new revenue to…well, everywhere probably. See, with him joining Kathleen by the wishing well, there will be more opportunities for photos, and that equals even more money for the shelter."

"Hear, hear!" Hugging his arm, Berkley said, "You're used to Kathleen being there now. And you have to admit, vacationers adore her."

Oliver agreed. "They often come into your shop for a souvenir T-shirt."

Lawson shrugged at Oliver. "That, at least, is a perk."

"I was thinking that if anyone put in a big enough print order, you could offer to have Kathleen and Kingston wear their stuff for a day."

"They're not my dummies." Still with dislike, Lawson eyed the picture again. "The town enjoys playing with them."

"So in the evening, you can throw their regular gear back on them."

"Meaning I'll spend every morning and every evening dressing dummies?"

Feigning indignation, Lark stopped. "Quit calling Kathleen that."

"It's what she is."

"It sounds insulting." Putting her nose in the air, she affected a chiding tone. "If you can't refer to her by name, call her a mannequin."

Taking her side, Berkley said, "I seriously thought you were getting used to her."

Trying and failing to maintain his scowl, Lawson gave up. "Guess I could put Will in charge of changing out the clothes."

"Oh!" Another great idea occurred to Lark. "Announce what time they'll be changed. Folks would love to see that."

Appearing truly scandalized, he shook his head. "No way. Betty would have a fit and you know it."

Yeah, she probably would. Still, the idea made Lark chuckle. Oliver draped his arm over her shoulders and got them all walking again. "I love the idea of a plastic man wearing my fitness center's logo gear."

"Or a Love Shack T-shirt, like the ones we're selling at the shelter," Berkley said. "We could put one style on Kathleen, the other on Kingston."

Wincing, Lawson took her phone to study the image once more. "I'll have two dummies—er, *mannequins*—staring at me all day."

"Nope." Lark knew she'd already won him over, but to tease him, she clasped her hands beneath her chin. "They'll be staring lovingly at each other."

Even Lawson had to laugh at that, and during their dinner, he went ahead and ordered a male mannequin, but he bypassed the one Lark liked and went for one of higher quality.

"Good choice," Oliver pointed out. "At least this one has muscle tone."

"And a package," Lawson added dryly, making Berkley almost spit out her drink.

"He's missing a few parts." Oliver eyed the "package," which was really no more than a slight molded bulge.

"But he does have a six-pack." This mannequin was far sexier than the one she'd chosen. "Kathleen will like that."

"Women and their expectations," Oliver lamented.

She patted his very firm stomach and smiled.

It was late by the time they finished dinner, followed by dessert and then coffee. After leaving generous tips to the servers for occupying the table so long, they headed back to their respective cars.

Sneaking in a hug for Berkley, Lark said, "Not to be a worrier, but after that creep's call, I hope you invite Lawson to stay over."

"I am," Berkley confided. "Not because of Chad, but because it's getting harder and harder to say goodbye each night."

"For him, too, I'm sure." When Berkley looked at Lawson,

everything she felt was there in her eyes. No one deserved happiness more.

Lark knew that because of her past, Berkley was more cautious than most, determined to never again be the topic of gossip. This, however, was a battle she didn't need to fight.

"I'm applauding you," Lark whispered. "I know everyone else will, too."

They parted ways, and Lark felt certain that tonight was a turning point for her friend. No idea how they'd work out two houses, and the occasional conflict of their jobs, but she knew they were the forever kind of couple.

Now she only had to worry about her own relationship, but with Oliver making it so easy, all she could do was smile.

15

Lawson woke for the fourth day in a row with Berkley wrapped up in his arms. Any second now, her alarm would go off. His girl worked far too hard, for too many hours, but it was one of the things he loved about her.

Done doubting it, he'd admitted to himself that it was 100 percent love. He'd been around enough to know the difference. What he didn't know for certain was how she felt. This was all new for her.

As he thought of how badly she'd been hurt, his arm automatically curled her closer and he pressed a kiss to the top of her head. Nose to his chest, warm breath stirring him, she mumbled lightly and resettled herself.

Now, today, and always, he wanted to take care of her. To lend a hand physically when her workload piled up, to defend her against creeps like Durkinson and applaud the loudest whenever the town heralded her.

The heralding was bound to happen again and again, because everyone here appreciated her. She thought he was the only one who really saw her, but they all did. Beautiful Berkley, inside and out.

So far, she'd resisted his efforts to help. *You're not a Love Shack employee.* Who cared? He wouldn't have to be at his shop for a couple of hours yet, and he'd rather stick around here than head home just to get a little more remodeling done.

Slanting his gaze toward the clock, he prepared himself for her screeching alarm.

Somehow wrapped around his head like a cat hat, Cheese stretched awake, then agilely leaped from the bed and padded out of the room, no doubt heading for her litter box.

Lawson flexed his toes. The way Hero used his right leg for a pillow left it numb. Grumbling, the dog threw a paw over his shin as if to stifle his movement, and then let out a huff. Berkley swore that the dog and cat rarely slept in the bed, but they'd crawled in and gotten comfortable each night that he'd stayed over.

"Mmmrrmm." A small fist stretched up past his face, narrowly missing his nose, and her entire body arched as she slowly came awake.

"Good morning."

Every morning, her eyes popped open as if shocked to find him there. Today was no different.

Vivid blue eyes met his, took a moment to focus, and then she softened all over.

Every. Single. Time. He'd never tire of it, and he'd never tire of her.

She snuggled in closer. "The alarm should be going off any—"

Before she could finish, it started blaring. Lawson fumbled, reaching for her phone on the nightstand, and silenced it. "Why do you put yourself through that when you always wake up before it?"

Using her hand to smother a jaw-breaking yawn, she stretched again, then sat up. The sheet fell to her lap.

"What if I didn't wake up?"

Hero gave a *woof* in agreement, then lumbered off the bed and looked at her expectantly.

With the back of one finger, Lawson stroked her bare breast. "You are beautiful in the morning."

"Like sleep-puffy eyes and tangled hair, do you?"

"I like you." Words burned in his throat.

I love you.

But he figured one big step at a time was all she should have to handle. He wasn't going anywhere. She wasn't going anywhere. He'd have more than enough time to show her before he told her.

Still a little shy about her nudity, she immediately pulled on a loose T-shirt when she left the bed, tugging the hem down below her bottom on her way out of the bedroom to the bathroom.

Her house was smaller than his, only two bedrooms and a single bath, but it was next door to the shelter. That meant she would never move.

Not a huge obstacle.

Sitting up, Lawson considered some of the options he could offer her. He'd thought of that, of being with her forever and how to make it all work, a lot over the last few days. Used to her daily routine, he quickly pulled on jeans and a T-shirt, tucked his own phone into his pocket and stepped into his sneakers.

The second she returned for the rest of her clothes, he drew her up and kissed her. "Take your time. I'll walk Hero out."

Very used to her independence, to doing it all on her own, she fretted. "Are you sure? It'll only take me a second to—"

He kissed her again. "Make some coffee if you want." She drank it each morning anyway. "I'll be right back."

Sticking his head in the door with a reminder *woof*, Hero waited.

Lawson grinned. "I do love your dog."

She gave him a big smile for that.

Taking only thirty seconds to dart into the bathroom, Lawson quickly had the dog headed through the house to the side door. He noticed that Berkley had laundry piling up. Probably because he'd taken up all her evenings.

Maybe tonight he could handle some of that for her.

At the very least, he could help her in the morning, and then later with getting dinner together.

Loosely holding Hero's leash, he enjoyed the gray haze of dawn. All around, birds sang to greet the morning. He was lost in thought when his phone buzzed.

It was still so early, he couldn't imagine anyone calling him, but the second he got his phone from his pocket, he saw that it was Oliver.

"What's up?"

"Am I waking you?"

He answered with "Everything okay?"

"No one is hurt," Oliver said, making that clear up front. "There's an issue in front of your shop, though. Nothing critical, no damage to the building or anything like that."

Well, hell. "What issue?"

"I was out jogging or I wouldn't have seen it. Luckily, no one else is around this early, but... Someone vandalized Kathleen."

"Vandalized?" Jaw locking, shoulders bunching, he turned to face away from Berkley's home. The last he'd seen Kathleen, she'd been absurdly dressed like a cheerleader, pom-poms in her hands. "How bad is it?"

"I think it's just red paint, but someone made it look like she'd been cut up." A brief hesitation, and then, "Why would anyone do that?"

Good question. He'd already learned to trust Oliver. Would

his thoughts mirror Lawson's? Only one way to find out. "What are you thinking?"

"Kathleen's a part of your place now. If she disappears, it's never long before someone brings her back to the wishing well. Anyone who's in this town for a few hours knows about Kathleen—and by association, about you."

Through Kathleen, his name got mentioned a lot. The town enjoyed heckling him with her.

"Can you imagine anyone from around here doing this?" He didn't wait for an answer. "Most likely it was an outsider."

An invisible fist tightened around his heart. Yes, his thoughts had immediately gone to Durkinson, but he'd wanted to convince himself he was wrong. "You think this is about Berkley?"

"You don't?" Then he asked, "Or did you piss off someone and not tell me?"

"No." He knew Chad, and if he was here looking for Berkley... Rather than ask more questions, Lawson said, "I'll be on the road in less than ten minutes."

"If I wasn't on foot, I would have taken her to my place, but the best I could do was move her around back of your shop. I'll wait here for you." Another pause, and then, "Bring a tarp."

Ending the call, Lawson thought of how Durkinson had reacted when Berkley told him to lose her number, and that the bastard had dared to call her again.

She'd blocked Chad's number, but Lawson wasn't convinced that would end it. If he was in town, that'd mean— Hero lightly butted his head against him.

Drawn from his thoughts, Lawson looked down to see the dog's worried frown. "I'm okay, buddy, just annoyed—but not at you." Lawson knelt down to reassure him. "You're more than just a great pooch, aren't you? Did someone train you as a therapy dog? You need someone to rescue?" Wouldn't be Berkley. She'd rescued herself long before she and Lawson had met again.

She'd done enough, been through enough, and now he wanted to protect her.

"Hey."

Looking up, he found Berkley standing there, her hair in a haphazard ponytail, fingers laced together in front of her, gaze watchful. Clearly, she'd heard his side of the call.

This was going to upset her. Hell, it wasn't even 6:00 a.m. yet. No other helpers were around, and he'd have to take off. Frustration rode him hard.

Instead of asking about the phone call, she nodded at Hero. "He tried to rescue Erin the other day."

The last thing Lawson wanted to do was alarm her, or further worry Hero. He could spare two minutes. "Yeah? What happened?"

"Erin's scarf blew off and caught at the top of the fence. She couldn't yank it down without tearing it, so she'd dragged over the bench and climbed up on it. She still had a difficult time, and was on tiptoes to reach over the fence and unsnag it. Hero didn't like seeing her up there, precariously balanced."

"Not sure I would have liked that, either." He gave the dog a pat.

Wearing a slight smile, Berkley said, "He whined and danced around her, and even barked a few times. When that didn't work, he pulled the same stunt on her that he'd used on you."

"Ah, the old 'grab the shorts' move?"

"At first, Erin laughed—until he almost pulled her off her feet. I had the difficult job of explaining to him that she was fine."

"How'd that go?"

"You know Hero. He's a worrier. Luckily, Erin is wonderful, and she knows Hero well, so once she liberated her scarf, she gave him some affection, and all was forgiven."

Abrupt silence swelled around them.

He should have explained the phone call right off, not left her to wonder about it. Drifting his fingertips over her jaw, he said, "That was Oliver on the phone." He quickly explained about the mannequin. "I'll get her cleaned up before anyone sees her."

"Thank you. I know how you feel about her, but the town loves her."

And he loved Berkley. "I don't want you here alone."

"I have Hero," she said. "I'll call you if anything happens, but the sun will be up soon and then the day will be in full swing."

Left with few choices, Lawson said, "I'll call once I get things in order, just to update you."

A smile flickered over her face, there and gone. "Promise you'll be careful, too."

Oh, how he'd love for the chickenshit to try something with *him*. He wasn't a helpless mannequin. That thought nearly had him rolling his eyes. Clearly, he was starting to like Kathleen. "I promise."

"Go. I'm fine." Taking the leash from Lawson, she stepped back.

In a rush, he jogged through the woods to his house, grabbed a clean shirt, ignored his bristled jaw and was on the road in under five minutes.

Since he always parked in back of the shop, that wouldn't look different to anyone who might happen to see him pull up, and fortunately, it was only Oliver there, hands on his hips, head down as he paced a tight circle in running shoes, loose-legged shorts and nothing else.

He looked up when he heard Lawson's truck and immediately approached. "I have her tucked behind the big garbage bin, just so she wouldn't be seen."

Two plastic feet, smeared with red, stuck out from behind the bin. Temper tightly leashed, Lawson nodded his thanks. He got the tarp from the back of his truck and handed it to Oliver. "I'll get the door unlocked and turn off the alarm."

He'd barely finished when Oliver crowded in behind him. "I've got her."

"Damn." With Kathleen wrapped in the tarp, only the top of her head and the tips of her toes visible, Oliver had his hands full. "It looks like we're hiding a body."

"We are," Oliver said, his expression grim. "A plastic one."

"You can set her on my worktable there." The stainless-steel table, more like a workbench, was used when he sorted inventory, or to set aside freshly printed products. On the back wall, he had a utility sink and some heavy-duty cleaner.

When Oliver peeled back the tarp, Lawson cursed. Poor Kathleen. Someone had really done a number on her.

Oliver eyed the paint-marred mannequin. "Half the town would cry if they saw her like this."

"I still remember how they pampered her when she got rained on." That day at Saul's restaurant had been a game changer for him and Berkley, and maybe for Oliver and Lark, too.

"Her wig is ruined."

Yeah, the hair was a mess, but it might wash up. He tipped his head at Oliver. "Do you have to be somewhere?"

"No, I cut my run short, thinking you might need some help. I'm free for a few more hours."

Mind-boggling. "You run for hours?"

Oliver shook his head. "Not usually. My routine is more of a run, then a jog, then a walk, home to shower and get ready for work. Lark, however, doesn't have to be awake anytime soon, and if I'd stayed..."

"You'd have woken her up." Lawson grinned. "Got it." He went to the sink to fill a small bucket with mild cleaning solution. With any luck, the wig would survive, at least until he could replace it. "For me, it's the opposite. Berkley is up before the birds. I had hoped to stick around and lend her a hand this morning."

"Damn, man, I'm sorry. If I could have figured it out on my own—"

"I'm glad you called." A glance at the clock told him they had about an hour before people would start showing up at the wishing well for souvenir photos. Handing Oliver the bucket and a cleaning rag, he said, "How about you start on her body while I get her hair off." He'd try soaking the ends of the hair in the solution, and if that didn't work... Well, they'd find her a hat.

Making a face, Oliver worked the ruined cheerleading skirt down Kathleen's legs. "This is perverted."

"Years from now, we'll laugh."

"Ha!" He wrestled her top off next.

Her arm came off, and Oliver looked so horrified that Lawson couldn't help snorting. "Here." He held open a large plastic lawn bag. "There's no salvaging that outfit."

With distaste, Oliver stuffed it into the bag, then manfully reattached her arm.

It took them over an hour to get the mannequin clean again. A slight tinge of pink remained in some spots, but hopefully no one else would notice. Since Oliver was the hero of the day, spotting Kathleen early, Lawson offered to re-dress her in clothes with the fitness center logo.

"I have a better idea." He nodded at a new shirt for The Love Shack. "Let's showcase that. It's cute, the women will love it, and Berkley deserves it."

Especially if this was Durkinson stirring up trouble. Neither of them said the words, but they were both thinking it, so Lawson agreed.

The shirt was pastel hues blended together, with *The Love Shack* in bold font across the front. In a smaller, more stylistic font, were the words *Where love waits for you*. Paw prints in different sizes framed the message.

The shirt had turned out really well. Locals would love it, especially since the design was created by a Cemetery artisan.

With Kathleen's hair still wet, he and Oliver did their best to give her pigtails, but…yeah. Neither of them was great at braiding hair.

Stepping back and eyeing the mannequin critically, Oliver asked, "What do you think?"

"That Lark would have a heart attack."

They both laughed.

"She's crooked." When Oliver tugged at one braid, the mannequin's entire wig slid.

"Yeah—not better."

He straightened her up again. "It'll have to do." Checking the time, Oliver said, "Lark could have fixed her hair in five minutes, but I hate to interrupt her now. She's probably just getting ready for work."

"Again, one day we'll laugh." Bright sunlight poured through the big front window. Lawson needed to get Kathleen out there. "I'm going to check in with Berkley, just to make sure everything is going okay."

"Good idea." Getting out his own phone, Oliver walked to a corner of the shop, presumably for privacy.

Lawson propped a hip against the front counter and hit Call. Four rings sounded in his ear, and he was about to straighten in alarm when she finally answered.

Breathless, she asked, "Everything okay?"

"Yes. Got the paint cleaned off Kathleen, she's re-dressed and ready to go. I just wanted to check in with you first."

"So she's not destroyed?"

"No," he said gently, realizing that she had expected the worst. "I promise she's fine. Don't laugh, but Oliver and I had to give her a bath, re-dress her and even fix her hair."

Of course, she laughed, just as he had intended. "Sounds like she's having more fun than me."

The ribald joke surprised a snort out of him. "I'm not sure I like you saying that."

"Well, in my mind, Oliver was out of the picture."

"Better." Low, to ensure Oliver wouldn't hear, he said, "Tonight, I promise to reenact it all on you."

She drew in a dramatic breath. "Now, see, that makes my day better already."

The teasing couldn't hide her tiredness. "You sound beat."

"I'm fine, just scrambling. Whitley called in sick. Poor girl has some kind of flu. Erin is coming in early, but not for another hour."

Damn. He looked around his shop, seeing everything he hadn't yet done, and still said, "How about I—"

"Nope." She sent him a smooch through the phone. "Love that you want to help, but you have your own place to run. I'm used to stuff like this happening. I have everything under control."

The amount of work she covered every day boggled his mind. "It's going to be a scorcher. Don't overdo. And remember, call me if anything happens."

"I will." In the background, he heard some happy barking as the dogs played, and assumed she'd stepped outside. "Lawson?"

"Hmm?"

"I like this. Us, I mean. Thank you for being in my life."

"There's nowhere else I'd rather be." It was where he hoped to stay—forever.

16

Each time Berkley left the shelter, she relocked the door. Until Erin arrived, she didn't want to risk leaving it open. Most people now knew her hours, but that didn't mean someone wouldn't drop in, and with cats still in the building, including the mother cat and her kittens, she continued to use precautions.

It was a pain, leading Hero back and forth, but then finally he was ready for a nap. She now had laundry going at the shelter and in her own laundry room. Double duty, necessary because she'd put off her own personal chores to spend all her free time with Lawson.

He was a new priority for her, but then so was Betty, and Lark, and the town itself. The tea group had been so much fun, she now looked forward to the next. Ditto on the town council meeting, especially since Lark had declared it would be their official "double date" night. Actually, everything was more fun with new friends… And Lawson. Thinking of the coming night, she decided he was the most fun of all.

Today was one of the days for Betty to visit, and Berkley expected her later in the morning. They had many chats while caring for the dogs. Betty called it Gladys's playtime, where she got to visit with her friends and meet any newcomers.

Occasionally, she and Lawson would take dinner to Betty and stick around for a short visit. She wanted Betty to know that she valued her friendship, and it also gave her a chance to make sure the dog wasn't too much for Betty.

So far, she and Gladys were in perfect sync, napping together, walking together, sharing meals and watching evening shows snuggled together on the couch.

Berkley was down the hall putting away some clothes when the knock sounded on her front door. Hero came awake with a loud, startled bark, followed by a serious racket as he made his displeasure at the unknown visitor obvious. Betty wasn't due yet, and she never used the front door. Apparently, Hero didn't like this unexpected twist any more than she did. *Everyone* knew to use the back door closest to the shelter.

Everyone local, anyway.

That realization sent dread squirreling up her spine. Ducking into the guest bedroom, she peeked through the window, but at first all she could see was the side of a body. When the person shifted, a wave of horror shocked her system.

Chad is here.

A thousand emotions seemed to slam into her at once, making her stomach and heart sick in equal measure. Alarm vied with indignation. She couldn't do this. She shouldn't have to do it.

She'd left this—*him*—behind long ago. When he'd called, she'd made her disinterest clear. She'd flat-out told him to lose her number. That should have been the end of it.

This was her *new* life, her better life.

Her life with Lawson.

She was different, damn it, and she'd been working hard to move on.

A little voice in her head called her a liar. Sure, she'd let Lawson in—but only so far. It was a big step for her, but not the biggest. She needed to leap.

Seeing Chad on her doorstep made it all crystal clear.

She'd once thought she'd loved him, and it had almost ruined her life. But he was nothing like Lawson. Not even close.

Lawson would never hurt her like that.

While she waged that internal battle, Hero continued to go ballistic, and Chad did not retreat. No, he started around the house, likely to try another door.

Thoughts in turmoil, she belatedly remembered that she'd left her phone in the laundry room. She slipped away without bothering to try to quiet Hero. With any luck, his vicious barking would send Chad on his way.

Fortunately, the blinds on the laundry room windows were still closed. She grabbed her cell phone, ready to call Lawson… Yet a second later she changed her mind.

Before she imposed on Lawson that way, she needed to admit to herself, and to him, that she loved him. Real love. Forever kind of love. Not the wimpy infatuation she'd once felt for Chad.

Using one man to save her from another was not the answer.

A second, brisker knock sounded on her laundry room door, and she stepped back in a rush. Hearing it, Hero came charging in, skidded across the floor and stationed himself in front of her. "Shh," she said to him, not to silence him, but to let him know they were okay.

Lawson would have opened his shop by now, and Erin was already scrambling to rearrange her schedule to fill in for Whitley.

She'd be alone here for a little while yet.

Another knock, more firm, and Chad called out, "Berkley? I know you're in there. I can see your shadow moving around."

She wouldn't let him see her upset, but she refused to be alone with him, so instead she said loudly "Just a moment!" and hopefully, not a single hint of fear could be detected in her tone.

What to do? When her phone buzzed with an incoming call, she nearly jumped out of her skin. One look at the screen and she saw it wasn't Chad.

It was the strongest person she knew. Betty Cemetery.

She answered on the second ring, saying in a whisper, "Betty—"

"Good morning," sang Betty's chipper voice. "I'll be leaving here in about an hour, and I have a craving for coffee cake. Do you think you'd have time to sit for a bit and share a—"

"I'm so sorry," Berkley said, cutting her off. "I can't talk right now. I have a problem."

Going alert, with even an edge of danger in her tone, Betty asked, "What can I do?"

Emotion flooded through Berkley, a great wave of it, bringing relief and strength. "No animal is hurt," she thought to say, because Betty had proven to have a great love of all animals. "It's just that Chad has showed up and I don't know what to do." Ignoring him meant also ignoring the animals who needed her care. She didn't want to let him in. And telling him to leave probably wouldn't work.

Movement sounded through the phone, along with Betty's huffing. "I'll be there in fifteen minutes."

In that moment, she loved Betty even more. For everything. "I don't want you rushing around." At Betty's age, too much haste wasn't a good thing. "Thank you, but I'm sure it'll be fine."

"I'm on my way out the door right now."

Darn it, now that scared her. "Listen to me, Betty." She forgot to whisper, and it prompted more banging from Chad, and that meant more barking from Hero. Loudly, speaking over the noise, Berkley said, "I want you to take your time, drive slowly, be careful—"

"Yes, yes, of course. Love you, too."

As the call disconnected, Berkley blinked at the phone. *Love you, too.* Despite the current chaos, she felt a smile coming on.

This time, Chad's hammering rattled her door frame. "I can hear you, Berkley! Talk to me. You owe me that."

Owe him? *Owe him!* Indignation stiffened her shoulders, as well as her spine. Muttering to herself, she leashed Hero, admonished him to behave and opened the door a fraction to say, "I don't owe you a single thing." Her plan was to tell him to get lost, but her normally sweet-tempered dog wasn't having it. He strained against her, no doubt picking up on her mood, until he got his head past her.

"Hero," she said. "That's enough." She struggled to pull him back so she could close the door.

The second she moved away, Chad stepped in.

"Get out!"

He frowned at the dog. "What the hell, Berkley?" Quickly, Chad stepped partially behind the door to use it as a shield.

"Don't curse in front of my dog," she snapped. Really, Hero was laying it on a bit thick. "*Down*, Hero."

Because she rarely had reason to use that tone with him, he shot her a worried look, and marginally subsided by parking himself directly in front of her while continuing a low rumbling warning.

"Can't you put him in another room?"

"Not on your life." The nerve of the man, to even ask such a stupid question. "You, however, can get out of my house."

"We need to talk."

"I didn't want to talk to you on the phone." Determined to show him her strength, she managed to keep the incredulous screech from her tone. "What makes you think I'd talk to you in person?"

"Berkley." He visibly softened, saying her name with familiarity. "Look at how you've changed. All grown up and with this…" His hand gestured at her face, and his gaze dipped down her body. "You look so different."

"It's been years. Did you expect me to stay a gullible girl who'd believe anything you said?" There, that sounded blunt and controlled.

"You can believe that I've missed you."

She snorted, then said again, "I want you to leave."

"After we talk, but I can't think straight with that vicious animal between us."

Little by little, Chad made this easier for her. He was so smarmy, so insignificant, that the rest of her long-held angst faded away. "He's not vicious, he's protective."

"You don't need protection from me."

No, she probably didn't. Seeing Chad now, she realized that he was nothing. A sad little man with rounded shoulders, a puffy face and not an ounce of integrity. She'd once considered his wispy blond hair to be cute. His pale blue eyes kind. When she looked at him now, all she saw was his deceit and his audacity.

No longer so rattled, she regretted alarming Betty. "Listen closely, Chad. I'm not interested in talking to you."

"When would be a good time?"

She almost laughed. *"Never."* When he pulled an expression of hurt, incredulity had her shaking her head. "Chad, look…" How did you make it clear to someone that you not only regretted knowing them, you hated what you knew? Lawson would tell her to say exactly that. Betty would probably have a wittier way to put it. "You have absolutely no reason to come here."

"Babe." He reached out for her, but she sidestepped him,

and Hero shot back to his feet with a snarl of warning. Warily eyeing the dog, he said, "I had to see you."

"I am *not* your babe."

Appearing genuinely confused by her attitude, he frowned. "We were so good together, at least admit that much."

Was he deranged? Unwell? His absurd insistence made no sense. Berkley kept a tight hold on Hero's leash, and on her temper. "For the last time, I'm telling you to leave."

"You were happy with me." Annoyance edged into his tone. "Happier than you can be now with your dyed hair and smelly animals."

Her teeth ground together and she had to draw a deep, calming breath before she could reply. "I was happy with who I *thought* you were—basically, a good, generous, single man."

Holding out his arms, he stated, "I'm single now."

Berkley huffed out a breath. Well, whoop-de-doo. Did he seriously expect her to care at this point? How had she ever been so gullible? Even at seventeen, she should have seen through him. "You *lied* to me." Taking a forceful step forward, she said, "You cheated on your *wife*." It all came crashing in on her, and she stepped closer still. "Thanks to you, I was put through hell. Whatever relationship status you have now, it couldn't matter less to me. It wouldn't matter if you were the very last man on earth."

Proving the loss of her temper delighted him, he grinned knowingly. "You're still unmarried, Berkley. I think that speaks for itself."

That did it. "I didn't even date because you turned me off all men! My experience with you was *that* disgusting, *that* ugly and foul, and for the longest time I couldn't stomach the idea of any relationship." Yet, Lawson had changed all that.

Absurdly understanding, he said, "You're just hurting, but, babe, I'm here now."

Expanding with anger, Berkley had the awful urge to sock

him, right in the mouth. Or maybe laugh hysterically. He was different now, so dense and so very sure of himself when he had no reason.

Or maybe he'd always been that way, but at seventeen she'd been too naive to see it.

Hero snapped, backing Chad up. Berkley knew her anger wasn't helping, in fact was making Hero more protective. She had to get a grip, had to gain control…

Chad lifted his foot, as if to kick the dog.

That did it. "Touch him," Berkley whispered with very real menace, "and I promise you'll regret it."

Hesitating, Chad lowered his foot.

"Knock, knock." Lawson pressed his way in, his gaze sweeping over both her and Chad and, she could tell, making his own assumptions. "Hope I'm not intruding."

"You are," Chad said.

Hero went ecstatic, all wiggling body and whipping tail and slobbering glee. He probably saw Lawson as backup and was thrilled for it. He was such a smart dog.

She saw Lawson the same, and was equally thrilled… Though, admittedly, she was also a bit embarrassed. Her biggest mistake, *Chad Durkinson*, was right here in her house, and the guy she loved had just shown up to witness her shame.

Though she'd just claimed disinterest in relationships, Lawson had changed everything. He'd changed her. Romance, sex, friendship—she wanted all of it. Forever. *Only with him.*

So she swallowed her discomfort, stepped forward and stationed herself at his side. "Chad was just leaving."

Before either man could speak, Betty charged in with Gladys, both of them gasping from their rush. Poor Betty didn't look at all put together. She had a curler dangling from the back of her hair, her blouse was buttoned wrong, missing one button hole, and she didn't wear a speck of makeup.

Just like that, Berkley's problems seemed to disappear. Grinning, she handed Hero's leash to Lawson and stepped forward to embrace Betty. Laughing a little, she fought grateful tears, and even dipped down to hide her face against Betty's soft shoulder.

"There, now," Betty said, awkwardly patting her back.

Then she did the most amazing thing.

She pushed Berkley behind her and said to Chad, "Young man, this is a private party. No boys allowed."

Chad glared at her, then pointed at Lawson. "What about him?"

Startled, Betty finally noticed Lawson, but said to Chad, "He's a man, not a boy. Now run along and don't come back. You're not welcome here."

"This isn't your house," Chad stated.

"Oh, but this is my town, and you, sir, must leave."

Berkley couldn't stop grinning. And when she looked at Lawson, at the stupefied astonishment on his face, she grinned even more.

"Who the hell do you think you are?" Chad demanded.

Berkley stepped around her. "She's Betty Cemetery, descendant of the town founder, matriarch of Cemetery, Indiana, and she's my very dearest friend." She pulled the door wide, saying with a peace she hadn't felt in years, "Don't ever again bother me, Chad. Not for any reason."

He fumed, glaring at all of them, and then especially at Lawson. "This isn't the end of it!"

In evil delight, Lawson handed the leash back to Berkley and closed in on Chad, who had very little room to maneuver. "Oh, I think it is. See, I have you on my security cam, vandalizing Kathleen."

Betty gasped. "What's this?"

"She's okay," Lawson said. "Oliver and I cleaned her up and she's in front of my shop again."

Relaxing again, Betty said, "Clearly, he's a troublemaker."

For only a moment, Chad appeared stunned, maybe afraid,

then his gaze shifted to Berkley. His smile held only contempt. "Any time I heard your name around here, his came up, too. I haven't forgotten him, you know, how he butted in where he didn't belong. How he threatened me." He pointed at her. "And you, Berkley, *no one* has forgotten you."

Honestly, in this moment, she no longer cared.

"Press charges against me, and it'll all come back up again, I guarantee it."

Suddenly Betty surged forward, her small fist flying, and that got both dogs going. Berkley almost got yanked off her feet.

Aggrieved, Lawson caught Betty, gently swinging her up and back behind him before she could make contact with Chad's face. "No, Betty." *His* smile was blindingly sweet. "You'll bruise your hand, and he's not worth it."

"No," Berkley agreed, awed and a little amused by Betty's violence. "He isn't."

Expression dangerous, Lawson turned back to Chad. "If he says even a single word more that sounds like a threat toward Berkley, I'm going to take him apart myself. How's that?"

Harrumphing, Betty patted her hair, found the curler, and gasped as she pulled it out and tucked it into her purse. "That'll do, thank you."

There was a tick of heavy silence, before Lawson said, "It would be entirely my pleasure."

Without another word, Chad stormed away. With him gone, the dogs subsided.

Within that moment of peace, it struck Berkley that Chad could no longer hurt her. She hurried to the door and shouted out, "Do your worst, Chad. Tell the world." How freeing that felt. "In fact, I'll tell them!" Here in Cemetery, she had nothing to fear, because she had true friends. A community. A home.

She had Lawson.

Without haste, she quietly shut the door, then leaned back on it, facing her defenders with a heart full of emotion.

Betty slumped into Lawson. "Thank God you held me back. There's no telling what I might have done."

It was the nonplussed expression on his face that got Berkley started, and after the first snicker escaped, she didn't even try to hold back. Lawson grinned, and soon Betty was chuckling. Even the dogs got excited. Cheese, however, jumped up on the dryer and eyed them all with mere curiosity before leaping into Lawson's arms.

He caught her handily, without a single scratch. "Told you she loved me." As he stroked the cat, she purred and butted her head to his chin.

Watching the interaction, Berkley thought about how much she loved him, too. "It doesn't feel right that Chad just gets to walk away."

"He doesn't." Lawson cradled Cheese like a baby. "Oliver got hold of the county police. We'd already fixed up Kathleen, but we saw it all in the security feed, including his car. They'll have his name and his license number."

"He's toast," Betty crowed. "Even without legal charges, he'll never be welcome in this town." She leveled a direct stare on Berkley. "We protect our own around here."

"Thank you," she whispered. Contentment filled every corner of her heart, leaving no room for bad memories or regrets. She smiled at Lawson, loving that he was here. Loving that Betty was here. Loving that Lark and Oliver were friends, and the townspeople respected and supported The Love Shack.

These were *her* people, the family that she was meant to have in her life.

Her disreputable past, mistakes and worries were all now behind her. For good.

Lawson was very unsure of Berkley's mood. She wore the most beautiful smile, but she had to be upset, right?

She didn't look upset.

Actually, she looked incredible. Flushed from a busy morning, her hair a little mussed, no makeup yet. Strong, he decided. She looked strong, and capable, and God, he loved her.

Cheese wiggled free, bounded down to the floor and headed to the back of the couch in the living room. Hero leaned against his leg, demanding reassurance that Lawson gladly gave. Gladys, the poor old thing, just plopped down on the floor with an exhausted huff.

He should have held on to Chad, at least until the cops arrived, but with Betty fuming and the dogs so agitated, he'd thought it might be best to get things settled down.

That included his heart, because it was still clamoring around in his chest.

The rush to get Kathleen cleaned up before anyone noticed had effectively diverted his better sense. He'd thought only of how the town adored the mannequin, the turmoil it would cause if the peaceful community learned that their beloved mascot had been defaced.

When he and Oliver finally had her back outside to greet vacationers and locals alike, he'd finally remembered to check the security feed. Seeing Chad clearly, watching the vindictive way he'd marred Kathleen, had stunned and enraged him.

Getting to Berkley became his top priority.

Oliver had promised to stay at the shop until Will showed up. He'd wanted to talk to the police anyway, so Lawson agreed.

He'd been so damned afraid for Berkley, both because of any physical threat Chad might pose and because the problems he caused would likely have rumors resurfacing. Berkley had paid for that debacle more than enough.

He knew how the past still plagued her, how she continued to blame herself for things that weren't her fault, and the embarrassment she still felt.

Resurrecting all that would be painful for her, not that Chad cared. But Lawson did. So damn much.

At the very least, he had wanted to be with her so if Chad showed up, she wouldn't have to face him alone.

He'd raced to her rescue, only to arrive in time to catch her giving Chad hell.

Chad, the ass, had dared to threaten her dog. Huge mistake. The look on Berkley's face as she'd defended Hero was a sight to see. He'd been so proud of her. Still was.

Always would be.

Betty braced one hand on the dryer as she caught her breath, more wrecked than he'd ever seen her. "I'm glad I didn't have to tangle with him." She came forward abruptly and grabbed Lawson in a tight hug. "Thank you."

At first, he wasn't sure what to do. He'd never had a hug like this—from someone so short, elderly and frail. A motherly or grandmotherly figure.

Actually, it felt nice, and his arms came carefully around her. "I like how you threw him out."

"Yes, well…" Betty pressed back, her makeup-free face showing her age more than ever. "Sometimes brawn is better than brains. That fool had neither." She patted Lawson's chest appreciatively, then stepped away. "You, young man, have plenty of both."

"Yes, he does." Berkley studied him. "When Chad showed up here, I wasn't sure what to do. I thought about calling you."

His heart stuttered. "I wish you had." He'd have dropped everything in a heartbeat.

That little smile appeared again. "You came anyway."

Tugging her into his arms, he held her close. "Of course I did." Holding her felt beyond nice. Perfection, even. "You were both fierce."

"It certainly got my blood pumping," Betty agreed.

Against his chest, Berkley trembled—probably laughing again, but just in case, he drew his hand up and down her back, before cupping her nape and drawing her face up to his.

Her shining blue eyes reassured him. The quick kiss she gave him helped, too.

She turned her head to see Betty. "You are the most wonderful person I've ever known. But please, for my sake, don't ever again put yourself at risk like that. I already worry about you too much."

"I know." Betty primped. "And I'll admit, I like it. It's wonderful to be loved."

"You're definitely loved," Berkley assured her. "And appreciated, and valued for so many reasons."

"Good to know." Betty started away. "Now, I need to repair my hair, put on my makeup and then take a break. It's been a trying morning. Come on, Hero and Gladys. Let's go." She glanced back at Lawson with a wink. "Carry on."

"Yes." Berkley rested her hands on his chest and smiled up at him. "Carry on."

Mindful that Betty was nearby, they were in a laundry room, and the shelter would soon get busy, Lawson took her mouth in a kiss that, he hoped, was full of promise. He felt Berkley's small hands fist in his shirt, keeping him close.

Where he wanted to be.

When he finally forced himself to ease up, she put her cheek against him, then whispered something.

Smoothing a hand along her spine, he asked, "What's that?"

She tilted up her face to see him, and this smile was different, more powerful. "I love you."

Automatically, his arms tightened. He'd heard the words, saw them leaving her lips, and still he said, "What?"

The gaze softened, warmed. "I love you." She touched his mouth before he could speak. "It's real. Unconditional. You don't have to say anything back. No," she insisted, when he tried to speak. "Let me finish."

Reluctantly, he gave a nod, but now his heart was going like a jackhammer, and he was smiling, too.

"I know we haven't been reacquainted that long."

"Long enough," he said, because staying quiet right now was hard.

"I guess, because of our history, I feel like I've known you forever."

"Like we were meant to be." When her brows lifted, he gathered her close and kissed her again. A hungry kiss.

She drew back to say "Really?"

"You don't feel that way? Because I do. Almost from the start, I was drawn to you. We share more than most people ever will. An understanding of what it takes to move forward, how important the right people are. What love means. Really means." He cradled her face in his palms. "I love you, too, Berkley. I love your style, and your independence. How you treat animals and care for them. How you care for people, too." *How you care for me.* "I love that you're humble, but not a pushover. Bighearted but strong."

"Stop." Laughing a little, she put her hands to her cheeks, but he still saw her blush.

"When I came here, I thought what I needed was a place to call my own. A nice location to settle so I could put down roots."

"You have all that now."

"I do, but it doesn't matter, not as much as I thought it would, because all I really needed was you."

Tears welled in her eyes, and her fingertips covered her smiling mouth. "This is kind of incredible, don't you think? Chad shows up, and we're confessing love."

"At least the shmuck was good for something."

Laughing, she hugged him tight. "We have a lot of things to work out, and I have more to say, but the animals have been unattended too long already."

"And I need to get back to the shop." He grinned. "Kathleen's boyfriend should be arriving today. I figured I'd unveil him tonight."

Excited, she said, "I want to be there!" Then she glanced back and lowered her voice. "I want to make sure Betty is there, too."

"Oliver and Lark, of course." He hugged her. "Tell Betty to put an announcement on the town's social media pages. Say we're unveiling something fun at the beach. Maybe we could all meet there around seven o'clock."

With Chad all but forgotten, she said, "This is going to be so fun!"

Loving her was fun, but the silliness with Kathleen and Kingston would be a good way to put a period to a day that had started with shadows from the past...so they could see all the promises of tomorrow.

Only four people knew the plans, but the town buzzed about it all day. If she and Lawson could have kept it from Oliver and Lark, they would have, but they needed their help to pull it off. Between them, and with Betty's social media help, they were able to notify most of the business owners, who in turn notified their customers.

Lark finished work first, so she got to the beach to set up the area for the presentation. Without explaining why she needed them, she enlisted Emily to bring a few white flowers, and Yardley, the wedding planner, to lend a few props.

Lark said everyone was full of questions, but she didn't cave. Neither did Lawson, though he said people tromped in and out of his store all day, doing their best to get him to tell.

Only an hour ago, Oliver stealthily swiped Kathleen, and when locals chased after him, demanding to know why, he only laughed and hurried away with her.

Saul's restaurant was mobbed with people buying food early so they could bring it to the beach to see what was happening. He even took time away from the restaurant so he and his son could join Emily to get good seats for whatever the show might be.

It tickled Berkley to see everyone so interested.

Erin and Whitley, along with several volunteers, ensured the animals all got plenty of attention throughout the day before they were put up for the night in their individual kennels.

After all the excitement with Chad, Betty was sure it was a wedding, and it was even funnier that she thought it was Lawson and Berkley getting married. Claiming a protective man like Lawson and a smart woman like Berkley were bound to see the wisdom in settling down together.

Berkley wasn't sure how wise it might be, and she wasn't in a rush to make things official, but she loved Lawson and she knew she'd be happy to share the rest of her life with him.

Betty continued to wheedle for information all day, and Berkley continued to insist that she'd just have to wait like everyone else. Finally, Betty wore out and promised to be at the beach. Even then, she grinned like she had a secret.

When Lawson picked her up at six-thirty, Berkley was ready. She'd fixed her hair, applied her usual makeup and had changed into a cute, lightweight romper perfect for the beach.

"Wow," he said, leaning in for a soft kiss. "You're beautiful."

"I'm still not supercomfortable being in front of a crowd, so I wanted to look my best."

"The beach is packed," he confirmed. "Oliver went by there before he dropped Kathleen off to me."

"You have both mannequins now?"

"In the bed of my truck, hidden under a sheet. They'll stay covered until we unveil them." Frowning, he studied her face. "Did I push you into this? I know how you feel about being the center of attention."

"Actually, I'm happy to be included. Showcasing the mannequins will be fun." She blew out a breath. "The problem is that Betty will be disappointed."

His brows went up. "You think so? Why?"

"Well…" It was embarrassing to talk about, but she really

needed to forewarn Lawson what Betty thought. "See, Betty got it into her head that we were bringing everyone to the beach for, um, a wedding."

Grinning, he led her and Hero out to his truck. "Not sure mannequins can legally marry." Hero was used to riding along and curled up on the floor by her feet while Lawson went around to the driver's side.

Berkley patted the dog, sure that he was picking up on her embarrassment. Once they'd pulled away from the shelter, she explained with an apologetic wince, "The problem is that Betty thinks *we're* getting married."

To his credit, Lawson didn't blink. In fact, his expression comically froze.

Deadpan, Berkley said, "Breathe."

"I'm breathing."

Didn't look like it, until he deeply inhaled.

After several minutes had passed, and they were driving into the town proper, he reached his right hand out to her, palm up.

Berkley laced her fingers with his.

Steering one-handed, he said, "This is not because of what Betty thinks, okay?"

Uh-oh. That sounded serious. "What isn't?"

He sighed, retrieved his hand and pulled to the side of the road to put his truck in Park.

Waiting, Berkley took in his gorgeous profile, the dark blond hair that always seemed disheveled, the light brown eyes that held confidence and kindness in equal measure, the beard scruff that added to his overall sexy vibe. Tension eased away, and she said, "I love you." Then she laughed, because loving him was wonderful. "I love loving you, and I guess I love telling you, too."

Those devastating eyes locked on hers. "Good. Because I thought we could get engaged."

Honest to God, her jaw dropped. "Lawson," she sputtered, completely taken off guard. "You don't have to—"

"Back up. I already told you this has nothing to do with Betty's expectations. In fact..." He lifted a hip, dug in his pocket and took out a small box.

Eyes wide, she stared. Was that a jewelry box? It *was*. She covered her mouth with a suddenly shaking hand. Long, long ago she'd given up on imagining a scenario like this. She'd resigned herself to living alone, protecting her heart and what was left of her reputation. Then she'd moved to Cemetery, and he'd moved there, too, and now...

"I got you this today."

"How?" she asked with a burst of laughter. *"When?"* His day had been as busy as hers. Their entire schedule had been upended by Chad and his nonsense.

"Will helped out a lot while I ran over to Albee."

Her jaw loosened again. "The next town?"

"Don't say it like I left the state." He held the small box against his thigh. "Albee isn't that far away, and I found what I liked within minutes—but if *you* don't like it, we can get something different."

Curious, she licked her lips. "I have to actually see it before I can decide."

"Right." He flipped it open with his thumb, gently took her hand and slipped a delicate five-stone ring onto her finger. Keeping her hand, he said, "I mean it, Berkley. If you don't like it—"

She whispered, "I *love* it." Seeing the ring, she wondered how he could doubt that for a single second. A moderate center diamond had two smaller diamonds set on either side of it. The bright, late-day sunlight through the windshield made it sparkle.

As if searching for the truth, Lawson's gaze stayed on her face. "I was thinking in practical terms, which probably wasn't the best move when telling a woman how much you care. It's just that you're always working with animals. I thought something big would maybe get in the way, but if you want something bigger, I swear that wouldn't be a problem."

She curled her fingers protectively around the band. "I love that you were practical, that you took into consideration my work." Her eyes were again drawn to the ring. "It's so beautiful, I never would have known that factored in."

He started to relax. "It's platinum, so it looks silver like the rest of your jewelry."

Lightly, she touched the different stones, then smiled up at him. "It's perfect."

He rubbed the back of his neck. "When we got home tonight, after showing off Kathleen and Kingston, I was going to ask you. Then you said Betty had expectations."

"Betty is so wise."

He laughed. "I'll be sure to tell her you said so." He took her hand and kissed her palm. "I love you, Berkley. I want to be with you, but there's no rush. We can have a short engagement or a long engagement. We can marry tomorrow, or a year from now. Whatever works for you."

"For us," she clarified, because Lawson's business was important, too. "There's a lot we need to think about. I mean, you have a house, I have a house."

"And you want to be close to the shelter. I get it. When you're ready, I don't mind selling mine."

Giddiness bubbled up. Sleeping with Lawson each night, waking with him each morning… Sign her up. "But you're on the lake." There was so much to consider.

Touching a finger under her chin, he tipped up her face. "We can keep both places if you want."

She frowned. "I want you with me."

"That's where I want to be." He glanced at Hero, who patiently watched their interaction. "You, Cheese and this astute fellow, you're all important to me. If you're ready for me to move in, I'm there."

"I'm ready."

His grin was lazy and sexy and full of satisfaction. "The houses aren't far apart. The shelter is growing already, and if one day you get a full-time employee, maybe your house would work as a perk and we could live in mine." He cupped her cheek. "Or we can stay in yours and use mine for time away. I promise, it doesn't matter to me."

"As long as we're together," she finished for him, knowing that was his thought.

He nodded. "Now that I've found you again, I don't want to let you go. Ever."

A car drove by, giving them a friendly honk as they passed. Smiling, Berkley said, "We need to get to the beach." She threw her arms around his neck and hugged him. "Let's present Kingston, and tonight, as you planned, we can talk things out."

"Should I put that ring back in the box for now?"

Laughing, she held her hand to her heart. "No way. Let's just wait and see if Betty notices. That might be even more fun."

Agreeing with a grin, he gave Hero a few pats, kissed her once more, then got them on their way.

A few minutes later, they arrived to find the beach packed. Umbrellas were set up, lawn chairs and beach towels spread over the sand. Every available picnic table along the perimeter of the lot was occupied. Cars had filled all the parking spots.

Fortunately, Oliver waved them over to a cleared space that he'd saved for them. Since he'd come by earlier to get Handsome, the dog was at his side, crooked teeth and all.

Lawson backed in. Berkley took Handsome for Oliver, then he and Lawson, accompanied by Berkley, Lark and the dogs, carried their hidden cargo to a small platform. Lark had arranged the setting, surrounded by flowers and, thanks to Yardley, some decorative poofs of netting.

It was perfect. Like a backyard wedding, except they faced a beach full of onlookers.

Betty hustled up to them, bringing Gladys along on a leash. The three dogs happily greeted each other, but Betty wore a frown. "Young lady," she said, while pulling Berkley aside. "What are you up to?"

For once she wasn't in her usual wardrobe. No business dress or low-heeled shoes. Betty wore a lightweight, flowing caftan in beach colors, and she was barefoot! Berkley stared at her small feet, a little spellbound by the sight.

"They're called toes," Betty said, reclaiming her attention.

Seeing the flush on her face, Berkley couldn't stop the grin. "The hat is cool."

"It shades my face. At my age, in this heat, too much time on the beach is not ideal."

Oh, no. She hadn't considered that. "I'm so sorry. I should have—"

Betty sniffed. "I'm enjoying it." She flexed her toes, then leaned in close, conspiratorial. "Shocked a lot of people, seeing me here, dressed casually, so it's been worth it. Now, what—" Suddenly her eyes widened. She stared at Berkley's hand, then up to her face, then back at her hand. "Is that an engagement ring?"

"Shh." Berkley crowded closer still. "I swear, I'll tell you all about it later, in private. But not here, okay?" She didn't want to draw attention.

With tears in her eyes, Betty said, "Your mother would be so pleased." She gave a quiet, sniffling laugh. "*I'm* so pleased."

Proving he'd been listening in, Lawson leaned near to Betty's ear and said, "I'm pleased most of all." Then he gave Betty a hug, and really sealed the deal by adding, "Maybe this week you could join Berkley and me for dinner, with Oliver and Lark."

"And the dogs," Berkley said, knowing that Betty now took

Gladys everywhere, and Handsome could always use more interaction.

Betty bloomed. "I would love that. Thank you." In the next second, she turned cross again. "Now, what are you young people up to?"

He deferred to Berkley, and she said, "Maybe Betty could do the honors. After all, she is the namesake of this town."

"Great idea," Oliver said, joining them.

Then Lark came close, too. "The crowd is getting restless, and everything is ready." She handed a megaphone to Betty. "What do you say?"

Beaming at each of them, she agreed. "I'd be honored—if someone would tell me what's going on!"

They quickly clued her in. Delighted, she agreed to make the announcement. The men helped her up to the small stage, where the covered mannequins waited.

Lark stepped back with the promise that she'd take plenty of photos for Betty to use on the town's social media pages.

Holding the leashes for the dogs, Berkley moved to the side, included but out of the limelight, as she preferred.

Oliver and Lawson stood ready for the unveiling.

In a clear voice made louder by the megaphone, a very colorful version of Betty said, "Quiet, quiet. I have an announcement."

A hush fell over the beach.

Going off script, she said, "Most of you don't know that our very own Kathleen was vandalized."

Gasps filled the air, along with heartfelt exclamations. Groaning, Berkley inched farther back. Eventually, everyone would know what Chad had done, but she would have liked to be a little more prepared.

But Betty continued without mentioning him, or Berkley, at all. Instead, she gestured at Lawson and Oliver. "Cemetery also has two very fine heroes who stepped up and saved our Kathleen."

Abashed, both men scowled, but it didn't matter.

With a loud, shrill whistle, Lark got the cheers going and soon everyone on the beach was applauding so loudly, even the dogs got excited. Seeing the guys' expressions had her laughing out loud.

"After ensuring that the miscreant—an outsider, by the way—was turned in to the Albee police, they not only bathed Kathleen and washed her hair, they dressed her and..." Her gaze moved over the crowd, building the expectation. "They got her a *friend*." Turning to Lawson and Oliver, she said, "Gentlemen, if you would."

Lawson huffed a breath.

Oliver smirked.

In unison, they removed the sheets.

Kathleen was dressed entirely in apparel that advertised the shelter, but affixed to her hand was a sign that said *He's such a lucky guy.*

Next to her, Kingston wore a shirt advertising Lawson's print shop. His head was turned to face Kathleen, his fixed gaze on her.

While everyone exclaimed in excitement, Lawson and Oliver left the stage so Betty could continue her show.

Oliver went to Lark, who applauded him again, at least until he lifted her in his arms and swung her in a circle.

Through the megaphone, Betty said "You young people" to the laughter of the crowd. She added, "But you can see what that fitness center of his does. Even I'm feeling more fit."

"Looking it, too," Saul called out.

Followed by Emily saying "Love the outfit."

Yardley yelled, "You're going to be front-page news, Betty."

Everyone cheered.

Wearing a smile, Lawson reached Berkley and said, "I'm feeling damned lucky myself."

In that moment, she no longer cared if anyone looked at her. Laughing, she put her arms around his waist and smiled up at him. "Ditto."

When he kissed her, the cheers escalated, and it wasn't until then that they realized Betty had switched from talking about the mannequins to focusing on them, which had everyone else doing the same.

Into that megaphone, Betty said, "You're all now truly a part of Cemetery." Gaze landing on Berkley, she smiled. "You're home."

Yes, these were her people, Lawson was her love, and she was a part of it all.

Accepting the position of director at The Love Shack was clearly the best decision she'd ever made. Here, she'd found everything.

Most of all, she'd found home.

★ ★ ★ ★ ★